"You're A Witch, Do You Know That?" Ian Murmured

His firm mouth continued to nibble and tease against her heated skin. "You make me do things I've never done before. I've never met a woman like you. One minute I want to send you packing—and the next, I want to carry you to the nearest bed and ravish you for a week."

Alex caught her breath at these bold words. The sudden mental image of them entwined was so powerful it hit her like a blow to the chest.

"Oh, Ian," she whispered into his hair, which smelled faintly of some kind of spicy soap. "This is crazy. We don't even know each other."

Dear Reader:

Romance readers have been enthusiastic about the Silhouette Special Editions for years. And that's not by accident: Special Editions were the first of their kind and continue to feature realistic stories with heightened romantic tension.

The longer stories, sophisticated style, greater sensual detail and variety that made Special Editions popular are the same elements that will make you want to read book after book.

We hope that you enjoy this Special Edition today, and will enjoy many more.

Please write to us:

Jane Nicholls
Silhouette Books
PO Box 236
Thornton Road
Croydon
Surrey CR9 3RU

REBECCA SWAN
Love's Perfect Island

Silhouette Special Edition

Originally Published by Silhouette Books
division of
Harlequin Enterprises Ltd.

To Mom and Dale, who never doubted I'd do it;
to my husband, Karl, who is my romantic
inspiration; to my brother, Don, who cheers and
supports; and to Teresa and Stephanie, two dear
friends who share my Aleutian memories.

*First published in Great Britain 1986
by Silhouette Books, 15–16 Brook's Mews, London W1A 1DR*

© Elizabeth J. Rogers 1985

Silhouette, Silhouette Special and Colophon are Trade Marks
of Harlequin Enterprises B.V.

ISBN 0 373 09281 4

23–0485

*Made and printed in Great Britain for
Mills & Boon Ltd by
Richard Clay (The Chaucer Press) Ltd,
Bungay, Suffolk*

REBECCA SWAN

is happiest when she's writing, traveling or reading, and her life reflects her favorite pursuits. She grew up in a career Navy family and has traveled extensively throughout the world. She's currently teaching language arts and careers at the junior-high-school level and is a free-lance writer in her spare time. Her articles and photographs have appeared in many national magazines. She lives with her husband, Karl, and her cat, Beatrix, in the foothills of Mount Rainier in Washington State.

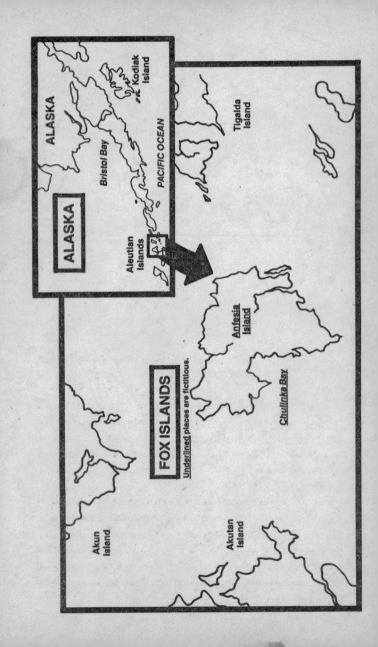

ALASKA

ALASKA

Bristol Bay

Kodiak Island

PACIFIC OCEAN

Aleutian Islands

Tigalda Island

FOX ISLANDS

Underlined places are fictitious.

Anfesia Island

Chulinka Bay

Akun Island

Akutan Island

Chapter One

"Who's up there?"

The terse question was delivered in a deep, masculine voice. Although the words were uttered softly in what sounded almost like a low growl, Alexandra Gilbert had no trouble hearing them in the otherwise silent warehouse. As she lay hidden eight feet above the man, she cursed herself for having chosen the moment before to stretch her cramped leg. The subsequent overturning of a can of nails had alerted him to her presence on the open balcony.

The words were more of a command than an inquiry and Alex, feeling very much like a criminal, stirred on the pile of fishing nets and tried to will herself to stand up and face the stranger. But before she could do so, he repeated his question. This time he spoke louder and with a hint of controlled impatience that gave his voice a dangerous quality.

"I said, who's up there?"

He sounds the way a coiled snake looks, Alex thought, and caught herself before she laughed nervously. His voice carried such a timbre of confidence and authority, she found it impossible to resist. Trying to swallow her embarrassment, she moved on the shadowy balcony. She knew that upon standing she would be fully illuminated by the shaft of sunlight that poured through one of the few high windows. Her face burned with shame at the thought of being exposed like a thief, but she knew that the stranger below left her no other choice.

Before she could rise and face him, the nets beneath her gave a sudden lurch. With growing alarm, Alex realized that she had hesitated an instant too long. The man below her was pulling on a corner of the nets that hung over the edge of the balcony.

"Fine, we'll do it the hard way, then," he said softly.

Before one word of protest could escape her trembling lips, he again yanked the nets roughly, pulling them and a startled Alex over the edge.

The fall was a short one to a relatively soft landing on a pile of canvas and netting she had noticed earlier. Fortunately nothing seemed bruised but her composure. A confusion of nets covered her, encasing her head and body in the webbing like a trapped salmon. She let out a small squeak of panic, surprise and anger before the man threw himself on top of her struggling form.

"Just hold it right there," he growled as he pinned the full length of her body under his own.

Alex was too astonished by this sudden turn of events to respond immediately. For a moment, time seemed to stand still as several sensations flashed through her. The pleasant, salty tang of the sea filled her nostrils from the nets that tightly embraced her. Another scent wafted from the stranger. Spicy and pleasantly male, it penetrated the nets and washed over her in heated waves. She could feel the lean hardness of his body pressed on top of her own slender form. His warm breath brushed delicately against her cheek. The only sounds she was aware of were those of her own panting and the pounding of her racing heart. She felt hot, flushed and, to her amazement, oddly excited in spite of her irritation.

"Get off me!" Alex exploded angrily through a layer of net.

She squirmed beneath the man's solid form, but her efforts to free herself served only to bring her body into closer and more intimate contact with his.

"Well, I'll be damned. It's a woman," he drawled in a tone of pleased surprise. He ignored her heated demand and brought his face close to hers. His voice was teasing as he purred down at her, "Let's see what kind of mermaid I've caught in my net today."

Their eyes met through the webbing. Alex was immediately struck by the intensity of the periwinkle-blue pair that gazed languidly into her own. They were like twin pools drawing her into their depths, compelling her to swim in their inviting waters. Humor and intelligence flickered there. At the moment, keen interest in her creased their outer corners.

Alex fought the spell those attractive eyes cast over her. Remembering her awkward predicament, she spoke in a husky voice, trying to keep it from trembling.

"Look, I'm a trespasser. You've caught me, whoever you are. Now get off and let me out of this mess."

She was all too aware of the pleasant and very disturbing weight of the man's legs and hips pressed against her own. Although clothing and fishing nets were sandwiched between them, she could feel heat flowing from his body to hers and back again like an electric current or waves on a beach. Excitement mounted within her, and she fought unsuccessfully to keep it down.

The man raised himself on one elbow. He kept Alex's body securely pinned beneath him as he plucked at the net that lay over her face and head.

"Hold still, little mermaid, and I'll get you out," he drawled.

He freed her head at last and looked down at her. His steady appraisal unnerved her, and she felt her already warm face flush even more deeply. She knew that her eyes were sparking with indignation, and she was aware that her long, mahogany-colored hair framed her face in tousled disarray. A soft strand from the silky mass tickled her cheek. The stranger reached down and gently brushed it from her face, his hand lingering just a shade too long in the process. The touch of his fingers was a burning brand on her skin.

He cocked his head to one side, and his full mouth curved into a wolfish smile. "A very pretty mermaid," he said. "I guess this is my lucky day. You even have gray-green eyes to match the color of the sea. The freckles on your nose are a nice touch, too." He dipped his head closer to her and breathed. "Is that rose I smell? Rather unusual for a mermaid, but I like it."

As he teasingly itemized her physical traits, Alex took in his appearance. He looked to be in his midthirties, and had to be a bit over six feet tall, judging from the way his athletically built frame fit against Alex's five-feet-nine-inch body. A perfect fit, an imp within her murmured. She felt a blush stain her cheeks as the shameless thought flickered through her mind. She hoped the man couldn't read in her eyes what she was thinking.

He was wearing snug, faded blue jeans that hugged his narrow hips and well-built thighs. His black-and-red plaid shirt was rolled up at the sleeves and open at the throat, where it exposed a triangle of dark, curly chest hair. His shoulders were broad, his neck and face tan. Here was a man who spent a lot of time outdoors, she surmised. Perched on his head at a rakish angle was a black wool watch cap. His casual attire appealed to Alex; it was a pleasant change from the suited university professors she was used to.

From beneath his cap spilled thick, black, wavy hair. His was not exactly the face of a matinee idol, yet it was handsome and arresting in an indefinable way. Alex assumed he was a fisherman although, unlike most of the others she had seen today, this one had no beard or mustache. His jawline and broad forehead framed a face that intrigued her and she felt a strong desire to know him. She couldn't explain her reaction; in all of her twenty-six years, this was a completely new one to her. Its intensity surprised her.

Again Alex struggled beneath him. Her arms remained entangled, but her shoulders broke free of his hold. His eyes traveled to the top of her pink shirt, which was gaping open, revealing a fraction of her lacy bra and just a hint of the top swell of her full breasts. She felt herself coloring as he raked her chest with his intense blue gaze. His wolfish smile broadened into a grin. To her dismay, he seemed to be thoroughly enjoying her predicament. Although he had her at a distinct disadvantage, for some strange reason Alex wasn't frightened. Perhaps it was the playful expression in his eyes that told her he wouldn't do anything to truly discomfit her.

She tried to keep her voice calm as she spoke. "Stop calling me a mermaid and let me up. This is ridiculous."

"If I can't call you mermaid, what can I call you?" he breathed down at her. His eyes were faintly mocking, yet curious. "Come on, what's your name?" He raised his eyebrows in a parody of open innocence. "Don't you want to know mine?"

What nerve he had! There was no way Alex was going to cooperate with this insufferable man. In spite of the physical excitement she felt, she forced herself to glare up at his taunting face.

"I have absolutely no interest in who you are, what boat you fish on, or anything else about you," she snapped up at him. "Now let me up," she added, and squirmed ineffectually beneath him.

"Wait just a minute," he said, a look of mock sternness on his face. "You've admitted that you're a trespasser so it's my duty to hold you for questioning." He leaned toward her until his lips were just inches from hers. His breath was warm and soft on her trembling mouth. "In fact," he said in a soft, husky voice, "I think I should fine you for being where you're not supposed to be."

Alex swam in those compelling blue eyes, then turned her face to one side. She knew exactly what form the "fine" would take, and was surprised to find herself wondering what it would be like to be kissed by him.

She pulled away from such thoughts. "You won't collect any fines from me," she said tartly. "Now get off me!" With that, she tried to lurch away from him, but only caused him to smile with sensual pleasure.

"Oh, do that some more. I love it!" He moaned softly and closed his eyes. Then he opened them and grinned down at her. Alex could see that he was having great fun at her expense, and it infuriated her.

Her emotions must have shown on her face, for the man's grin faded to a wry smile as he said, "Okay, I'll let you up. Calm down, little mermaid."

He rolled off her and helped pull the net away until Alex was able to sit up and brush off her jeans.

"May I help you?" He smiled at her, the outer corners of his eyes crinkled in mocking amusement. He reached over to brush some dust off where her jeans fit snugly over her thighs. His interested eyes again raked her slender form as she pushed his hand away.

"That's okay," she remarked dryly. "I can handle it."

She adjusted her shirt and pushed her heavy hair back from her face. Her cheeks still felt flushed from her exertions and from the conflicting emotions that had rocketed through her.

Trying to regain her composure, she glanced around the large room that she'd impulsively entered thirty minutes ago. Fishing nets and cork lines hung from horizontal poles, and boxes of supplies and tools lined the walls. A pile of crates with "McLeod's Seafoods, Inc.," stenciled on them stood in one corner. Stout beams crossed the room overhead, the space above them dim and covered with cobwebs. She could hear and actually feel the muffled hum from the salmon cannery next door vibrating through the wooden floor. She hoped that its regular rhythm would help calm the fluttering of her heart. Through the one open window high above came the piercing cry of gulls and the clatter of a forklift as it rolled along the dock.

She could also hear the regular breathing of the fisherman a few feet away from her. It irritated her that he could be so poised when her composure had been so thoroughly shattered. She looked over at him. He had lolled back on the nets and propped himself up on one elbow. His posture and his mocking, confident expression reminded Alex of a potentate relaxing on a mound of satin pillows as he inspected the latest addition to his harem. The image did nothing to soften her mixed reaction to him.

"Hot?" The sound of his low voice startled her.

"What?" she managed to say.

He growled his response, a slow smile lifting one corner of his full mouth. "I asked if you were hot. You look a little steamy." Did nothing miss his scrutiny? His eyes were appreciative. Something in them told her that he was taking all of the credit for her discomposure. "It becomes you," he added.

"Y—yes," she stammered, fearing that her voice would give away her aroused emotions. "It's a very warm day, but then, I was told the Aleutians could be hot in June."

"This is your first trip to the islands?" he asked.

"That's right. I've never been to Alaska before."

His eyes narrowed slightly. "How do you like it so far?"

Caught off guard, Alex answered with candor. "I only arrived about two hours ago, but from what I've seen, I think I'm in love. It's beautiful here."

A glance at his teasing face reminded her of their recent intimate tussle on the nets. She was suddenly aware that his question had not referred only to the emerald-green mountains and azure waters of Anfesia Island.

"You enjoyed that!" she accused him, putting her hands on her hips. She leaned a shade closer to him to drive her words home.

One eyebrow rose as he smiled rakishly. "You mean our little roll in the nets? Of course I enjoyed it, lady. And," he added, "something tells me you did, too."

What an arrogant man, Alex thought to herself. "Enjoyed being held down and toyed with? Is that how you think women like to be treated?"

A warning look flickered in his eyes, which were suddenly hooded with partially lowered lids. Alex had the distinct impression that pushing him would be a waste of time.

"Normally I don't treat women like that, but you had it coming. You're up here where you shouldn't be, and I meant to throw a scare into you."

Begrudgingly she said, "Well, you did, but you had no right to take advantage of the situation simply because you're stronger than I am."

He laughed a low, throaty chuckle that thrummed pleasantly against her senses. "Okay, next time *you* can be on top." His eyes twinkled with amusement.

With a sharp intake of breath, Alex opened her mouth to toss back a sharp retort, then thought better of it. He was openly baiting her, daring her to respond. She decided to ignore his obvious gambit.

"No, I don't approve of your methods at all," she remarked coolly to him. "But," she added sardonically, "I suppose Ian McLeod would applaud your style."

The man raised one eyebrow questioningly at her and smiled faintly. "Why do you say that?" he asked.

Alex was immediately sorry she'd mentioned the cannery owner. "Look," she said, one hand fidgeting nervously with the net beside her, "I haven't even met him yet, so I don't think it's fair to repeat what I've heard about him. Besides," she said, her eyes avoiding his, "it was just someone's impression."

"Which was?" he pursued.

He seemed terribly interested for some reason. She had better be careful about what she said to him. Maybe this fisherman was a good friend of Ian McLeod and would repeat her comments to him. It was obvious that he was not going to drop the issue, so she looked levelly into his eyes, pretending a confidence she didn't feel, and took a deep breath. "I've heard he's somewhat of a ladies' man, and that he's handsome and charming and is used to getting what he wants," she said in a rush. She decided to skip the part about his apparent dislike for environmentalists.

The man smiled. "Yes," he said, "that's all true, especially the handsome and charming part." He nodded sagely. "He's also sensitive, witty, highly intelligent and very well-read. Not only that, he's a great cook, and—"

Oh, for heaven's sake, Alex thought to herself, is this man going to go on and on about his employer, this paragon, and expect her to remain entranced while he did so? Incredible. Impatiently she rose to go.

"I'm really not interested in all this," she interrupted him. "I'm leaving," and with that, she started toward the door.

Before she knew what had happened, he had stepped between her and the door as swiftly and silently as a hunting panther. She felt the male power in him as she looked up at his face so close to hers.

"Wait a minute," he drawled down at her. "You haven't told me why you're up here. You walked right by the No Trespassing sign at the foot of the stairs. Don't you know you're supposed to get permission to be in this warehouse?"

Alex felt her mouth harden into a line as she replied, trying to keep calm and patient. "I believe we've already established that I trespassed and that you caught me at it. Tell your boss, if you like." Then she tossed her hair in a gesture she hoped would imply more boldness than she felt. "In fact, I'll tell him myself," she said lightly.

She breezed by the tall man and reached for the doorknob.

"By the way, who were you meeting up here?"

His voice was overlaid with insinuation, and his face had a knowing look when she turned to gaze back at him. He stood with his hands on his hips, his legs slightly apart. Just looking at his well-proportioned figure, which emanated confidence and male strength, made her heartbeat quicken.

"What do you mean?" she asked, her curiosity aroused. "I wasn't meeting anyone." She was confused and sounded it.

"Oh, come on, now." He shook his head. "You don't have to play dumb with me. You're a big girl. There's only one reason why a good-looking woman would be lying hidden on a dark balcony on a very convenient pile of nets. Granted," he said with a wave of his hand and an imperious nod of his head, "they aren't the same as a nice, soft bed, but they'll do. You were obviously meeting your lover up here."

His arrogant, all-knowing expression made Alex almost twitch with annoyance. She felt her jaw stiffen with anger as she said to him, "How dare you imply such a thing!"

He broke into rich, suggestive laughter that seemed to wash over her in palpable waves. But even though he was laughing, something in his eyes told Alex that he was all business, and that he would brook no attempts on her part to be less than truthful.

"Don't try to pretend you don't know that this is a favorite meeting place for fishermen and sweet, young things from the cannery," he said. "Why, romantic trysts up here are practically a tradition." He glanced around at the shadowy corners. "It even used to be tolerated until someone dropped a cigarette in here last summer and almost burned the place down." He looked back at her with a steady gaze. "It happened during the heat of passion, so to speak."

Alex felt her cheeks flush slightly at the double entendre.

"You can imagine how touchy people are about fire in such a remote area as this," he went on. "I mean, the cannery compound is the only thing on this island. It would take the Kodiak Fire Department a week to get here," he said wryly. "So, up went the sign. You'll have to meet your boyfriend somewhere else, I'm afraid."

"You're making a mistake," she flung at him. "I told you I arrived just two hours ago. How could I be meeting someone? I don't even know anyone here."

He shrugged and partially lowered his lids over sardonic eyes. "So you're a fast worker, or you met the guy in Seattle before you came up." He ignored her gasp of outrage and grinned at her. "Who is the lucky man, anyway?" He folded his arms across his chest. "Wait, let me guess. Is it Arnie on the *Doris M.*, or Jess on the *Caryl Dyane*, or is it big bad Tony on the *Betsy Joan*?"

Alex's hands clenched at her sides as she fought an urge to slap his smirking face. She ground out her words. "I told you I wasn't meeting anyone up here, and I resent your nasty accusations."

"Nasty?" His eyebrows went up in mock surprise. "Is that how you view healthy lust?"

"It's no business of yours how I view lust, or anything else, for that matter." She was aware of seeming huffy and prudish, and she hotly disliked this man for making her sound that way.

She considered trying to step around him, then decided to simply brazen her way out of this awkward mess. There was that cloaked look in his eyes that told her she wouldn't be allowed to go until she explained her presence. He certainly takes a lot upon himself, she mused angrily as she composed what she would say to him.

"I came up here to look at some birds."

Even though she tilted her chin up when she said it as a way of giving herself a confident air, she knew the words sounded foolish. She immediately regretted saying them, especially since the two barn swallows she had been watching earlier were nowhere to be seen or heard.

The man threw his head back and exploded into laughter again, as she knew he would. "Birds? You came up here to see some birds?" He chuckled. "Sure you did, lady." His mirth faded, and a no-nonsense look flickered in his eyes. "You expect me to believe that?"

Alex rushed ahead with her explanation. She didn't know why she was even bothering to clarify her statement to this offensive man, but yet she felt compelled to tell him more.

"You're going to feel very foolish when you learn that I'm telling you the truth," she threw at him coolly. "My name is Alexandra Gilbert, I have a Master of Science degree in ornithology..." She paused. "That's the study of birds," she said to him in an aside that sounded more imperious than she had intended.

"Don't patronize me, lady," he growled at her. "I know what ornithology is. Go on."

She took a deep breath and continued. "I was sent here by the University of Iowa to help conduct a census of the bird species that nest on Anfesia Island. My supervisor, Dr. Lily Harper, flew up a month ago and persuaded Mr. McLeod to let us locate our base of operations here, at

Chulinka Bay. The rest of the team will be arriving in a couple of days. So you see," she continued as she gazed up into his handsome face, "birds are very much my business. Whether or not you believe me is entirely up to you."

The man seemed to relax somewhat. He commented, "I remember about the bird people coming up, now that you mention it."

Alex decided not to challenge him on his use of the somewhat undignified term "bird people." "Oh," she asked instead, "did you meet Dr. Harper?"

"Indeed I did," he answered. "A very feisty lady. Must be sixty if she's a day, and has the energy of a twenty-year-old—amazing woman." He again narrowed his gaze at her. "Now, she looks like an ornithologist—you don't." He quickly swept Alex's body with frankly appreciative eyes. She felt exposed and restless beneath his appraising glance.

"Well, life's full of surprises, isn't it?" she retorted with spirit.

"Sure is," he drawled, "but none of this explains why you entered an off-limits area without permission."

Trying to remain as patient as she could, Alex continued. "As I told you, I arrived by seaplane a couple hours ago. I went down to the dock to look around and get my bearings. I noticed two barn swallows flying in and out of that broken window up there." She pointed, and he turned to look up at the square where there was a pane of glass missing.

Then he turned back to her, a look of disbelief on his face. "This is getting better and better. I may not be an ornithologist, Ms. Gilbert, but I know what barn swallows are, and I can tell you that there aren't any in these parts."

"Wrong," Alex countered. "They aren't supposed to be here, but they are. In many parts of North America they're very common, but here in the Aleutians they're listed as casual or accidental. Birds can and do show up in the most unlikely places. When I saw the pair that was flying in and out of that window, I knew I had to see if they were nesting inside. Here they'd be considered rare, and if I can document that they're actually nesting out of their normal range, I can write up my findings for a professional journal.

"They've built a nest up on that rafter," she informed him as she nodded toward one of the beams. "You can't see it from down here, but you can from the balcony. And that's what I was doing when you came in," she said firmly, "looking at a barn swallow nest, not waiting for my lover, as you claimed. I was nervous about being here, so when you came in I decided to stay hidden until you left. That's when my foot overturned some nails and you realized you weren't alone."

He didn't respond but continued to look at her with a half smile.

She went on to say, "I know I shouldn't have entered without permission. I'm a little impulsive at times, but I'll explain the whole thing to Mr. McLeod when I pay him a courtesy call. I'm sure he'll understand my excitement at finding some rare birds to head up my census list."

The birds in question still hadn't put in an appearance. Alex silently scolded the swallows for vanishing just when their busy chittering in the vast room could have lent credence to her story.

She suddenly felt as if she had the upper hand at last in spite of the absence of the birds. Smiling at the man, she said, "Now, don't you feel just a little bit foolish for having been wrong about my reason for being here?"

"No, Ms. Gilbert, I don't feel the least bit foolish," he said, breaking his silence at last. "And I'll tell you what..." He took a step toward her. "I'll believe your swallow story if you'll believe I caught a mermaid up here today and want to take her home with me. Is it a deal?" He teasingly held out his hand as if to shake hers.

"Oh, I give up!" she exploded. She ignored the tanned hand with the long fingers and pivoted on her heel. "You are an incredibly obnoxious and arrogant person," she tossed over her shoulder at him, and with that, she yanked open the door and stormed out. The clatter of her feet on the wooden stairs could not quite block out the sound of the rich, throaty laughter that drifted down to her from the open door.

Hoping no one had seen her hasty departure from the warehouse, Alex glanced around warily at the foot of the stairs. To her right was the end of the dock. She could hear the calm waters of lovely Chulinka Bay lapping at the pilings and at the several fishing boats that were moored alongside.

Her breath caught as she once again drank in the scene that had so entranced her upon arrival. It reminded her somewhat of pictures she had seen of Norwegian fjords. Treeless, velvety mountains, their creases deeply shadowed now, almost completely encircled a small bay dotted with fishing boats. Overhead was a flawless blue sky dappled with the moving white specks of crying gulls. Glaucous-winged, she automatically identified to herself.

It felt good to be out here in the open. She paused for an instant and let the soft breeze ruffle her loose shirt and thick hair. She breathed deeply of the fragrant air that was touched with the pleasant tang of salt water.

She turned left, away from the picturesque scene, and started to walk purposefully down the dock. It must be coffee-break time, she thought as she strode past the cannery. About a dozen cannery workers had emerged into the slanted sunlight of late afternoon. They were eating sweet rolls and drinking from steaming mugs. The women wore white aprons, plastic sleeve guards and black rubber boots over their jeans and T-shirts. Some lounged against the railing, while others chatted and laughed with fishermen who were working on one of the boats tied alongside the dock.

As Alex passed through their midst, a couple fishermen cast her approving glances, and some of the women said hello to her. Not wishing to pause and get acquainted while she was still smarting from her encounter with the handsome stranger, she returned their brief greetings and walked on.

Her long legs covered the length of the dock quickly, and she turned left at its end and headed down a path. It led to the old cabin that Dr. Harper had gotten permission for them to use during the several weeks the team would be working on the island.

As she walked, Alex fumed to herself. Something as innocent as looking at some barn swallows had somehow evolved into a scene of embarrassment and anger. She felt frustrated and insulted by the fisherman. His teasing remarks had been uncalled for, even though part of her thought they may have been provoked by his apparent attraction toward her. How she would love to get back at him! His comments had been so inappropriate.

She had to admit, though, that her explanation for being in the warehouse must have been difficult for him to believe. Her reason would sound strange to anyone not used to looking for birds in all sorts of unlikely spots. If that really was the cannery meeting place for lovers, as he'd told her, it would seem plausible that she *was* lying in wait for one of the fishermen.

And yet, why hadn't he just accepted her reason for being there? Why assume that there could be only one explanation for her presence in that room? It rankled her to think that he may have bought her story but had pretended not to just to tease and annoy her. She hoped that the offensive man would be kept very busy out on his boat, and that she wouldn't bump into him again.

A rich tangle of tall grass and wildflowers grew beside the small porch of the cabin. Thinking about all the work that awaited her inside, she paused at the door and sat on the porch railing. She would compose herself before going inside to the task of unpacking all that gear.

It occurred to her that the fisherman might report her trespassing to Mr. McLeod, after all. That would be all right, she reassured herself, since she planned to tell the cannery owner herself anyway. No, she finally decided, the stranger had had his fun at her expense, and that was probably enough smug satisfaction for a man like that.

A man like what? Why couldn't she get him off her mind? Her heart had finally stopped its wild fluttering, her knees again felt solid and weren't quivering as they had when she had been with him. How could anyone have such an impact on her? It had never happened before. Alex was confused over feeling such an immense attraction to someone who had so thoroughly vexed her.

Not a very good beginning, she sighed to herself as she watched the scene before her. The sun was dipping toward the horizon. Shadows had lengthened on the mountains, and gulls were rising in screaming flocks from the many roofs of the cannery compound. She was apprehensive about meeting Ian McLeod, and now this incident had further unsettled her. She remembered what her supervisor had told her about him, that he was attractive and forceful, and that he was not easily swayed. It was only through some very diplomatic and persuasive talk that Dr. Harper had gotten him to agree to let them stay at the cabin. He didn't want "a bunch of environmentalists up here underfoot," he had told her. But in the end, he'd said he would tolerate their presence.

Alex wanted to be composed and quietly assertive with Ian McLeod. She would clear her troubled mind at once and stop thinking about the disturbing incident with the blue-eyed stranger. She must consider, for instance, just how she would tell McLeod that Dr. Harper was no longer the team leader, and that she, herself, was. She was worried about how he would receive the news of that recent, and unexpected, development.

A breeze blew off of the bay. It caused her to reach automatically for the soft gray sweater she had draped loosely around her shoulders when she'd gone out to explore. She sighed with annoyance as she realized that she didn't have it anymore. It must have slipped off while she was struggling in the nets, and in her haste and confusion she had left it in the warehouse.

She stood up to go back and retrieve the garment. It had been made by her mother and was one of Alex's favorites. Then she stopped. She didn't want to risk running into him again. She would have to get the sweater tomorrow.

What a frustrating hour she had just spent. She certainly was in no mood to meet the prickly Mr. McLeod today. First thing in the morning she would put that dreaded chore behind her. Squaring her shoulders with determination, Alex turned to enter the cabin to start unpacking.

Before she could close the door behind her she heard the sound of running feet. She looked out and saw a boy of about seventeen sprinting down the path toward her. His wheat-colored hair was disheveled, and he was panting from his exertions.

"Are you Alexandra Gilbert?" he asked when he had caught his breath.

"Yes," she replied. She was somewhat alarmed by his haste and his agitated manner.

"Come with me right away," he said. "There's an urgent message for you at the radio shack."

Chapter Two

I see you found her, Sonny," said the portly, older man from his swivel chair in front of a bank of radio equipment. His head was bald with a fringe of gray hair. A pair of glasses with smudged lenses rested halfway down his sunburned nose.

He waved his hand at the boy. "You can leave now. I won't be needing you again tonight. Go have yourself some supper."

Sonny smiled at Alex and the older man, then said, "Thanks, Dan. See you in the morning." With that, he left.

Dan looked at Alex and motioned her toward an old wooden chair near his desk. His voice was kindly, his manner fatherly. "Please sit down, Ms. Giblert. I'm Dan Barnett. Just call me Dan."

"I'm happy to meet you, Dan," she said as she reached out to shake hands with him. She sat down on the chair he had indicated. "Your helper—Sonny?—said you have an urgent message for me."

He clucked his tongue. "I'll have to tell him not to get so riled up. He makes it sound like someone died." He glanced over at her. "No one died, that I know of, young lady, so you can relax."

Alex sat back in the chair and breathed more easily. She had assumed that there was trouble at her parents' farm in Iowa. Her imaginings about what the message contained had left her feeling a little shaky.

She quickly looked around her. The room in which she sat took up the whole interior of a small cabin that was near the dock area and the company store. Its walls were lined with bookcases stuffed with dozens of loose-leaf binders, card-file boxes and manila folders from which papers protruded. The bare, wooden floor was deeply pitted in places. Several pictures of fishing boats decorated the walls. The frames were black and the photos hung askew at various angles.

Dan's scarred, wooden desk appeared to be as cluttered and disorganized as the rest of the room. Several In and Out baskets brimmed with papers and folders. A mug sat amid countless coffee rings. Taking up one whole corner was a cardboard box containing radio gear, spare parts and wires that coiled over the edge and down to the desktop.

As Alex inspected her surroundings, Dan leafed through a sheaf of papers, looking over the top of his glasses as he did so. His chair squeaked as he swiveled around to hand one of the sheets to her.

"Here it is, Ms. Gilbert."

"Please call me Alex," she said as she took the paper.

A male voice suddenly crackled over the CB. It said through a smattering of static, "There's a hot game of cribbage starting up on the *Dorothy Lea*. Are you interested, Travis? Over.''

More static, then a different male voice responded. ''Roger, the *Dorothy Lea*, I'm on my way. And this time, Skipper, I'm providing the refreshments. Over and out.''

Alex barely registered the words from the radio as she looked down at the message. She read it several times, her heart sinking. Finally she looked up to find Dan staring at her, deep concern lining his kindly face.

''I can tell it's disappointing news for you, Alex.''

''You can say that again,'' she said in a stunned whisper.

She looked down at the paper in her lap, her eyes skimming the brief message again, although she could have, by now, recited it from memory. It was from Dr. Harper.

> Grant money canceled. Rachel and David took other positions. Come back immediately.

She fought back the tears as the significance of those few words sank in. Crushing the paper to her side, she rose and walked across the small room to a window in order to hide her intense disappointment from Dan.

The window looked out on Chulinka Bay. The water was already starting to darken with the approaching dusk, and the sun was sending flares of crimson and bright apricot across the western sky. Lights twinkled on several of the boats that bobbed at anchor, adding a magical quality to the scene.

Alex felt her heart ache with sadness. How could she be asked to leave this place she already loved? And what about the bird census? What would happen to it? After months of preparation it just wasn't fair to be told to come home before the project had even begun.

Another thought flashed unbidden through her mind. The only good thing about this was that she would never have to chance running into that disturbing fisherman again. But to her surprise, rather than finding that idea reassuring, she found it disquieting. A part of her wanted very much to see him again. The realization gave her the same feeling of inner turmoil she had experienced earlier.

The peaceful scene before her blurred, and she hastily wiped away tears and turned back toward Dan. She was determined to pull herself together. This wasn't the end of the world, after all. Might as well be, another little voice whispered in her brain.

"Is there anything I can do, Alex?" Dan's voice was full of solicitude as he looked over at her.

"No, I suppose not. Thanks anyway," she said as she walked back to the chair and sank onto it. "I'm just very, very disappointed that the project I've worked so many months to organize and prepare for has been canceled before it can even begin."

"What project is that?" he asked with interest shining in his eyes.

Briefly Alex filled him in on the bird species census. He nodded attentively as she spoke.

"We've had funding problems all along the way," she said. "I just never dreamed that our grant wouldn't be renewed."

"How many people were in your team?"

"Originally, there were four of us," she said. "Rachel and David are undergraduates who were going to assist in the data gathering. Dr. Harper was the leader, of course, then she had to drop out. Last week she broke her ankle while visiting another project, so she named me as the leader in her place. I've worked in the field before, but I've never been more than an assistant. I was really looking forward to this.'' She sighed ruefully and tried to smile at Dan's sympathetic expression.

"Oh, well," she continued, "at least now I won't have to explain all this to Mr. McLeod. He wasn't too thrilled about our team coming up here in the first place."

Dan coughed slightly and crossed his hands on his broad middle. "Yes, he told me about that. I think he finally gave his permission for you university folks to stay in that old cabin because he was impressed by Dr. Harper's reputation. He knew she was a real pro."

"Well, she is one of the country's leading ornithologists," Alex said. "She said, though, that he was still reluctant to let us work here."

Dan said, "It's because of the crab plant he wants to build near the seabird colony."

Alex was instantly alert. "You mean the rookery on the north side of the island?"

"Yes, that's the one."

"But," she said, "the rookery is the main reason that we wanted to study the bird life here. It's a very important breeding ground for several seabird species. If we can gather enough data on that area, the Department of the Interior will add Anfesia Island to the Aleutian Islands National Wildlife Refuge."

Dan nodded and responded, "Yes, I know. And Ian knows that, too, and he's not about to let some environmentalists come up here and spoil his plan."

"But he already owns—what is it?—fourteen canneries all over Alaska. Why does he need another one?"

"It isn't so much a matter of need, Alex. His family has been involved in the seafood industry for many years, and expansion is part of any business. Besides, crab will be a new line for him. This cannery handles salmon in the summer and is closed up during the winter. The tanner and spider crab markets are just starting to open up, so it'd be a whole new ball game." He chuckled. "You should see how excited he gets when he talks about it."

Things were beginning to become clear to Alex. Now she understood why Ian McLeod had been so reluctant to have the scientists here. She was surprised he had given his permission at all in light of what he planned to do. It rankled her that she would now have no part in preparing a report that might have swayed the government to name the colony as a protected area. Progress, she thought ironically. Progress for those driven by the profit motive, but not progress for an important natural area and its wildlife.

She sighed deeply and got up to leave. "Is there a seaplane tomorrow, Dan?"

"Yes. It comes in around noon," he answered.

"I guess you'd better save me a seat," she said ruefully. "Looks like I'll be on it, much as I hate to leave." She walked toward the door. "And thanks for listening," she said as she turned back in his direction. "I needed a sympathetic ear."

"That's okay," he replied. He looked a little sad. "I'm just sorry things didn't work out for you. I can tell you're a very dedicated scientist, and I would've enjoyed having you around this summer."

She smiled at him. "Thanks. Good night, now."

As she walked slowly down the path, she thought to herself somewhat bitterly that it was the same old thing. There was never enough money to do the really important things, like study wildlife or set aside sanctuaries. Because a grant had not been renewed, an ambitious cannery mogul, who was undoubtedly worth millions already, would get his way. Ian McLeod would build his crab plant near the seabird cliffs, thus driving the birds away forever. There would be no input from the environmentalist side as a kind of balance in deciding what happened to such an important area.

It just wasn't fair! Alex fumed, feeling helpless. She looked at the scene before her. Lights had winked on among the many small fishing boats that rocked on the gentle swells. She could hear random male voices shouting jests and light banter from boat to boat as the fishermen prepared to eat and relax after a hard day's work. Having spent her entire life in Iowa's corn and soybean belt, this complete change of surroundings enchanted her. How she hated the idea of having to leave tomorrow. Just because there was never enough money!

She suddenly stopped. Wait a minute—how much money would the project take, anyway? All of the gear and most of the food had already been paid for and sent up. It rested in boxes and duffels in the cabin, waiting to be unpacked. The small grant had been meant to support the four team members while they were here for several weeks. One person could live on the supplies for much longer.

Alex snapped her fingers and turned on her heel. She felt hope blossom in her breast as she raced back to the radio shack. It was a crazy idea, but it just might work.

She burst in on Dan, who turned in his chair to look at her, an expression of surprise on his kindly face.

"Back so soon? What can I do for you, Alex?"

She was a bit breathless as she asked him, "Dan, can you send a couple of messages for me?" She stood beside his desk, her hands flat on it, leaning forward with excitement.

"Sure I can," he said, picking up a pencil and getting ready to write on a piece of paper. "Okay, shoot."

A few minutes later, Alex was again walking down the path toward her cabin, but this time her step was light and bouncy. She gazed around with great pleasure and satisfaction, feeling exhilarated by the somewhat daring decision she'd made.

Dan had sent two messages for her. One was to Dr. Harper, telling her that, with her permission, Alex would stay on Anfesia and conduct the bird census by herself. The other was to Alex's sister in Des Moines, asking Monica to loan her some money. If she had to pay all the expenses from now on, Alex thought to herself, that was what she would do in order to see this project completed.

A feeling of warm affection spread through Alex as she thought about her sister. Monica would be only too willing to send money so that Alex could continue her work. The two sisters had been close since childhood and had always depended on each other. It was older sister Monica who had taught Alex how to swim and how to ride a horse, after helping Alex overcome her fear of the big animals. Then later, when Alex was in college and their parents' farm had lost money for a couple of years, it was Monica who had paid Alex's tuition.

After Alex received her degree, she had returned the favor. Monica had needed money to do something she'd long dreamed of—opening her own art gallery. Alex remembered how Monica had cried with joy when Alex had placed the large check in her hand. "You made sure that I got an education," Alex had told Monica, "now let me help you make your dream come true." Using Alex's money, Monica had opened a fabulous art gallery, and in a few short years she had become a successful businesswoman. Yes, Alex thought confidently to herself, Monica would gladly loan her the money she needed now.

As she neared the cabin, Alex looked around once more. The sky was still awash with bands of deep crimson and orange from the setting sun. The waters of Chulinka Bay reflected the colors, blending them with the cooler tones of blue and green. Shadows had deepened on the flanks of the surrounding mountains and a balmy breeze ruffled her hair, caressing her neck with silky fingers.

Alex smiled with contentment and optimism. She would give Ian McLeod a run for his money. She would do such careful field work and write such a complete and accurate report that the Department of the Interior would be sure to grant protection to the seabird cliffs. Any development nearby would be strictly forbidden.

Suddenly aware of how late it was and how long it had been since she'd eaten, Alex turned toward the cabin. She felt her stomach growl in anticipation of a hot meal.

As she reached for the doorknob, her hand brushed a piece of paper. It was jammed into the crack of the door, and she clutched at it with curiosity as she entered the cabin and switched on the light.

She unfolded the paper and read the brief message. It was addressed to her and had been written in bold, impatient strokes with a black felt-tipped pen. It was from Ian McLeod.

Ms. Gilbert, please come to my office sometime this evening before ten. We need to discuss your field project.

In spite of the "please," the note read like a command. Alex let out a sigh. So she was going to meet him tonight, after all. Oh well, better to get it over with. She glanced at her watch. Deciding that she had plenty of time to eat, do some unpacking and clean up before she had to face the cannery owner, she tucked the note into her pocket and set about her tasks.

The three-room cabin was small and old but serviceable. A tiny kitchen and an even smaller bathroom had obviously been added after the original building had been erected. Some well-worn rugs and faded curtains at the windows gave the place a cozy feeling. The kitchen was stocked with several pots and pans that would come in handy during her stay. She selected the most comfortable bed as her own, made it up and put away the binoculars, notebooks and field guides she would need in her work.

After a relaxing dinner and a shower, Alex walked toward the long building near the dock, a shadowed hulk which she already knew contained the company store, a laundry room and Mr. McLeod's office.

She had changed into a cream-colored blouse and fitted corduroy slacks the hue of ripe wheat. A soft wool shirt in a deep shade of teal blue was flung over her shoulders. The night air felt cool and refreshing after the heat of the afternoon. A multitiude of stars pricked the ebony sky. The only sounds were those of softly rustling grasses that grew beside the path, and the muffled hum from the cannery.

She hesitated at the office door. It was open a few inches, allowing a stream of golden light from within to fall onto the porch. Her heart sped up a bit as she heard movement inside. Telling herself to be as composed and professional as possible, Alex took a deep breath and rapped lightly on the door.

"Come in," a deep masculine voice said. It sounded vaguely familiar to her, but she couldn't place where she'd heard it before.

She pushed the door open and stepped into a comfortable room paneled in wood. It was furnished with a couple of brown leather chairs, a full bookcase and a large desk. Brass boat fittings gleamed from one wall, and a ship's clock and several nautical maps decorated another. An antique brass lamp with a green shade stood on the desk, casting a cozy pool of light onto the rich oak surface.

A dark-haired man sat behind the desk, his back to her as he searched through the open drawer of a handsome oak filing cabinet.

"Have a seat," he said, without looking around. "I'll be with you in a second."

He was wearing jeans and a black wood turtleneck that was molded to the contours of his broad back. Alex caught a glimpse of his profile, and time seemed to stand still for her. To her amazement she suddenly felt as if the room were spinning. The man before her was the fisherman from the warehouse.

But why was *he* here in Mr. McLeod's office? And where was Mr. McLeod? She stood rooted to the spot and her breath became ragged. This *is* Ian McLeod, she realized, and he had played a mean joke on her this afternoon by letting her believe he was just a fisherman.

Her surprise quickly turned to anger as she stared at the back of his handsome head. How dare he! She felt like an absolute idiot and swore to herself that she would never forgive him for his deception.

Ian extracted one of the file folders, closed the drawer and swiveled around in his chair. He laid the folder on his cluttered desk and looked up at her. His blue eyes twinkled with amusement, and that same wolfish smile played around the corners of his mouth.

"We meet again, Ms. Gilbert. Please, have a seat," he said and motioned toward the soft leather chair in front of his desk.

Alex almost stumbled as she hurriedly stepped forward and sank down into the cool leather. Her body was tense and her knees were shaking. In a voice that was low and grating, she said, "Why did you pretend you were a fisherman?"

"Don't put words into my mouth," he answered. "At no time did I say I was a fisherman. You assumed it."

"But the way you're dressed..." Her voice trailed off.

"As you yourself said, Ms. Gilbert, life's full of surprises. Since this is your first time in Alaska, you don't know that people tend to dress casually up here. It fits the image of the last frontier." He chuckled. "Besides, it's much more comfortable." He leaned toward her across his desk, his hands loosely clasped on the papers. "I did try to tell you my name, if you'll recall, but you were very clear about not being interested. So—" he shrugged "—I let you draw your own conclusions."

Alex grasped the smooth arms of the chair. "I feel like a fool."

His expression softened. "Please don't. I'll admit that I knew what you were assuming and did nothing to change your impression. Oh, and I want you to know that your phantom barn swallows flew in just after you left. Your story sounded so wild I had trouble believing it, so I guess I owe you an apology."

How appealing he looks, how handsome, Alex thought as she gazed over at him. One moment he's aggravating, the next disarming. Her heart fluttered as she realized how drawn she was to this man.

She shrugged and allowed herself to laugh softly. "That's okay. In my business, I'm used to people having all sorts of misimpressions about what I do. Birds can be unpredictable, but that's one of the things I like about being an ornithologist."

He leaned back in his chair and looked at her with an expression of keen interest. "How did you get into this field? Like I said earlier, when we...er...bumped into each other, you don't look like an ornithologist."

Alex squirmed in her chair as she felt her face grow warm at the vivid memory of being pressed against his lean, hard body. She answered hurriedly, hoping to hide the emotions his reference had aroused.

"There's a stereotype about bird-watchers and ornithologists, I know. People picture little old ladies in pith helmets and tennis shoes."

"That's it," he said.

"Actually," she continued, "ornithologists come in all shapes, sizes and ages, just like in any other profession. And I've never seen a pith helmet among them."

"So, why you?" he pursued.

"Well, I started out as a high-school biology teacher. I did that for two years," she said.

"In Iowa? You were a farm girl, I'll bet."

"That's right. I grew up on a farm where we raised soybeans and corn, and after college I taught in a town about a hundred miles from home." She was beginning to relax as she answered his questions.

She went on. "I became restless. Being a teacher just wasn't for me. I like to spend lots of time outdoors, and the routine of teaching got to me. I went back to college, earned an M.S. in ornithology—a field I've always been drawn to—and here I am."

"Are you going for your doctorate?" Alex noticed that his intensely blue eyes quickly swept her body as he asked this. It occurred to her that his mind was not entirely on her professional goals. The pace of her breathing increased as she became aware that the atmosphere in the small, intimate room had become charged with excitement. It was as if an electric current were passing from him to her and back again.

Her heart felt as though it was thundering inside her. This must be some sort of instant chemistry, she thought to herself. Did he feel it too? She was stunned by the intensity of her reaction to him. Never before had she felt so sensually aroused by a man, by a stranger who was not even touching her.

"My doctorate?" she repeated. "Yes, that's the next step, then I hope to continue with field research and writing."

"Have you decided on the topic for your thesis yet?"

"No," she said, "I was thinking I'd get some ideas while I was up here. I'm particularly interested in seabirds. This seemed like the perfect place to do an in-depth study."

Ian leaned forward. His words were spoken in a soft, honeyed tone. "I'd like to do an in-depth study of you, Alexandra Gilbert. I find you very attractive."

The air sizzled. An icy-hot shiver shot down her spine.

"Alex." Her voice was a whisper as she stared at him, mesmerized by his intense gaze. "I go by Alex."

"Alex," he repeated, making it sound like a silken caress. "And you must call me Ian. There," he said as he stood up, breaking the spell, "now that we've properly introduced ourselves, I suggest we go up to my cabin."

Her body stiffened in sudden apprehension. Had her ears deceived her?

"I...I beg your pardon?" she choked.

He chuckled. "Take it easy, Alex, I'm not going to se-duce you...yet," he added, giving her a significant look. "Besides, I like to think that I'm a little more subtle than that. Your sweater is at my cabin and I thought you might like to get it."

She was somewhat wary, but his smile was so ingen-uous, his manner so casual, she put aside her doubts. She rose to meet him as he silently came around the desk.

"Okay," she said. "I'll come with you, but I can only spare a few minutes. I've had several long plane rides in the past couple of days, and I'm afraid jet lag is starting to set in."

Ian took her by the elbow and steered her toward the door. She liked the feel of his firm grip on her arm; it al-most seemed like an embrace. The same spicy scent she had noticed in the warehouse wafted to her as he moved beside her. Mixed with it was the fragrance of warm wool from the sweater he wore, and a pleasant, masculine smell that was all his.

Outside Alex noticed that a full moon had risen to just above the horizon. It cast a glimmering streak across the still waters of the bay and infused the air with a silver sheen. She was very aware of Ian's presence as he guided her toward a dark shape perched alone on a rise.

A plaintive cry split the air. It came from the beach near the dock.

"Black-bellied plover," she told him.

"Identifying birds at night by their calls." He whis-tled. "I'm impressed."

She shrugged. "It just takes practice, like anything else."

"Let's talk about your project," he said easily as they walked along.

"Okay, where do you want to begin?" she asked.

"First of all, when is Dr. Harper arriving?"

Uh-oh, Alex thought to herself, here we go. "Well, actually, Ian, that's something I need to talk to you about," she said somewhat nervously. Just get it over with, a little voice in her muttered.

"She's been delayed?"

"Not exactly," said Alex. She took a deep breath and plunged on. "She's not coming at all. She named me leader in her place."

Ian dropped her arm, and they both stopped walking. He turned to face her, his dark head close. His hands were on his hips, his feet apart.

"What do you mean? What happened?" His tone was impatient and she knew he wouldn't like her explanation.

She rushed on. "Well, last week she was visiting a puffin colony on an island off the coast of Maine. She broke her ankle when she stepped into a nesting burrow. She'll be laid up for several weeks. And, rather than cancel the project up here, she put me in charge." She smiled hopefully at him, but she wasn't sure if he could see her expression, and she didn't feel reassured. "I've worked with her for two years. I know I can handle it."

Ian snorted. "She broke her ankle in a puffin burrow. Whatever happened to the good old days when women stayed home and had babies instead of traipsing around the world studying birds and God knows what else!" He shook his head.

Alex bridled at his comments. "Just a minute," she said tartly. "Women have just as much right as men have to pursue anything they like. In fact—"

He cut her off with a wave of his hand. "Calm down, Alex. I agree with you. Let's not have a battle of the sexes out here. I only meant that life was easier when women were a little bit more predictable."

"Easier for men," she said, "but not easier for the women who wanted and needed different things from life than doing housework and taking care of children. I'm glad women have more choices these days."

"Yes, and so am I. Are you listening to me? I said I agree with you. As a matter of fact, I personally find women who are excited about their careers interesting and...provocative." The way he rolled the last word around on his tongue made her catch her breath. "I guess I just feel caught off guard by this development," he continued. "She probably told you I wasn't wild about the idea of your group coming here."

"Yes, she told me," Alex said dryly. She felt her cheeks grow warm as she recalled with some embarrassment Dr. Harper's assessment of Ian, which she had unwittingly quoted to him in the warehouse.

As if reading her mind, he dipped his head closer to her, making her heart flutter, and said, "So she thinks I'm a ladies' man who gets what he wants, does she? Is that what you think, too?"

"Let's just say that I think she's an accurate judge of character, and leave it at that, shall we?" Alex commented with a touch of sarcasm in her tone.

She wished he wasn't standing so close to her. It was unnerving. On the other hand, part of her wished he would fold her in his arms. Such images kept flickering unbidden through her mind, making it difficult for her to concentrate on what he was saying.

He turned from her and looked toward the glittering bay. "The only reason I said yes was because she would be in charge. Besides—" he laughed "—I think that woman could sell combs to bald men." He sighed. "Oh well, I suppose you can handle the job, if she thinks so."

He turned back toward her and again placed one hand on her arm. "Let's grab that sweater and see that you get some sleep tonight."

In a few moments they were standing in the deep shadows of the porch of his cabin. His was the highest cabin in the compound. It commanded an unobstructed view of Chulinka Bay and the slopes that embraced its shores. The ebony sky twinkled with diamonds. His voice came softly from just a few inches behind her. His breath stirred her hair faintly, sending a thrill through her.

"Beautiful," he murmured.

"Yes," she responded a bit breathlessly.

"The view of the island isn't half bad, either," he said. There was laughter in his voice, and she realized that his first pronouncement had been about her, not the scenery. She felt slightly flushed as she realized that he was flirting openly with her. Better keep this relationship businesslike, she warned herself.

Just then, more soft calls drifted up from the shore below.

"There's that bird again," he said. "Do you suppose it's calling its mate? This is a night made for lovers, and it sounds a little lonely to me."

Was it her imagination, or had a slightly wistful tone entered his voice, Alex wondered. She had the impression that he had just revealed more about himself than he'd meant to.

"These particular birds do a lot of their feeding at night, and yes, this one could be calling to its mate," she answered him. "They're probably migrating north, although it does seem late in the season."

She turned toward him and found him standing only inches away from her, his lean frame looming in the darkness.

"I...I'll take my sweater now and leave," she said.

He opened the door for her, reached in and flicked on the light, then motioned for her to enter ahead of him. She glanced around the room and saw that it was small and cozy, like his office. The few pieces of furniture were in earth tones of rich brown and warm rust. Two cream-colored area rugs in a thick, fuzzy pile partially covered a polished hardwood floor. The larger of these rugs lay in front of a stone fireplace. Brass lamps and framed nautical prints completed the decor. Through an open door she could see a small, tidy kitchen. Several copper pans hung over a cream-and-blue tile counter. Another door revealed a large bed covered with an orange-and-brown plaid spread and surrounded by a sea of cream-colored rugs. The bedroom walls were of golden knotty pine.

"Want a tour?"

He smiled engagingly at her. He had obviously caught her staring at his bed. Didn't those piercing blue eyes miss anything?

"No, thanks," she remarked airily. "I can see you have a very comfy place here."

"Oh, it's better than you think," he said. "Through that bedroom is a bathroom with the only tub on the island. If you ever get tired of showers, just tell me, and I'll let you come up here and use it. And," he added with a boyish grin, "I'll let you have the place to yourself. Unless, that is, you want me to stick around to scrub your back."

"You're shameless, do you know that?" She smiled back at him.

"That's me," he agreed. "By the way, your sweater is right behind you on top of that bookcase."

Alex turned and picked it up, then reached for the doorknob. "Well, thanks for saving it for me. I'll say good night now."

It was then that she remembered the events at the radio shack. She'd better let him know about those developments as well. "By the way, there is one other thing you ought to know about our project."

His eyebrows rose slightly. "Oh? And what's that?"

"I'm the team."

"I don't get it," he said, a puzzled expression on his handsome face.

Alex quickly outlined the events of that afternoon.

"Let me get this straight," he said. "Your grant money was canceled, the team disbanded, and you are going to conduct this...this bird count, or whatever it is, all by yourself?" His tone conveyed that he was clearly flabbergasted.

"That's right," she said lightly. "Well, good night." She turned to make a fast exit, but before she reached the door, his hand closed on her arm, stopping her progress.

"Hang on," he said in a low voice that was almost a growl. "This changes things. Stick around a few minutes—we need to talk."

He guided her to a seat, then gently pushed her down onto it. Alex was annoyed. It was getting very late, and all she could think about was crawling into bed for some much needed sleep. What did he have in mind now?

"Want some wine?" he asked as he headed for the kitchen. Without waiting for her to answer, he opened the refrigerator, extractd a bottle of Chablis and poured two small glasses.

He crossed the living room in several long strides and handed a glass to her.

"Cheers," he said, and took a sip as he looked at her over the rim. Then he sank down onto a chair that was a duplicate of the chocolate-brown one she was rigidly sitting on.

"Please make this as brief as you can," she said. "I really am very tired, and I want to be up bright and early tomorrow so I can get out to the seabird cliffs." She sipped the cool liquid and found it just to her taste.

He watched her in silence, sipping his wine. His long legs were stretched out casually in front of him, his ankles crossed. He seemed to be deep in thought. Finally he spoke in a controlled voice, his words measured.

"You're not going to like what I'm about to tell you, Alex, but it needs to be said. You're leaving on the plane tomorrow."

The silence in the small room was almost palpable. Alex thought she'd heard incorrectly. There was some mistake here.

"No," she said, "you don't understand. My sister will lend me money, and I'm sure Dr. Harper will give her okay for me to stay on alone. I'm not going anywhere tomorrow except out into the field to begin my work."

"You seem pretty sure about all these last-minute arrangements." He made a short, impatient sound.

"Yes, I am," Alex said confidently. "Monica and I have always been able to count on each other, and I know there will be absolutely no problem with the money.

"As for Dr. Harper, she put me in charge, so she obviously believes I can handle the job up here. I'm sure she'll say yes because it's such an important project. I think she'll be pleased to learn I'm willing to stay on and do it alone."

Ian's voice took on a too-patient tone that rankled her. As if explaining something to a child, he said, "Alex, as much as I'd love to see you stay for my own selfish reasons, I'm afraid I must insist that you be on that plane tomorrow." Calmly, he sipped his wine.

It was too much! He was actually telling her what to do! He had no right to do that. The incongruity of his attitude suddenly struck her, and she threw back her head and laughed.

"What's so damned funny?" he asked her in a tone of some annoyance.

"You are," she said, looking over at his frowning face. "You can't order me around. I told you I've arranged to continue the project, and that's just what I intend to do. Period."

His blue eyes narrowed, and he gave her a look that told her he wouldn't take being crossed lightly—by her or anyone else. She braced herself for what was to come. He put his glass down and leaned forward.

"You're talking like a fool. Have you any idea what you're getting into up here? Do you know how difficult it would've been for four people to do what you have in mind, let alone how dangerous it would be for you alone? Ever hear of the williwaw, for example?"

"No. Don't tell me you're going to try to scare me with an Aleutian version of Bigfoot?"

"Very funny, Ms. Gilbert," he flung at her. "We'll see who's laughing when the weather changes suddenly, as it tends to do up here, and the williwaw catches you out in the field all by yourself. It's a hurricane-force wind that blows in off the Bering Sea, with gusts up to one hundred fifty miles per hour. I've seen williwaws tear roofs off buildings, toss barges up onto beaches like they were so many toys, and knock people right off their feet." He leaned farther forward. "Last summer one blew in and three boats disappeared in it. Never did find out what happened to them, or to their crews." His voice dwindled to a whisper. "They just vanished."

"You *are* trying to scare me," she said, attempting to make her voice sound scornful.

"You're damned right I am," he said heatedly. "I can't be worrying about some greenhorn wandering all over this island by herself. When the salmon really start coming in, this place gets very busy, and I get busy right along with it. I can't be responsible for what could happen to you.

"And there's more," he continued, ticking the items off on his fingers. "You could fall off a cliff. That happened to a guy a couple years back. We found his broken body the next day. If you go out in a boat, you could be swept out to sea, overturned, lost, blown away. The terrain around here is spongy and full of holes. You could step into one of those holes and break an ankle—just like Dr. Harper—making it impossible for you to get back here. One night spent outside, especially if a storm blew in, would finish you off. And if you fall into the water, your chances of survival are nil. The water's so cold up here, even in summer, that an average person can last *maybe* twenty minutes. That is, unless a heart attack from the shock of the cold doesn't kill you first.

"A four-person team was one thing, three were okay, but you all by yourself? Uh-uh. Pack your stuff and be ready to leave tomorrow."

Her voice was husky as she responded to him. "Quite a speech. I wonder if you act like such a mother hen toward your employees."

"My employees don't run around by themselves on this island!" he exploded. "If they wander away from the compound, they go in groups. It's too dangerous, too isolated here to do otherwise, and they know that.''

Alex could see that Ian's mind was definitely made up. Her only hope of staying lay in the plan that had formed in her mind while he had been itemizing Anfesia's many hazards. Taking a deep breath, she made her bold suggestion.

"I see your point,'' she said calmly. "I'll hire a guide.'' Silently she wondered how big of a dent the fee for such a service would put into her finances. "If I had a guide,'' she continued, "you wouldn't have to worry about my safety, would you?''

His eyes narrowed as he appeared to consider her idea. "Just where are you going to get a guide?'' he challenged her.

"Well, I...'' her voice faltered. "I'm sure I can find someone in Kodiak who'd be willing to...''

Ian snorted. "On your severely restricted funding, believe me, Alex, you can't afford to pay any of the professional guides I know of. Besides,'' he said with an impatient wave of his hand, "none of those guys would even consider taking on the kind of job you have in mind.''

"Well, then, what about someone from right here?'' she pressed, beginning to feel a little panicky. "Couldn't I pay one of your workers to show me around the island, at least part of the time? I know we can work something out, if you'll just—''

He cut in. "No. Absolutely not,'' he said with a firm shake of his head. "When this place starts jumping, I need every single pair of hands and then some. I couldn't possibly spare anyone.'' His face took on a placating expression. "Face it, Alex, your project is canceled. There will be other chances for you to lead a field study.''

He paused, staring at her when she failed to respond. "Am I getting through to you?"

Alex slowly put down her wine and stood up. She slipped on her jacket and walked to the door. Then she turned to face him.

"Oh, you're getting through to me, all right, Mr. McLeod." She ground out his name as she looked up into his eyes, for by now he was on his feet, too. "This whole discussion has been a smoke screen, hasn't it? If you were really concerned about my personal safety, you'd make sure I had a guide. Instead, you find every excuse you can think of to prevent my staying. I offer solutions to the problem, and you throw up roadblocks." She hesitated, then pressed on before she lost her nerve. "You know that my report on the seabird cliffs could prevent you from building the crab plant you have in mind, and that's what *really* worries you. You don't care what happens to the environment, as long as you're making money."

"Now wait a minute," he snapped back. "You've got this all wrong, damn it. I make my living off the environment. I have to care about it, and I do. But that doesn't change the fact that this is a very dangerous place, and I don't—"

Alex held up her hand, "You've convinced me, okay? So I'll be very careful." She paused, then continued confidently. "You'd like to see me run scared, leaving an important wild area to its fate, wouldn't you? Well, you can't frighten me that easily. I came to do a job, and I intend to do it. Thanks for the wine. Good night."

She walked out the door, but before she could get off the porch, he caught up with her. He grabbed her by one arm and swung her around to look at him. Her heart began to race wildly at being this close to his tensed, lean body. He exuded power. There was a dangerous look on his face, and she wondered if she'd pushed him too far.

"You're dreaming," he said in a low voice that had leashed fury in it. His eyes narrowed, glinting at her like shards of blue glass. "I already own the land near the cliffs. Don't you know that I'll build that plant whether or not you or anyone else writes some half-baked report about those seabirds? I was trained as a lawyer, Alex, and I know how to get what I want. I said I was concerned about your safety, and that's exactly what I meant. I don't like having other interpretations given to what I say. I expect to be taken at face value."

Alex felt tremors of heat where his tightly gripping hand held her arm. Suddenly she knew he meant every word, but only to herself did she admit that his impassioned speech had awed her.

He gave her a little shake and drew her closer to him. His breath was on her face. Her senses reeled at being so close to his broad chest and angular face. Her breathing was rapid and shallow.

"You'll be on that plane tomorrow if I have to put you on it myself." His promise was almost a whisper in the charged atmosphere created by their two battling wills.

Recklessly she flung up at him, "Then I guess you'll have to, because I'm not leaving."

"Why, you stubborn little—"

He grasped her firmly with both hands and pulled her to him. His mouth was on hers before she knew what was happening. His lips demanded that she respond. They bore down upon her mouth, coaxing her lips apart to allow his questing tongue entrance. She felt her knees become weak and unsteady as he explored the moist interior in a way no man had ever done. She had never been kissed like this, and she felt herself becoming unbearably aroused. Her hands reached up to grasp him around the neck and she felt his strength beneath his sweater.

Still his mouth moved on hers, his teeth nipping gently at her lips, a low moan rumbling from deep in his throat. One hand moved slowly, touching her intimately and firmly in the small of her back, causing her to bend like a willow wand into the curve of his body. His mouth was a burning brand as it trailed kisses along the column of her throat.

"You're the most aggravating woman I've ever met," he growled against her temple. Then he buried his face in her hair. "See what you do to me, Alex?" he said huskily, his hands caressing her lower back and hips.

She was panting as she pushed him away from her. Thoroughly shaken by his intensity and by her eager response to it, she looked up at him with a feeling of wonder.

He said to her, "I only spend the summer up here. The rest of the year I live in Seattle. Promise me you'll meet me there in the fall. I hate to see you leave, but I'm sure you can see it's for the best."

Gathering her courage, Alex stepped out of the circle of his arms and replied, "I'm staying, Ian, and neither scary stories nor romantic pressure will keep me from doing what I came here to do. Good night."

Before he could respond, she stepped off the porch and hastened down the dark path toward her cabin.

"We'll see about that," his voice rumbled to her on the soft breeze.

Chapter Three

It was chilly the next morning when Alex's alarm clock jangled her awake at five o'clock. No sooner had her feet hit the little rag rug beside her bed than she recalled the events of the night before. She touched her lips as she played back in her mind the way Ian had kissed her. Shivers ran up her arms, not entirely from the coolness of the room. Her instincts told her there would be some kind of confrontation with Ian today. She hastened out of bed, eager to get away from such unsettling thoughts.

Forty-five minutes later she was striding down the path that led away from the compound toward the north side of the island. Binoculars hung around her neck. Her small pack contained food for later, for she meant to stay out all day, getting her bearings and deciding how best to conduct her research. Also in her bag were dark glasses, a spotting scope and collapsed tripod, two field guides and a notebook and pencils. A rain poncho and some emergency flares were stuffed into the side pockets. Her camera gear was in another bag that hung down at her side.

She'd dressed in layers so she could strip off the sweater and jacket later if the weather warmed up. She wore a yellow Shetland wool sweater over a cotton shirt, jeans, wool jacket and hiking boots.

She had tied her heavy hair in a loose ponytail, but already several strands had worked themselves free and were blowing across her cheeks and forehead. She brushed them away, looking up as she did so. Although it was still chilly, the sky was clear and blue. A few wispy clouds hung far off on the horizon. No williwaw today, she mused wryly. That man is a real alarmist.

She consulted the map Dr. Harper had drawn for her. The trail to the seabird cliffs was a short one, less than two miles. It was obvious that not many people came out this way. The path was faint and hard to follow in places. It was heavily edged with a dense thicket of tall grass and other wild plants. Alex knew there were no trees on the island, but some of the willow shrubs and fleshy plants grew to above her head. Moisture clinging to leaves dampened her jean legs as she pushed her way past the branches and grass blades that hung over the trail. Heather and tiny purple violets bloomed in profusion, adding spots of color to the lush green foliage.

Soon she had thrown off her early-morning feeling of fatigue. She had not slept particularly well last night. Her two encounters with Ian, especially the second one, had left her shaken and unable to relax. The clean, pure air that blew off the water refreshed and revived her. She took deep breaths, savoring its tangy fragrance. It was great to be alive and out in the field at last, doing what she loved best.

Alex heard the seabird colony before she saw it. A babel of raucous calls and piercing cries reached her ears while she was still on the trail and behind a hillock. She rounded a bend and saw the source of this tumult of combined bird voices.

In the near distance, the land ended abruptly, falling off to the sea that stretched to the far horizon. An expanse of flat stone, dotted with boulders of all sizes, marked the boundary between land and air. The gray of the stones was heavily splashed with the whitewash left by the comings and goings of tens of thousands of seabirds. Alex could see that the air above the cliffs was a swirling mass of gulls, kittiwakes and puffins. Never in all her life had she witnessed such a spectacular concentration of wildlife. For many moments she was breathless, entranced, unable to move.

Near the cliffs, she dropped her pack and camera bag and took off her jacket. She had warmed up during her trek, and the sun had climbed higher in the sky and was heating her back and head. She walked closer to the cliffs until she could look right over the edge. As she did so, the seabirds increased their clamor. Hundreds more rose into the air, beating their slender wings and calling at the top of their lungs. Their myriad voices echoed against the stone walls.

She peered down to the foot of the cliffs. She estimated it to be more than a hundred foot drop. The precipice ended in a jumble of jagged stones below. Those would make for a nasty landing, she thought to herself, and moved back a step. Heavy surf crashed onto the rocks, sending driftwood and huge clumps of kelp up onto the boulders with each wave. Her face was soon dampened by spindrift, which was carried to her on the breeze.

Off to the left, the rocks thinned out, leaving a small, curved beach of sand and gravel. The water nearest the shore looked dark blue to Alex, indicating great depth. She knew that this was where Ian meant to build his crab plant. The thought made her sigh with irritation.

Turning her attention back to the rookery, she sat down to watch the colonizing birds. Hundreds of seabirds circled above her head or flew out to the water to feed. The cliffs were comprised of many deep canyons of rock and earth. The walls were thickly dotted with nests. Every available niche and toehold, every grassy clump, had been claimed by a pair of black-legged kittiwakes or common murres.

This incredible abundance of life would be placed in terrible jeopardy if Ian McLeod went ahead with his plan, and it appeared that he had every intention of doing so. She had to do all she could to make him see what a dreadful mistake it would be to develop a site that was of such importance to so many seabirds.

There were good reasons why seabirds nested in remote areas, she reflected to herself. Human encroachment spelled a colony's doom. Once the crab plant was in place, the noise and activity would agitate the birds and might even affect the egg-laying cycle. Alex could also imagine workers, innocent in their curiosity, hiking up to the nearby colony on their coffee breaks. The frequent pressure from human visitors would surely disrupt the colony's natural routine. Then there were the idiots who couldn't resist throwing a rock or bottle to see the birds' reaction....

Alex set aside these disturbing thoughts and gazed out at the ocean. She could see some fishing boats on the horizon, presumably heading out for a day of purse seining for salmon. She could smell a pleasing combination of fish, kelp and salt tang as she breathed deeply of the cool breezes.

Her reverie was suddenly interrupted. "Alex," a male voice called out from behind. Looking around, she saw Dan ambling down the path toward her. She rose to meet him and walked back from the cliff edge.

She could see that the older man was a bit winded from his exertions. He stopped a few feet away from her and mopped his forehead with a red hankie. Patting his wide middle, he laughed and said to her, a bit breathlessly, "Whew! I'm not used to this much exercise, especially early in the morning. I need to lose about fifty pounds before I become a hiker."

Alex smiled at him. "I'm pleased that you came out, Dan. I didn't know you were interested in birds."

He coughed slightly and shifted his weight from one foot to the other. "Well, actually, Alex, I'm not here for the birds. I came out to give you a message from Ian."

She was instantly alert and on guard. "What kind of message?" she asked warily.

He glanced away from her with a nervous look. "He ran into me this morning as he was coming back from your cabin. He was pretty upset to find that you'd already gotten up and headed out here. I guess he thought you'd sleep later than you did."

"I always get up early when I'm doing field work."

"Yeah, well, he wanted to catch you before you could do that, and tell you about the change in today's seaplane schedule."

She turned and looked out to sea, folding her arms across her chest. "That won't affect me, Dan. I'm not going to be needing a plane for several weeks."

Another nervous cough. "Look, Alex, Ian told me that he ordered you off the island. I'm really sorry about it. You seem like such a nice person." He paused. "Well, anyway, I can see his point, I guess. This is a pretty dangerous place for someone to be all alone day after day. I mean, what if you fell off one of these cliffs? You'd never sur—"

She turned toward him, cutting him off. "Now, don't you start on me, too."

He put up a hand and shook his head. "Okay, I won't. You probably know what you're doing and can handle the solitude. I'm just saying that I can see why Ian's concerned about your safety."

Dan continued despite Alex's glower over his last words. "There's something you should know about Ian. He feels responsible for everyone on this island. For years he had his own law practice in Seattle and came up here only for visits. His parents built this business from scratch. His dad was one of those self-made men, if you know what I mean. Anyway, his folks died in a plane crash just about three years ago, and Ian made the decision to take over running the canneries."

He paused in his narrative. For a few moments, the only sounds were those of the crying seabirds and the crashing of the waves below. Alex squinted against the glare of the sun on the water and tried to absorb what Dan was saying. She found herself deeply interested in hearing about Ian and his background.

"Go on," she said.

"Well, Ian was pretty broken up when his folks died. He didn't show it to most people, but I've known him since he was a little guy, and I could tell their deaths hit him pretty hard."

Alex felt a stab of sympathy for Ian and nodded, silently asking Dan to continue.

"He'd never shown much interest in running the business, but when they died he jumped right in and took over. I think it's because he thought so much of his mom and dad—admired them, you know—that he really threw himself into this work. He left the running of his law firm to his two partners, and he's been doing this ever since. He told me that it's kind of grown on him and that he's come to love it. He's good at it, too." The admiration in Dan's voice was apparent.

"And he believes that doing a good job, being a success at this, extends to being responsible for his workers and anyone else who happens to be here?" Alex asked.

"Yes, I think he does," Dan said. "He wants nothing to go wrong, and he won't take chances with other people's lives, if he can avoid it. Too many accidents can happen in this far-off corner of the world for a person to be anything but very cautious."

"All right, so he worries about the people here." She sighed a bit impatiently. "What was the message he wanted to give to me?"

"Oh, yeah. The seaplane will be a little early today. You only have about two hours to pack up and get ready to leave."

Alex felt her jaw tighten as she said to him, "Dan, you can go back and tell Mr. Worrywart that I have a right to be here, and that I'm staying until I finish this project. Someone needs to do an adequate report on this incredible seabird colony. And I think I'm just the person to do it."

"You're probably wasting your time trying to get this place—" he waved his hand to indicate the cliffs "—made into a special sanctuary. Ian is determined to see that his dream becomes reality. He's not a person you'd want to cross."

"Neither am I, Dan," she said in a soft voice. "Neither am I." In spite of her brave front, she trembled inside to think of what Ian might do when he learned that her determination to work on the project alone had not diminished.

Dan gazed out to sea, a thoughtful look on his face. "You know, I'll never forget when Ian first came up with this dream of his. He and I were sitting in the mess hall late one night talking to some crab fishermen. They were commenting on how much money could be made in the new tanner and spider crab markets." Dan chuckled. "You should have seen Ian's eyes light up—just like his dad's used to when he got a bright idea. I could almost see the wheels clicking away in his head. Ian's a born businessman. He's the kind of person who sees possibilities, Alex. The next day he flew to Kodiak to talk to some contractors. And he's been planning and looking forward to this project ever since."

Dan put a kindly hand on her arm. "Look, Alex, take a little friendly advice. Be on that plane today. It's for your own good."

She chuckled ruefully. "There are times when I don't do what may be for my own good, Dan." She patted his hand. "Thanks for dropping by. I've enjoyed your company, if not the message from your boss. See you later." And with that, she turned and walked back down toward the cliffs.

"Okay, Alex," he called after her. "I hope you know what you're doing."

She spent the next hour deciding where she would set up her portable blind for some in-depth studies of particular nests and their inhabitants. She explored several of the promontories and shot a couple of rolls of film with various lenses. The longer she was there the more

excited she became about the work that lay before her.
Intruding upon her concentration from time to time were
thoughts of Ian. Her stomach fluttered each time she
imagined what his reaction would be when Dan told him
he'd been unable to persuade her to catch that plane.

The sun had warmed the land considerably, and she
had peeled off her sweater, letting the cooling sea breezes
waft among the folds of her thin blouse. She was sitting
on a grassy bank writing in one of her notebooks when a
different noise caught her attention. It sounded like a
motor.

Shading her eyes with one hand, she looked left, in the
direction of the sandy beach. A small motorboat was
headed her way. It looked like it was being driven at full
throttle, for it sped along in the water, its front end al-
ternately rising and slapping down hard on the surface.
Someone's in a big hurry, she thought. A lone man was
in the boat. As Alex watched, he cut back on the engine
and slewed the boat around until it was nosing in toward
the sandy crescent. She lifted her binoculars and peered
down at her visitor. It was Ian and he looked angry.

She lowered her glasses and jumped to her feet. For
one panicky moment, she considered running up the
path, away from the cliffs. If she hurried, she could
probably pack just what she needed for the trip and still
be on that plane.

Then she scolded herself. How ridiculous. She wasn't
going to bend so easily. Calm down, she told herself.
How bad can this be? Pretty bad, said a small, frightened voice within her. Her fingers gripped her binoculars until her knuckles showed white.

She took a couple of deep breaths to ease her jumping
nerves and to slow down her increased respiration. She

forced herself to look at Ian's lean body as he leapt into shallow water and dragged the boat onto the beach. The hull made a grating sound as he slid it across the coarse sand and gravel. He tied the boat's rope to a large rock, then turned in Alex's direction and looked up, one tan hand shading his eyes. Alex felt that intense gaze pierce her like a bolt of lightning. He began taking long, purposeful strides up the beach toward the earthen bank behind it. He was headed right for her, and coming fast.

Alex felt her stomach lurch with apprehension. She'd never liked confrontations of any kind, but the two she'd already experienced with this assertive man had shown her that all of her previous ones had been child's play. He meant business, no doubt about it. She felt her knees go wobbly, so she sat down, laid her binoculars down, and fumbled with her notebook. She wanted to appear busy and unconcerned when Ian reached her.

Within moments he was standing over her, his breathing ragged from climbing the bank and rushing over the rough terrain to the cliffs. His tall shadow fell across her notebook.

She looked up and managed a shaky smile. "Good morning. I was just—"

"Get up."

His growling voice was low and menacing. There was a grim look on his face, and his lips were set in a hard line. A muscle in his jaw twitched with tension. The breeze had mussed his hair. Alex couldn't help but feel a surge of attraction toward him, in spite of his obvious irritation. Those locks of wavy dark hair falling onto his forehead gave him such an appealingly disheveled appearance.

He stood with legs wide apart, hands on hips. His athletic thighs looked firm under his snug jeans. He wore a forest-green wool shirt with rolled up sleeves revealing tanned forearms and strong wrists. The sight of the curling dark hair visible at his open shirt neck and on his arms hit Alex with a thump of desire, almost causing her to forget why he'd come. She stared transfixed at him for a moment, unsure of what to say or do.

"I said, get up, Alex. We're through playing games."

He reached down as if to haul her to her feet, and she flinched away from his grasp.

"Thanks," she said icily. "I can manage."

She rose up and found herself staring into cold, blue eyes that were only a few inches away from hers. They were hooded, and they flickered with warning. She felt her heart speed up at being this close to the man who had kissed her with such intensity the night before.

He turned from her and glanced around. "Is this all your stuff?" he asked gruffly as he nodded toward her pack and camera bag.

She nodded in assent.

"Fine, then. Pack it up and let's get going."

"Now, just a minute—" she started, but he cut her off with a wave of his hand.

"We don't have time to debate this, Alex. The plane will be here ahead of schedule today, and you will be on it."

"I'm not going, Ian. Can't you get that through your stubborn head!" Her voice had risen with determination.

"Like I said," he continued in an even, low voice that only hinted at the strong emotions he held in check, "we don't have time for discussion. Pick up your stuff and follow me to the boat."

As if he fully expected her to meekly pad after him, he turned and started striding toward the beach. Alex watched his broad back without moving.

When he glanced behind him and found her still rooted to the spot, he frowned and started back. Her body tensed with dread. Something told her she had gone too far.

"I...I'm not going, Ian." she stammered when he stopped a few feet away from her. Reckless courage swept over her. Looking him straight in the eyes, she flung her words at him. "I told you last night, the only way you're going to get me on that plane is if you carry me. Now, if you'll excuse me, I have to get back to my work."

She turned away from his glowering face and took a step in the direction of her pack. Without warning, he had reached her in a silent stride and grabbed her from behind.

"Have it your own way. I've never been one to ignore such an obvious challenge. Up you go!"

Alex felt her feet leave the ground as Ian grasped her with powerful arms and swung her easily across one broad shoulder. She found herself suspended unceremoniously, legs dangling down his chest, her rear poked up into the air. Her top half hung down his back, and she found herself staring at his firm buttocks and narrow hips.

"Put me down!" she screeched at him, hitting ineffectually at his broad back and kicking her feet.

He had already started to walk toward the beach. His strong hands firmly held on to her thighs, and Alex felt an electric shock travel through her at his intimate touch.

"Stop kicking," he ordered, not in the least perturbed by her struggles.

"This is absurd!" she protested hotly. "You can't get away with this! Let me down immediately, you bully!"

"I've never used force on a woman before," he retorted calmly, "and I'm not sure I approve of it now. But you shouldn't dare me, Alex. I'll always call your bluff."

"I...I didn't," she panted.

He chuckled throatily. "Oh, yes, you did, lady. You wanted me to pick you up. I think you like sparring with me."

Alex suddenly felt her already hot face flush even more as she realized that there was a grain of truth in what he said. Something in her became excited by the power of his personality. All previous men in her life seemed bland and passive compared to him. She was stunned by her insight and knew that it was accurate. But she wasn't about to let him know that. She wouldn't give him the satisfaction.

She was about to open her mouth to hurl more protests into the air when he stepped into a hole and lost his balance. Holding her firmly, as if to cushion her fall, he tumbled to the ground, taking her with him. They rolled together into a grassy depression that was sheltered from the wind.

Seeing her chance to escape, Alex scrambled to her hands and knees and started crawling over the edge of the soft bowl. A band of firm fingers grasped her ankle and hauled her back. Ian flipped her over so that she was looking up. She was potently aware of his long length stretched out beside her. She felt overheated, and they were both panting.

For many moments time seemed to stand still as she stared up at one of the most appealing sights she'd ever seen. A perfect blue sky stretched overhead, dotted in many places with calling birds. Lush plants leaned in all around the edges of the depression, forming a protected, hidden spot that was lined with spongy heather and soft moss. And mere inches above her heated face loomed Ian's head. His blue eyes gazed down at her with such smoldering intensity that her heart raced. She felt her mouth soften into a smile in spite of her lingering annoyance with him.

With a low moan, he dipped his tousled head and lightly, gently kissed her at the base of her throat. She looked down and saw that the top button of her blouse had come undone, exposing the upper swell of her breasts. As if unable to resist, Ian dropped his head lower and pressed warm kisses there, causing her to grasp his hair with both hands and twine her fingers in its thickness.

"You're a witch, do you know that?" he murmured as his firm mouth continued to nibble and tease her heated skin. "You make me do things I've never done before. I've never met a woman like you. One minute I want to send you packing, and the next I want to carry you to the nearest bed and ravish you for a week."

Alex caught her breath at these bold words. The sudden mental image of them entwined was so powerful, it hit her like a blow to the chest.

"Oh, Ian," she whispered into his hair, which smelled faintly of some kind of spicy soap. "This is crazy. We don't even know each other."

He lifted his head from where it had been buried between her breasts and gazed deeply into her eyes. "Some people might think it's crazy, Alex, but I don't. Can't you feel the attraction we have for each other? Didn't you notice it the first time we were together, in the warehouse? You can't tell me you didn't."

As if to punctuate his words, he brushed his mouth back and forth against hers, causing her lips to part in a low moan of desire. He teased her lips farther apart, then lightly touched them with the tip of his moist tongue, sending flashes of heat through her. He rolled over on top of her and she arched her back, pressing up against him.

Her body was covered by his lean frame. He held her head, one hand on either side. Her hair had come undone; she could feel that it formed a soft pillow that framed her face. Just when she thought she couldn't stand any more of his teasing movements on her mouth, he fastened his lips to hers, biting gently and thrusting his tongue inside. He seemed to be unable to get enough of her mouth as he explored its sweetness with a fervor that fanned her with desire.

Her head swam with the many exquisite sensations that coursed through her. Is this what she had been missing all of her twenty-six years? What on earth had she ever seen in the other men who had passed through her life?

"Sweet," he murmured. "So sweet."

She could feel the male hardness of his urgency pressing against her thigh. But this is too fast, too fast, she told herself. With an effort, she dragged her mouth away from his.

"If I'm a witch, then you're a sorcerer," she said huskily. "You must have put something into the drinking water up here to make me act like this. I think we should get up."

He groaned, disappointment apparent in his voice. "As you like, but don't think you've heard the last from me," he growled into her hair, sending shivers down her spine.

He moved off her and leaned back against the bank. She sat up, brushed her hair from her face and adjusted her blouse.

Alex took a deep breath and latched on to the first sane thought that entered her numbed brain. "Remember, Ian McLeod, we're still adversaries. Nothing has changed. I'm determined to fight you all the way about that crab plant."

A dark cloud seemed to cross his face as he looked out over the edge of the grassy bowl toward the seabird colony before his gaze returned to her.

"And you're wasting your time trying to stop progress, Alex. Has it occurred to you that you may be completely wrong about things? I think those birds will keep right on nesting there even after the plant is built."

"Well, I don't," she retorted. "This kind of area is so fragile. The noise and activity would have a very damaging effect on the rookery."

He brushed off his hands and stood up, then reached down to help her to her feet. The roughness of his palms and fingers felt warm and familiar. He leaned down and pressed a final kiss on her lips.

"One last try," he said. "Are you coming with me so you can catch that plane?"

"You're absolutely unbelievable!" She laughed. "Not even your caveman tactics have changed my mind, Ian. I'm staying, and that's final."

For a moment she thought some of his old anger was returning, then his expression softened with resignation. "All right, I'll let up on you about it for now, but I think you're making a big mistake."

He climbed up out of the depression, and Alex followed suit. He turned toward her, his attractively mussed hair silhouetted by the sun.

"I think you're being foolish. You have no idea what it can be like up here in this wilderness."

"I'm willing to learn," she responded.

"Oh, you'll learn," he said grimly. As he turned away and started back down the bank, he added, "And you'll regret your decision; I can promise you that, Alex."

Chapter Four

True to his word, Ian did let up on Alex during the next several days. They ran into each other occasionally, but not once did he try to persuade her to give up her project. She felt deeply grateful for that and relieved. It felt good to have the pressure of his insistence gone from their encounters. Perhaps he had finally accepted her decision.

In the meantime, the money had arrived from her sister, and Dr. Harper had sent a message for Alex to proceed with her plan. "The best of luck to you," the great ornithologist had added.

Alex settled into a pleasant routine. Each day she got up at dawn, ate a hasty breakfast, then headed into the field. She spent a great deal of her time at the seabird colony, taking copious notes while she observed from the blind, and photographing particular nests and their downy babies. At the end of each day, she sank into bed happily exhausted and instantly fell asleep.

Anfesia was a small island so it was easy to explore it on foot. She covered its length and breadth, taking notes on the bird life she encountered in its many habitats. Every day was an adventure.

Although her experiences in the field were wonderfully stimulating and absorbing, Alex began to feel a certain restlessness. At first the sensation merely tweaked at the outer corners of her mind. Sometimes she attributed the feeling to hunger or fatigue, but soon found that taking a break from her work did nothing to quell the sensation.

One sunny afternoon, as she sat on a bluff overlooking Chulinka Bay, she tried to pinpoint the cause of her restlessness. Was she homesick? Maybe a little, although letters flowed pretty regularly between her and her parents and sister Monica. While it wasn't the same as dialing the phone and hearing their voices, the letters did keep her in touch with the happenings back home. No, she felt sure that homesickness wasn't what was nagging at her. What could it be, then? She did feel a little lonely, she admitted to herself. Although she loved her work, the solitary aspect of it did have its drawbacks.

She gazed down at the bay and the cannery compound clustered on its shore. She could see people walking on the dock. Two women in white aprons stood on an outside catwalk washing the cannery windows, and some fishermen carrying grocery bags were emerging from the company store. Idly Alex wondered where Ian was right now. She noticed with some interest that her pulse quickened at the thought of him. She stopped to think about her reaction, and realized that she recognized it. Whenever she thought about Ian, her interest level rose a few notches. Maybe her "restlessness" wasn't that at all. Maybe she was wishing she could see Ian and was looking forward to their next meeting, whenever that might be. It felt as if a lot of time had passed since she'd heard the sound of his deep voice or felt the rough texture of his hands and the warmth of his mouth.

She wondered when she would see him again. She knew he was busy. The salmon season was now in full swing, and Chulinka Bay hummed with the comings and goings of boats as they delivered fish, then chugged out for more. The cannery seemed to be operating virtually around the clock. Workers and engineers scurried about getting the fragile product processed and packed safely in cans.

Ian seemed busiest of all. On the few occasions she'd seen him, he'd been able to spare only a minute or two to exchange some hurried words. Then off he'd dash, usually heading down the dock to the loading area. Twice he apologized for being in such a mad rush and Alex saw, or imagined she saw, a look of regret and desire pass across his face. She wondered if he thought about her as much as she thought about him. She also wondered if his apparent preoccupation with work was because of the sudden spell of heavy fishing, or if he was trying to avoid her. Thoughts of the latter possibility made her unhappy. He might be trying to stay away from her because he was still displeased with her decision to cross him and stay on.

Standing up and brushing herself off, Alex shook such musings from her mind. She must put all of her energy into her work, she told herself sternly. It wouldn't do to become emotionally involved with a man with whom she had such basic philosophical clashes.

It rained hard most of the day. The wind howled and whipped the bay into a froth. At first Alex thought the storm might be a williwaw, but some cannery workers assured her that it wasn't. She spent many hours in her cabin, typing her notes and mapping out which areas of the island she would cover when the weather cleared.

When the sun came out in the late afternoon, heating the roofs of the compound buildings until they steamed, Alex walked along the dock to stretch her legs which were cramped from the long hours spent at her typewriter. Gulls arranged themselves on the pilings, screaming loudly at the workers as they spilled out for a coffee break. She stopped to chat briefly with some young women who were tossing pieces of cinnamon rolls to the begging gulls. Then she saw a familiar figure at the end of the pier and her heart skipped a beat. It was Ian.

He was talking to one of the fishermen. Seeing her, he motioned for her to join him. The fisherman finished what he was saying, then swung his rubber-booted legs over the edge of the dock and climbed down a ladder to his boat. Almost immediately, the boat, a trim little craft named the *Maryanno*, had its engines gunned and was chugging out into the bay.

As she walked toward him, Alex was reminded of how much Ian looked like a fisherman. Today he wore snug, faded jeans that rode low on his narrow hips. His leather belt was fastened with a plain brass buckle. A black watch cap sat amid his mass of wavy, dark hair, and a red-and-yellow plaid shirt completed the picture. The shirt was open at the neck and rolled up at the sleeves. Very sexy, she observed to herself. She knew he'd also have terrific presence in a three-piece suit. In fact, he was a man who could pull off any style with aplomb and dash.

"Hi there, witch. I've missed you," Ian said when she was within a few feet of him.

Her heart seemed to skip a beat when she heard the endearment. In her mind's eye, she could recall in sharp detail their intense kisses at the seabird cliffs.

He was smiling down at her with a wicked grin, and for a moment she thought he might sweep her into his arms right there in front of all the cannery workers. But the moment passed. Part of her was relieved, part of her disappointed. Once again, her emotions warred within her. It happened every time he got near her, she thought ruefully.

"Good afternoon," she said to him, smiling.

His eyes swept down her body and up again, quickly, appreciatively. "You look fantastic," he murmured, roguish humor twinkling in his eyes. "Did you dress that way for me?"

She glanced down at her clothes. She wore fitted tan slacks that hugged her long legs and a teal-colored turtleneck, whose vertical ribbing accentuated the fullness of her breasts. A wool jacket was thrown loosely over her shoulders.

She could feel her cheeks color slightly at his words. Trying to cover her mild embarrassment, she swept some strands of hair from her face. She was wearing it loose and had brushed it until it shone. She wondered if her unusually careful preparations, just to take a stroll, had unconsciously been because she'd hoped she would run into him.

"You flatter yourself, Mr. McLeod," she replied with mock archness. "I suppose you're used to having women fall down at your feet."

"I've had my share," he said in a low voice, that same wicked grin creasing his face. "But it's funny—I can't remember even one of them anymore."

Alex suddenly felt flustered, and she hastily changed the subject. "I've noticed that the cannery's been pretty busy the past few days."

"That's right. But things will slacken off now for a day or two because of the storm. The boats can't fish in weather like that."

"Will the cannery stop altogether?" she asked.

"Oh, no, we've still got plenty of fish. We store them until we can get them cleaned and processed." His face lit up. "Say, if you're really interested, I could give you a tour."

"You mean, right now?"

"Sure. This is the first real break I've had in days, and I'd love to spend it with you, Alex."

Her heart increased its pace as she listened to his words. All thoughts that he might have been avoiding her vanished. She smiled happily at him. "Thanks. I'd enjoy that. Lead on."

Just then she heard the excited twittering of the barn swallows. Looking up, she saw one of them fly out through the broken window.

"Oh, by the way," she said, "do you mind if I go back up there to check on the swallows? I'd like to get some pictures of their nestlings."

He took her by one arm and leaned close to her. "Lady, you have my permission to go anywhere you want to at this cannery." He smiled down at her with a playful grin. "And don't forget, you have a standing invitation to use the only bathtub on the island. My offer to scrub your lovely back still goes."

Alex felt her face grow warm at his suggestion. She had to admit, it appealed to her.

"I haven't forgotten, and thanks for the offer," she said. "I'll have to think it over," she added dryly. "Now, about that tour..."

"Ah, yes, the tour. Step right this way, madam."

He guided her across the dock to the off-loading area. A boat called the *Elizabeth Anne*, its name painted on the bow in calligraphic style, was being cleaned by several crew members. The men shot appreciative glances at Alex. Two of them were using stiff-bristled brushes with long handles to scrub the deck, while a third person—a woman—sprayed water from a hose onto the slick planks.

"Are there many women working as crew members?" Alex wanted to know.

"Quite a few," Ian answered. "In fact, there are more and more of them every season. I can remember when it was rare to find a woman working on these boats. Some skippers used to believe in the old superstition that having a woman on a boat would bring bad luck."

"You're kidding," she exclaimed. "In this day and age?"

"I'm afraid so," he said, shaking his head and chuckling. "Then the *Teresa Jane* changed all that."

"What happened?"

"The *Teresa Jane* was a boat with an all-female crew, including the skipper. It showed up about six or seven years ago and was high boat for the season," he said.

"High boat?"

"That means they caught more salmon and made more money than any other boat fishing for us," he replied. "Those women really worked." He laughed as he leaned on the railing. "You should have seen the looks on the grizzled faces of those old-fashioned skippers who wouldn't hire women. I was up here visiting my folks, and I really saw the sparks fly. One old guy nearly bit off the stem of his pipe when he heard his boat had been pushed into second place by the *Teresa Jane*.

"But," he continued, "I have to hand it to him. That same guy now has two women in his crew, which proves you *can* teach an old sea dog new tricks."

Alex studied him closely for a moment, then said, "Dan told me your folks are dead. Was it very difficult for you to step in and take over?"

She thought she saw a brief look of sadness flicker in his eyes before he answered. "Well, yes and no. I'd spent all of my summers up here, so I knew what the business was like. Dad had always wanted me to take over for him, but I went into law instead. And he was happy for me, I'm sure of that. But I think he was always a little disappointed that I hadn't followed his lead."

"But you did, eventually. There must be something about life up here that really appeals to you."

"Oh, you bet," he said with enthusiasm. "I love it up here. And, being an only child, it just seemed natural for me to take over. There was no one else to do it. Dad's employees helped me a great deal, showing me how everything worked and answering all of my questions. And it helped that Dad had let me work here during the summer. I used to think it was such a kick to be in school all year, then come up here and relax." He laughed. "Mind you, 'relax' in this context means putting in sixteen-hour days sometimes."

"What kinds of things did you do?" she wanted to know.

"Absolutely everything. I worked in all areas of the cannery, I crewed on some boats, I spent some time in the office—I've done it all. Dad thought it would be a good idea for me to at least know the business." A far-off look came into his eyes. "You know, I've often wondered if he did that because he knew that somehow, sometime, I *would* be in charge."

He leaned toward her where she stood with her back against the railing. "Say, you don't want to hear my life story."

"Oh, but I find it interesting," she responded truthfully, warmed by the exciting nearness of him. "This is all so different from the life I led back in Iowa. The closest water, for example, was Mud Lake." She chuckled. "And it lived up to its name, too, believe me. It was nothing like these pure, clear waters. You're lucky up here."

"Yes, and don't I know it," said Ian. "Well, on with the tour."

He took her by one arm and steered her through a door in the building on their right. They entered a cavernous room whose ceiling soared a full two stories above their heads. It contained huge bins and was painted throughout with glossy white enamel that reflected the illumination pouring in from the many skylights.

Ian suddenly pulled her to him. He pressed her body against his and murmured down at her, "Do you have any idea what it does to me to be close to you, Alex?"

Her body flamed at his touch. Where his hands and arms clasped her, she felt warm and tingly. "Is this part of the tour?" she chuckled nervously, surprised that she could get even those few words past her trembling lips.

One of his hands caressed her lower back, causing her to curve into him. She could feel his lean hardness through the fabric of her slacks. Her breasts were pressed against his broad chest, and she could feel his heartbeat through the layers of their clothing. Her nipples hardened as he teasingly moved his body so that it brushed erotically against her.

"Oh, Alex," he murmured, his voice a husky whisper. "You don't know what you do to me, witch."

He dipped his head, placing his firm mouth on hers and kissing her with a studied intensity. Hungrily, she returned his embrace. Her arms encircled his narrow waist, then moved up to cling to his back, feeling the lean, hard musculature there. An excited thrill passed through her body, causing her to tremble against him. Her response seemed to arouse him further, for he pressed her even more urgently to him. Her instantaneous response to his maleness awed her.

A man's voice above them abruptly called out, "Hey, Bill, let's start in on this other bin."

The unexpected sound of the man's voice echoed in the vast room and surprised her. She pulled her mouth away from Ian's and he moaned softly.

"It's my foreman, Ray. You can't see him because he's in one of the bins." He grinned down at her, blue eyes twinkling playfully. "Maybe we can continue this later. Come on, I'll show you more fish than you've ever seen in your whole life."

During the next couple of hours, Ian introduced Alex to every step in the salmon canning process, beginning with the holding bins where hip-booted men waded in a sea of silver-bodied fish.

As Ian explained each step to Alex, she began to get a clearer picture of this man who intrigued her so. Obviously his parents hadn't spoiled him, in spite of the fact that he had been their only child and heir to a vast cannery empire. He'd spent his summers learning the business from the bottom up, then had gotten his education.

His parents had been humane and considerate models, and their influence had created a man who treated his employees well. It was apparent that he had respect for his workers and they for him. No wonder McLeod's Seafoods was one of the biggest and most successful companies in Alaska.

They stopped at a conveyer belt where women were inspecting cans before the lids were put on. Alex noticed that the group was shooting numerous secret glances in Ian's direction. She was once again acutely aware of how good-looking he was, and of how attracted to him these women might be, judging from the wide smiles that were flashed his way. She felt a stab of pride at being seen in his company.

A couple of workers seemed to sit up straighter on their stools, almost as if they thought he might notice them if they just sat a little taller. He smiled in a friendly manner at the women, making small talk and joking with them. They gave Alex some curious glances, but as far as she could tell, there was no indication that he was involved with any of them beyond the employer-employee relationship.

Alex suddenly felt her face burn with guilt and embarrassment. She was actually feeling some jealousy, thinking that Ian might be interested in one of these women. He was so obviously an appealing ladies' man, she was sure he could have had his pick of any of the women who worked here each season. How many summer affairs had he indulged in, she wondered, and was distressed to discover that she didn't care to speculate about that.

Then she mentally chided herself. After all, she had absolutely no claim on him. She was up here on university business, and she would leave in a matter of weeks. Had he meant what he'd said about meeting him in Seattle in the fall? Or had he said that just to soften her up on the subject of the seabird colony? In any case, she shouldn't care a bit about it, one way or the other. It was true that she and Ian seemed to have a strong physical attraction for each other, but she didn't want to read more into their relationship than seemed to be there. Banish your jealous thoughts, Alex, she scolded herself.

They walked past another woman, who was feeding can lids into a machine. She was perhaps in her middle fifties and looked like a former burlesque queen. Her eyes were outlined in dark pencil, and her hair was a flamboyant bouffant of stiff, red curls beneath her hair net. She sat almost coquettishly on her high stool, and smiled broadly at Ian as they passed.

Ian said, close to Alex's ear, "I'll introduce you to Velma some other time. When you meet her, you'll want to stay and talk for hours, she's so interesting. She's the best storyteller up here. She used to be in show business, and she has some great yarns." He paused. "Say, do you know anything about art?"

"Just what I've learned from my sister. She owns an art gallery in Des Moines. Why?"

"Well, Velma paints lovely watercolors. I think they're good enough to sell, but I don't believe she's ever tried to market them."

Alex glanced back at the slender woman perched on the stool. Velma reached up and patted her tall coiffure, then adjusted one of her large hoop earrings. Somehow the black rubber boots and white plastic apron she wore did not detract from her aura of tinseled glamour.

There was something reassuringly familiar about Velma, and Alex searched her memory for the connection. Then she remembered—Aunt Irene! Velma reminded her of Aunt Irene. Alex's favorite older relative had always raised eyebrows in the family because of her flamboyant ways and raucous laughter. My, how the tongues had clucked when Irene quit her small-town job and went to New York to become an actress. She'd ended up marrying a director. The two of them later opened their own theater in Boston, where they still made headlines with their popular productions. Most of this was history by the time Alex was born. She and Monica heard "The Aunt Irene Story" many times while they were growing up, told sometimes by their mother, but more often by Irene herself.

The Gilbert clan had never stopped loving Irene, but the more conservative members simply didn't know quite how to take her, and thought of her as wild and impulsive. While they were growing up, Alex and Monica always eagerly looked forward to Irene's visits to their farm. She had such entertaining stories to tell, and she brought with her proof that there was a whole wonderful world out there beyond the fence at the bottom of the field. Alex still had the little red satin ballet slippers Aunt Irene had given to her the same Christmas she had given Monica a box of paints—a gift that had changed Monica's life forever, as it turned out, because it had kindled a lasting interest. It had been her first exposure to the world of art, a door that had led eventually to buying her own gallery.

Follow your dream, Aunt Irene always said. There was that same air of the dreamer, the risk-taker, about Velma. Alex felt strongly attracted to her and knew they could be friends. Furthermore, she knew Monica would feel the same attraction, and for the same reasons. Alex made a mental note to get to know Velma sometime, and to ask to see her paintings, as well. There might even be a chance she could sell some of her work through Monica's gallery, but that was being a bit premature....

At the end of the tour, Ian led Alex into a large, dimly lit room. To Alex it felt pleasant and soothing to be surrounded by the quiet of this out-of-the-way area of the compound.

Just then a sharp meow sounded from a shadowed corner near them. A lithe black cat stood up on a pallet of canned salmon and stretched itself sinuously.

"Hey, Toulouse! I didn't know you were in here, buddy, but I should have guessed," Ian said. He moved toward the cat, who had sat down and curled his long thin tail around his front paws. "Alex, I want you to meet the most pampered cannery cat in the whole world—Toulouse."

She scratched the pleased-looking cat under his chin, watching his eyes close to gold slits of contentment. A loud purr rumbled from his throat, and his front feet moved rhythmically in front of him, as if softly kneading the air above the cans.

"What a handsome puss," Alex exclaimed.

"Yes, he is," Ian agreed as he patted the rich ebony coat. "He's been in here taking a nap on the cans while they're still warm. At night he's on the foot of my bed, but during the day this is one of his favorite places."

Ian reached for a can opener on a shelf nearby. Toulouse rubbed his sleek body along Ian's arm as he opened a can and spooned the contents onto a little plate on the floor. The sinewy cat instantly leapt down from his perch and padded quickly toward the dish. As he ate, his thin black whip of a tail waved slowly from side to side in such obvious ecstasy that Alex laughed with pure delight.

"What a precious cat," she said. "I'm positively charmed."

She was suddenly aware of Ian's strong hands slipping around her slim waist as he encircled her from behind. He murmured into her hair, "You're not the only one who's charmed. I just looked at my watch, and I can hardly believe we've been together for more than two hours. You make me forget all about the time, witch. My mind was only partly on this tour. Mostly I thought about you and how good you taste and how right you feel pressed up against me. What kind of spell did you cast on me today?"

He nuzzled her neck, sending shivers of icy fire down her back. Her knees felt weak and watery, and her stomach began to flutter with excitement.

His hands roved up from her waist to caress her slowly and searingly through the clinging fabric of her turtleneck. A thumb brushed the bottom of one breast, sending molten rivers rushing through her veins. She could feel the solid columns of his thighs against the backs of her legs. His flat belly melded into her lower back and her bottom was neatly and snugly tucked into the lean curve of his torso. Heat began building between them. Alex felt her head becoming light. Her breath started from her parted lips in small pants. He had an instant effect on her, this man.

She felt herself being turned around and she looked up into his face. His eyes were half-closed, the lids lowered in apparent ecstasy. If he were a cat, he'd be purring right now, she thought giddily.

"*Did* you dress like this for me?" he asked her for the second time, slowly sweeping her body with eyes that gleamed with desire. "You have a wonderful body. Forgive me for being so blunt," he said, with a wolfish grin, "but I couldn't help but notice it. And," he added, "I'm a keen appreciator of the works of nature."

He scanned her again, then settled his gaze on her up-turned face. "I might add that I'm also intrigued by your mind," he said with a teasing smile as his lips drew near hers. "But it's not to your mind that I want to do the things I'm thinking about.... Darling Alex!" he exclaimed as he lowered his mouth onto hers.

His firm, full lips possessed her mouth, coaxing her lips apart until his tongue could seek out hers. She gave herself up to the moment, to the many exquisite sensations he was causing her to feel. She gloried in the silky moistness of his tongue, in the clean taste of his mouth as it teased and nibbled, and in the faint soapy-spicy fragrance that emanated from his skin and hair.

He released her mouth at last, leaving her slightly breathless. Immediately, he pressed his eager lips to her cheeks and the curve of her jaw, bending her head back as he imprinted her skin with a string of burning kisses. His hands never stopped in their urgent caresses along her back, across her shoulders and down to her hips.

Alex began to feel a gentle and insistent throbbing at the center of her being. Wild images of making love with Ian tumbled teasingly through her mind.

"Oh, Alex, Alex," he whispered against her hair while his strong hands drew her even closer to him. "Give up your ideas about the seabird colony and be my lover."

The whirlwind that had been churning in her mind slowed, then halted altogether. What had he said? She wasn't sure, and she drew back to look up at him. She placed her palms against his broad chest and gently pushed him away from her.

"What?" she asked in a near whisper.

"Sweetheart, give up those notions you have about that place." His voice carried just a hint of a pleading tone. "Or at least put them aside for now. You know they only drive us apart."

He dipped his head to claim her mouth again, but this time she snapped out of the spell he'd woven and broke from his arms. She felt her lower lip trembling.

She said, "I can't put aside my beliefs and my reason for being here. Can't you see that, Ian? It wouldn't work for me."

He reached for her. "I wish I hadn't mentioned it. Come back, Alex." But she stepped away.

"No, Ian, please. It suddenly feels as if you're kissing me just to soften me up on my position." She felt hurt and incredulous.

Ian made imploring motions with his hands and once more reached for her, but again she stepped out of range.

"Wait a minute, Alex," he said, "you don't understand. The only reason I'm kissing you is because I want to. Very much."

Alex shook her head as if to clear it of her tangled thoughts. Hadn't Dr. Harper warned her? Her words rang in Alex's memory, "He's a ladies' man who gets what he wants." Why hadn't she seen that he might use his charm and good looks to distract her from her goal? She felt like an utter fool. And yet, and yet....

Trying to regain control of her quavering voice, she said, "I believe you, Ian. At least, I think I do. But you've got to see that mentioning the colony while kissing me would give me reason to...well...doubt you. It's possible that *you're* confused about your motives, and I..."

His eyes had narrowed. He stood with his arms held slightly out from his sides, his hands in loose fists.

"Don't be an idiot, Alex," he said to her in a soft voice that held within it a warning of leashed power. "I think

I've taken great pains to tell you how much I'm attracted to you. I think you're a very sexy, arresting woman. You're unlike any woman I've ever met. You can't blame me for wanting to make love to you."

Alex felt an expression of skepticism cross her face. She took a step away from him.

"And don't give me that look, lady," he growled at her. "I remember how you returned my kisses, and how you pressed your luscious body up against mine. No one was forcing you to respond. You want it as much as I do. Don't try to kid me that you don't."

"It's true," she reluctantly admitted, "but I was mistaken. I never dreamed you'd use...lust as a weapon to get me to back off this project."

"Damn it, woman! I'm not using lust as a weapon." He raised his voice slightly as he ground out his words. "Holding you in my arms doesn't have a damned thing to do with your project."

Alex's disbelieving silence drove Ian to continue, his voice less strident.

"My point is that we're never going to agree on that issue. I'm going to build that plant, Alex, and you may as well drop this idea that you're on some kind of noble crusade to save wildlife that probably won't even be affected. This is the one thing that keeps coming between us. Don't you see that?"

Yes, she could see it, she thought grimly. The realization made her heart clench in a fist of pain. If this obstacle were only removed...but how could it be? In any case, the romantic mood of a few moments ago had been thoroughly shattered. Alex fought to hold back the tears that were suddenly burning her eyes. She didn't want him to see her cry, so she turned and began walking away from him before the tears could stream down her inflamed cheeks.

Just before she left the warehouse, she turned and spoke to him. Her voice was tremulous, but she held her head high, her back straight.

"You're right about one thing, Ian. We'll never agree on that issue. Thanks for the tour."

The hot tears spilled from her eyes as she almost stumbled down the dock and back toward her cabin. She felt angry and bitterly disappointed. She was much too vulnerable when Ian worked his romantic magic on her, she admitted to herself, but she would be on her guard from now on. Wiping the salty dampness from her face, she swore a silent oath that Ian McLeod would never again catch her at such a disadvantage.

Chapter Five

During the next few days, Alex made a point of avoiding the compound area. There was a dull ache in her breast, a pain that was almost physical, whenever thoughts of Ian crossed her mind. She didn't want to run into him and experience that familiar tug of desire for the feel of his strong arms around her, the brush of his lips teasing hers. It was clear to her that he was like any other coldly calculating businessman who was out to increase his empire. She and her project were in his way, and he would not rest until he had swept these annoyances from his path. It saddened her to think he was so single-minded. She hardened her heart by staying away from the cannery area and by spending every daylight hour out in the field.

Trying to lose herself in her work, she continued her exploration of the island. One day she sat atop a bluff overlooking the Bering Sea. She had set up her spotting scope and was eating her lunch as she looked out on the blue swells, which were tipped here and there with whitecaps. The endless expanse of tossing water disappeared into the distance. Somewhere over the horizon were the Pribilof Islands, and far beyond them, the Bering Strait, leading to the Arctic Ocean.

She took her eyes away from the scope and bit into her apple, squinting against the glare of the sunlight on water. She wondered if she would ever see the strength and fury of that monster of Arctic-bred storms, the williwaw. This time of year, she knew, foul weather was predictable and fairly frequent. Part of her wanted to experience one of these tempests, to see for herself one of nature's purest examples of unleashed power. Another part of her trembled inwardly to imagine what such a wind could do to anyone who was caught in it.

She spent the afternoon hours at the seabird colony, adding to her growing mass of data. Thoughts of Ian kept intruding on her concentration, and she brushed them aside with irritation. She was not about to let his presence on the island influence her work, no matter what conflicting emotions about him warred in her breast.

She packed up her gear a little early, meaning to return to the compound before dusk in order to buy some fresh produce at the company store. En route back to the cannery, she stopped to eat sweet, ripe salmonberries as she watched a plump female rock ptarmigan lead nine fluffy chicks along the trail and into a stand of brilliant fireweed.

A pang of unexpected longing swept through Alex as she continued her walk. What was it about that softly clucking mother ptarmigan that had played such a poignant chord within her? Was she feeling lonely again, she wondered? As much as she loved her solitary hours in the field, she knew there were dangers in remaining isolated from other people for too long. She had always been very independent and self-sufficient. Could it be that she was beginning to feel the need to share her life with someone else? It had certainly occurred to her before, but never with such intensity.

When she arrived at the compound area, she happened to notice a redheaded woman sitting alone on a log down on the beach. The woman was writing in a little notebook. She turned to look out at the water for a moment, and Alex recognized her as Velma, the former entertainer whom Ian had pointed out to her on the cannery tour. Alex hesitated. She felt drawn to this woman. Should she approach her and introduce herself? Velma seemed preoccupied with the work in her lap. Maybe she had sought out the spot on the beach so she could be alone and not be interrupted.

Alex took a few steps away, then turned back. Something about the ptarmigans she had just seen on the trail returned to her mind. What was it? A feeling, a kind of longing. She was lonely here and needed a friend, a woman whom she could talk to. Why hadn't she recognized it before? She'd been too busy perhaps to acknowledge such yearnings.

Velma again looked up from her writing and gazed out at the water, pencil to her lips, as if searching for just the right word. Then she dipped her head and wrote. Something told Alex that Velma was approachable. There was only one way to find out.

Alex walked down onto the beach, her feet making scrunching noises in the gravel. As she drew near, Velma turned to look at her. She smiled in friendly greeting. When Alex reached the redhead, she could see that she was writing on a stationery pad. Alex spoke first.

"Hi," she said, "I hope you won't mind that I've come over to introduce myself. My name's Alex Gilbert. I saw you on a tour Ian gave me of the cannery. Your name is Velma, right?"

The older woman smiled even more broadly at Alex. "That's right, Velma Larson. But let's not be formal with each other. Just call me Velma."

"I hope I'm not disturbing you...."

Velma laughed and shook her head, her big hoop earrings swaying wildly. "No, honey, you're not bothering me in the least. I was just writing to my son, Rory. He's a junior in college, and this summer he's working as a camp counselor. I gathered from his last letter that he's getting a little frustrated with all those young kids. So I'm giving him some advice on how to handle them." She chuckled. "Get them organized into some plays and skits, I'm telling him." She paused and gestured to Alex. "Take a load off your feet, honey. There's plenty of room on this log for two."

She scooted over and made space for Alex to sit down. Alex gratefully dropped her pack to the ground and settled herself beside Velma.

"How would you get a bunch of little kids organized into plays?" she asked. "That sounds like a real challenge."

Velma laughed again, her eyes twinkling. "The trouble with some of these kids he's describing is that they're not busy enough. So they're bored. They'll be happy to have something different to do." She rolled her eyes. "Can you imagine being bored? Why, I've never been bored a day in my life." She leaned toward Alex. "I'm a pretty good judge of character, and I'd guess that you haven't spent many moments in boredom yourself. Am I right?"

Alex felt flattered. It seemed as if Velma had just given her a wonderful compliment. It made Alex stop and look at herself. Did she really project an aura of self-reliance and the ability to use her time creatively? She certainly hoped so.

She answered, "Hmm, I guess I'd have to think about that one. I sure can't remember ever being bored, though, except when I've been trapped someplace by someone boring. I'm thinking of a professor who regularly put people to sleep. Now *he* was boring." She laughed and Velma joined in.

"But when you're in charge of the situation, you're not bored, right?" Velma said.

Alex nodded her head in the affirmative. "Oh, that is certainly right. There are just too many interesting things to do in this world to be bored."

"Well, now you've learned one of the most important lessons in life, I think," said Velma. "Self-sufficiency is such a valuable thing to have. You should be able to amuse yourself, and not need someone else to do it for you." She paused. "Anyway, like I was saying, I'm telling Rory to pick out some funny plays and have the kids put together their own simple costumes and props. They may not have enough time to memorize the parts, but they can read the plays and walk through them. You see, kids don't really know how to entertain themselves. They look to us adults to give them ideas and get them organized. They haven't learned self-sufficiency yet, like you have, so they're bored. What do you think of my idea?"

"I think it's great," replied Alex with enthusiasm. "Ian said you used to be in show business."

Velma looked out at the bay. "Yes, that's right. I used to be a full-time performer on the stage—dancing, acting, novelty acts—just about anything I could talk somebody into letting me try." She shook her head and rolled her eyes. "Honey, I've been sawed in half, I've kicked up my legs in chorus lines, I've played the straight woman to comedians, and I've been in more plays than I can name. Those were the good old days." Her face assumed a pleased expression as if she was savoring wonderful memories. "And I still do a few things in the little community theater near my house in Seattle. The greasepaint gets into your blood, if you know what I mean. I'm active now mainly in helping to raise money to keep the group going. I sell tickets now and then, and once in a blue moon I take a small walk-on part. It's a tremendous lot of fun."

She looked with interest at Alex. "Now, here I'm going on and on about myself, and I haven't even asked about you. I remember when you and Ian strolled through the cannery the other day. You set the place to buzzing, by the way. You make a handsome couple."

Alex wasn't sure if Velma meant her remark to have any special significance, but it flustered her nonetheless. She felt herself start to blush, and hastened to disguise her reaction.

"Yes," she said, "it was interesting to see how salmon is processed."

"And what brings you up here exactly? Ian said something about birds."

Briefly Alex outlined her project for Velma, who seemed fascinated by the explanation.

"You're actually counting the birds?" she wanted to know.

"That's right—among other things," said Alex.

"But, honey, birds fly away. How on earth do you get them to sit still long enough to count them?"

Alex laughed. "I know it must sound rather strange. There are several ways to do it. You can estimate the size of a flock as it flies over. Or you can count the number of birds in a section of a rookery, then multiply that by the number of sections you establish. Things like that. But sometimes it really is one, two, three—one bird at a time."

"It must be a real challenge, and I admire you for doing it, Alex. I suppose it's important work, or you wouldn't be up here in the wilderness."

"Oh, yes," agreed Alex, "it's very important work. Birds and their numbers tell us a great deal about what's happening in the environment. What affects the birds will proably eventually affect us and all other species."

"Have you always been a bird scientist?"

"No," replied Alex, "for a time I taught high-school biology. But the routine finally got to me, so I went back to school and studied ornithology."

"You wanted a little adventure in life, hmm?" Velma's eyes shone warmly at Alex. She seemed to be looking right into Alex's soul.

"That's right, Velma. I was hungry for something besides a nine-to-five job. I like travel and adventure. And I want to contribute something significant to the world of science. That must sound awfully stuffy and self-important, but there it is. I don't know how else to say it."

"Now don't apologize for having high ideals, Alex. That's a wonderful goal." Velma paused, a thoughtful look on her face. "You know something, I think you'll do it, too. You seem to have real backbone."

Again Alex felt pleased by Velma's attention. "It's nice of you to say that. Thanks. I just hope I can live up to my goals."

"You'll make it because you're a risk-taker. I can see that."

"It's interesting you should say that, Velma, because that's how I see you, too. In fact, you remind me of my Aunt Irene, my mom's sister. Aunt Irene took a risk and went to New York to be an actress. Mind you, that was years ago, when everyone in the small Iowa town where I grew up either became farmers or farmers' wives. I still love her for setting an example for me."

"Good for her!" cheered Velma. "And good for you, too. Here you are, having a real adventure while your old friends at the high school are correcting papers. That-a-girl!"

Alex laughed along with the high-spirited Velma. There was such warmth in the woman, such a positive outlook on life, that Alex felt refreshed just being with her.

Velma said, "There is one thing, though, that bothers me a little bit about what you're doing up here."

Alex felt a slight apprehension creep over her. "What do you mean?" she asked.

"It's terribly solitary work, isn't it? I mean, aren't you out alone in the boondocks all day? Don't you get lonely, Alex?"

"It's funny you should mention that," Alex said ruefully, "because just a few minutes ago I had a real wave of loneliness come over me. I don't know what brought it on. I'm usually so self-reliant. It surprised me to be feeling that way."

A sage look crossed Velma's face. "Just don't get to thinking you're too self-reliant, my dear. We all need strong attachments to other people."

"Yes, you're right about that. To be honest, that's why I came down here to introduce myself just now. I guess I felt the need to reach out and be friendly." She smiled at the redheaded older woman. "Thanks for being so approachable. I had a feeling you would be."

Velma chuckled. "'Approachable.' I like that. Yes, I like that very much, Alex. Thank you." She paused, then placed one hand on Alex's arm. "Listen, honey, if there's ever a time when you need to talk to someone, remember me, will you? When I'm not at that crazy lid machine I'm on my own time, and I'd love your company. Will you do that?"

"Yes, of course I will. Thanks. That means a lot."

"To me, too, honey. We all need friends."

Later, as Alex was once more walking toward the store, she realized that her loneliness had lifted entirely. With all of the worrisome things on her mind right now, she needed to be able to talk to someone who would understand her feelings. Velma had made her feel welcome and interesting as if she—Alex—had something to give in return. A warm glow came over Alex as she recalled Velma's words, *"We all need friends."* How true, how very true.

Before going to the store, Alex swung by her cabin to drop off her gear. There was a note on her door. Curiously, she opened it as she went inside and let her pack and camera bag fall onto her bed. Her heart skipped a beat when she saw that the note was from Ian.

I know you've been avoiding me, Alex, and that's your right, even though I'm sure your reason for doing so is completely off base. You keep pretty early hours, but perhaps you'd enjoy a little entertainment tonight. We'll be holding our annual Fourth of July dance in the mess hall, and there will be a fireworks display over the bay after dark. Please feel free to join us. Maybe you'll even save a dance for me. What do you say we call a truce for the evening?

                                        Ian

The Fourth of July! She had lost track of the passage of time. June had gone, and July had taken its place while she had been totally engrossed in her work. The Fourth of July celebrations back home had been among her favorites. She was strongly tempted to go tonight, but part of her was wary of Ian's motives for inviting her. She reread his note; it sounded innocent enough.

Alex sighed. She did need a break from her project, from the daily routine, the gathering of data, the nightly typing of her field notes. Okay, she'd go, she decided, but she made a mental note to proceed with extreme caution where Ian McLeod was concerned.

As soon as she'd made her decision, she felt fluttery and excited. What would she wear? How should she fix her hair? Did she still have some of that coral lipstick left, the shade that seemed most flattering with her mahogany-hued hair? She began opening her dresser drawers, pulling out clothes to see what struck her fancy for tonight's festivities. The reflection in the mirror above the dresser gazed back at Alex. She noticed that her face had become quite tan. Her cheeks bloomed with the pink of robust health. A long shower, a few strokes with her hairbrush and a dash of mascara and lipstick were all her face and hair needed tonight, she decided.

Suddenly she laughed aloud in the empty cabin, the peals of her somewhat rueful mirth sounding hollow to her ears. In spite of her valiant attempts to shake off her feelings of attraction for Ian, she had obviously been unsuccessful. Just the thought of seeing his rugged face and lean body was enough to send her into giddy spasms of sweet anticipation. Calm down, she told herself sternly. This was not even a date, and if he had made it sound like one, she was sure she wouldn't have gone. Maybe he was just trying to be friendly. Perhaps he wanted to smooth over the rough spots that had occurred during their last meeting. He was no doubt trying to get back into her good graces, and that was what made Alex feel wary. She couldn't forget the pain he'd caused by making love to her in one breath, then trying to change her mind about her project in the next.

It was all very confusing to Alex. She didn't like being suspicious of anyone's motives, so she shrugged to herself, deciding that she would once again take him at face value. She would keep a certain reserve about herself where Ian was concerned, but she would join him in a truce, as he'd suggested. She would go to that dance and have a good time!

A few minutes later, she was perusing the shelves in the company store. Boxes and canned goods were arranged in colorful displays. She passed the packaged mixes, cans of jam, bottles of pancake syrup and containers of fruits and vegetables. The supplies that had been sent up for the field project provided more than she needed in the way of canned and dried foods. What she craved on a daily basis was fresh produce, and at lunch today she had eaten her last apple.

The fresh fruits and vegetables were in the back of the room. Alex headed for that section. She knew that a supply ship had docked yesterday. Perhaps it had brought some tomatoes or cucumbers.

After making her selections, she took her purchases to the counter. An older woman Alex recalled seeing in the store the other times she'd shopped here was waiting on a fisherman. On the other occasions when Alex had been in the store, the older woman had been working at a desk, and a young Aleut woman named Jennie had helped Alex. Today Jennie was nowhere to be seen, and the older woman was working at the cash register.

Alex studied her as she waited her turn. The woman wore an avocado-green work smock over a pair of maroon polyester slacks. Her short, graying hair appeared to have been overpermed, for it had the dry, frizzy look of a scouring pad. The woman's face was thin and angular and lined with wrinkles that emphasized the downward cast at the corners of her mouth.

When it was Alex's turn at the counter, the older woman looked up sharply at her, her small, rather darting eyes squinting at the scientist. Alex began taking her purchases out of the basket and placing them on the worn counter. The woman shot her another curious glance and began ringing up the prices. They were alone in the store, and Alex was immediately struck by the woman's odd stares, but dismissed them as having no special meaning.

"I've seen you in here before," the woman said as she weighed some tomatoes. Her voice was high-pitched and not particularly pleasant. The younger woman thought she detected a querulous tone.

"Yes," she said, "I come here every few days to get fresh produce. I just can't live without salads."

"That right?" the woman remarked rhetorically, checking a price list. She shot Alex another glance. "You...uh...work in the cannery? Or on one of the boats? I don't think I caught your name."

"My name's Alex Gilbert," she said, "and, no, I don't work in the cannery or on a boat. I'm here to do a study of the birds that nest on Anfesia."

The woman laughed somewhat nervously, it seemed. She rubbed her hands together, then stuck out her right one to shake Alex's.

"I'm Hazel Newhall. I run the store, do the books, order the stock—that kind of thing. I hardly ever work behind the counter, but today is Jennie's day off."

Alex grasped Hazel's hand. It was dry and bony and her grip was weak, her fingers flaccid.

"So, you're here to study birds. That must mean you won't be here very long," Hazel continued as she tucked tomatoes and lettuce into a grocery bag.

Alex thought she detected a pleased note in the woman's high voice. She couldn't think of a reason why this woman would want her to leave so she dismissed the thought as a mistaken impression.

"I mean," Hazel continued, "this is such a small island. I'll bet a person could count all the birds in a couple of days." She looked up at Alex. Something about Hazel's penetrating dark eyes made Alex feel uncomfortable. "So why are you still here?" The bluntness of the question caught Alex off guard.

"Well, actually," she said, "my study involves much more than simply listing which species are here and counting how many there are of each kind. I'm also photographing the nesting birds, taking notes on feeding activities and preparing an in-depth report on the seabird rookery. All of that takes a great deal of time."

She found herself wishing Hazel would hurry up so she could leave. She had hours before the dance, but she wanted to type up her weekly report to Dr. Harper and answer her parents' last letter before she began her leisurely preparations for the festivities.

"Oh, you must mean those cliffs out where Mr. McLeod is going to build that new crab plant," Hazel commented.

Alex felt herself stiffen with mild irritation at this reference to Ian's proposed cannery. "Yes, that's right," she conceded.

"So, how long do you think you'll be here?" Hazel pursued. She darted a hooded glance at Alex, who was beginning to feel she was being interrogated.

"I really can't say. It all depends on the weather and on how much I can accomplish by myself. I honestly don't know how much time I'll need to complete my report."

"How, uh, well do you know Mr. McLeod?"

The quick change of subject threw Alex for a moment. Where was this conversation leading, anyway? Why should this woman ask her about Ian? It was baffling, but was no doubt just idle curiosity.

She shrugged. "I really don't know him well at all, to be honest. The first time I met him was when I arrived on the island, and that wasn't very long ago." She added lightly, "He seems like a very nice person."

"Oh, he's the nicest man in the world!" Hazel bubbled. "That's why I'm so glad he's interested in my little Sylvia."

Alex paused in the act of taking her billfold out of her jacket pocket. Sylvia? Who was Sylvia? She tried to ignore the nervous leaps her stomach was suddenly taking.

Trying to sound casual and not terribly interested, she asked, "Sylvia? Is that your daughter? I don't think I've met her."

Hazel's brows raised a fraction. "Yes, Sylvia is my beautiful daughter. You haven't met her because she isn't here."

She paused and Alex felt herself relax a little. Why she should care if Ian was "interested" in this Sylvia was a question she didn't want to pursue. It unsettled her to imagine him paying serious attention to another woman, and she was sorely vexed that such an idea could affect her this way.

Hazel continued. "No, Sylvia isn't here right now, but she will be in a day or two." She paused in the act of sacking up Alex's groceries and glanced at the younger woman as if to see what her reaction would be.

Alex again tensed up. She fumbled with her billfold and took out some money. "Well, that will be nice for you and for Mr. McLeod, won't it? You'll both be glad to see her, I'm sure."

"Oh, especially Mr. McLeod," said Hazel, rolling her eyes dramatically. "How he adores my little Sylvia! Well, who wouldn't? She's gorgeous. She could have any man she wanted, just like that." She snapped her fingers to emphasize her words. "She and Mr. McLeod had so many nice dates in Seattle this spring. Ah, the way they look at each other... Why, even a blind person could see how in love they are."

She leaned conspiratorially across the counter to speak in a loud stage whisper. "This is our little secret. Don't tell Mr. McLeod about Sylvia coming up. My little darling and I want to surprise him, okay?"

Mutely, Alex shook her head affirmatively. She could hardly believe her ears. Ian was apparently involved with another woman. And he had been kissing her—Alex—in that other woman's absence. She felt herself becoming furious, and her hand shook as she reached for her change.

Hazel caught Alex's fingers in one hand and clenched them as she dropped in the coins with the other. Alex

fought the impulse to jerk her hand away from the un-
welcome contact.

"I predict," said Hazel, "there will be a big wedding
in the fall." She let go of Alex's hand and winked. "A big
wedding, I can just feel it. See if I'm wrong."

"Yes, well, that's wonderful news, I'm sure," mum-
bled Alex.

More than anything else in the world, she wanted to
run out of the store. Fast, physical action was what her
body needed most to help calm the rumblings of apprehension and dismay that were coursing through her.

She picked up her bag to leave.

"You're not wearing a wedding ring. Not married?"
Hazel asked her.

"N-no, I'm not," Alex said unevenly. "Just haven't
met the right guy," she joked wryly, laughing weakly at
one of her least favorite expressions in the world.

Hazel seemed to be studying the young woman. Alex
felt herself squirm inside under that baleful gaze. Get
your imagination under control, she scolded herself.

"Are you going to the dance and fireworks display tonight?" Hazel wanted to know.

At the moment, the idea seemed much less attractive
to Alex than it had before she'd entered the store.
Nevertheless, she responded, "I think so, yes."

"Well, maybe you'll meet a nice fisherman tonight.
You could look quite pretty with a little makeup and a
different hairdo, if you don't mind my saying so." She
patted her own hair, which looked as if it had been crisply
deep-fried, and pursed her lips.

"Of course," she continued, "Mr. McLeod will be the
handsomest man there. Too bad my little Sylvia will miss
all the fun. She just loves to go to dances and parties."
She darted another glance at Alex. "I'm sure Mr. Mc-

Leod will be sorry Sylvia won't be there. I wonder if he'll even have much of a good time tonight, being spoken for, you might say, and not having his dear, sweet love right there beside him.''

Alex had the distinct impression that she had been warned off. She'd heard more than enough. ''Well, thanks for helping me,'' she said as she turned and headed for the door. ''Maybe I'll see you later,'' she said, fervently hoping she wouldn't.

As she stormed along the path, she was so upset she was clenching her jaws and gritting her teeth. How should she interpret this new and very unsettling development? If Ian already had a ''dear, sweet love,'' why had he been paying her such compliments and so much attention?

A wave of sympathy for the unknown Sylvia washed over her. If only that innocent young woman knew how her intended had been cavorting with another woman. Alex swore to herself that she would never reveal to Sylvia how Ian had misbehaved. She would spare her the pain of knowing that her man had been kissing another woman.

She was still fuming when she reached the porch of her cabin. She paused before going in, trying to calm herself. Did she really want to go tonight, knowing what she did about Ian?

She looked out over Chulinka Bay. Dozens of fishing boats bobbed at anchor. The crews had come in for the festivities, she realized. The encircling mountains were lushly green; their slopes were velvety and creased with hidden shadows. The air was fresh and clean. It was lightly scented with the combined fragrances of salt tang and the blooming wildflowers that dotted the landscape. Gulls and terns rasped high above, their wings startlingly white against the azure sky.

She made up her mind. She would go to that dance, and she would have a good time! She refused to let her muddled feelings about Ian McLeod ruin the first social event she had attended since leaving Iowa.

Later that evening, Alex arrived at the mess hall. Just before she went in, she smoothed some imagined creases from her yellow sundress. She was feeling positive and happy because she had spent the past two hours talking herself out of caring if she ever saw Ian McLeod again. She wasn't sure how long the effect would last, but she was willing to find out. Tossing her heavy, loose hair back from her face, which felt slightly flushed with excitement, she entered the room.

It was a large one, meant to feed more than one hundred people at a sitting. Most of the collapsible tables and benches had been folded up and rolled against one wall. The remaining ones had been placed in a rough circle, in the center of which several couples were already dancing. Rock music was playing on a stereo. All of the lights had been turned out and candles placed on the tables. The warm, quavering light from the many candle flames softened the utilitarian aspect of the room, creating an atmosphere that was actually romantic. Red, white and blue bunting festooned the walls, adding just the right patriotic touch.

There were about seventy-five people there already. They were sitting at the tables, dancing or taking food from the counter near the kitchen. Alex recognized several people who waved at her.

Members of boat crews stood around the room, talking or watching the dancers. Some were in slacks and sport jackets, but most wore freshly laundered jeans and open-necked plaid shirts. It appeared that the men had even trimmed their beards for this event. The young women from the cannery talked among themselves, casting secret glances at the clusters of rugged-looking fishermen. Every now and then one of these men would approach a woman, then draw her onto the dance floor.

Velma was having an animated conversation with two fishermen on the other side of the room. The men leaned forward, as if to catch every word, then threw their heads back in raucous laughter. As before, Alex felt drawn to this lively woman. She wandered over to join the group.

Skirting the busy dance floor, Alex walked up to Velma. She arrived at the table where Velma sat just as the redhead delivered what must have been another punch line, judging from the reactions of her listeners.

Hands on hips, Velma said, "So I looked right in that producer's eyes and kept my face perfectly straight as I told him, 'Honey, that wasn't part of my act, that was my dog Georgie.' And you know something, boys? I got the job anyway!" Velma laughed right along with the two fishermen, who slapped their thighs and roared with mirth.

"Hello, Velma," Alex said when the laughter died down a bit. "Mind if I join you?"

The older woman looked up and greeted Alex with a broad, inviting smile. She gestured to an empty seat.

"Please do, sweetie. Say, you look gorgeous, doesn't she, boys?"

Alex sat down and smiled back at Velma. "Why, thank you. I was about to say how stunning you look in that black dress."

"Thanks, honey, this is an old favorite of mine. Oh, these are Swen and Anchor," she added, nodding toward the two men. "Boys, meet Alex."

The two burly fishermen grinned at Alex, and each shook her hand.

"Alex is up here on a special unversity project. Alex, tell these two how you got into the bird-counting business."

Before long, Alex was laughing and chatting with the three of them as if she'd known them for years. With warm and genuine interest, Velma drew Alex out, encouraging her to tell the two fishermen all about herself and why she had come to Anfesia. She recalled her first impression of Velma, which she had acquired during the cannery tour with Ian, and knew that it had been soundly confirmed twice today. Here, indeed, was a woman with the same freewheeling spirit as her Aunt Irene, and with whom Alex knew she could be close friends.

Thoughts of the tour made Alex remember Ian's comments about Velma's watercolors. She was just going to ask the redhead about her art when a male voice spoke up behind her.

"Care to dance?"

She looked up to see a fisherman with a face that was scrubbed so clean it shined. He appeared to be about twenty-two or -three, and he strongly reminded her of the corn-fed farm boys she'd grown up with. Like most of the other men in the room, this one wore clean blue jeans and a plaid shirt.

She smiled at him. "Sure," she said. Turning to her three companions, she added, "Will you excuse me?"

"No problem, honey," replied Velma. "I knew it wouldn't be long before someone pulled you onto the dance floor. Enjoy yourselves, you two." She leaned toward Swen and Anchor. "Boys, speaking of dancing, did I ever tell you about the time I was late for a chorus tryout in Miami? Seems my luggage got mixed up with someone else's, and all I had to wear was this really big, baggy tuxdeo covered with green sequins. It was from some novelty act. Well, you can just imagine how that would've looked. So I ran around in a panic, searching for the wardrobe woman, but before I found her..."

Alex missed the rest of Velma's story as the young man led her into the center of the room for a slow dance.

"My name's Tom Lewis," he said. "What's yours?" His smile was warm and boyish, his brown eyes tinged with innocence. Alex liked him immediately.

"Alex Gilbert," she answered. "Do you work on one of the boats?"

"Yes," he said, "on the *Stephanie Lara*. Ever hear of it?"

"No, but then, I've only been on the island about three weeks. I'm sure I haven't even begun to see all of the boats that fish around here."

"And what are you doing on Anfesia? I don't think I've seen you before," said Tom.

Briefly Alex told him about her project. He listened with great interest.

"Hey," he said, "you should come out on the *Stephanie* sometime. You'd get some great pictures of birds out there where we fish. Tomorrow would be a good day, if you're interested."

She had been wanting to get out on the water for some time. Not only was she eager to get some close-up photographs of pelagic birds as they fed, but she was curious to see the purse-seining operation.

"Are you sure your skipper wouldn't mind having a visitor on board?" she asked.

"Oh, you wouldn't be the first person to come along just for the ride," answered Tom. "I'm sure he won't mind."

"Fine, then. Tomorrow would be a good day for me. Thanks."

"My pleasure."

The music stopped and they drifted back toward the tables. The seats near Velma were now taken, so Alex and Tom sat elsewhere.

"Care for some wine?" he asked.

"Yes, I would," she answered as she sat down on one of the benches.

When Tom returned with the two glasses, he told Alex that this was the first time he'd ever been away from the small Colorado town where he'd grown up and he was extremely homesick. He missed the trees, he missed his horse, and, most of all, he missed his girlfriend.

"We write every day," he told Alex. "Trouble is, the mail only comes twice a week up here, if that, and days go by when I don't hear from Susie at all." He hung his head, then looked up, his face brightening. "We're getting married when I get back. The money I'm making up here this summer is for the down payment on a little house I've had my eye on. It's right near where Susie and I grew up, so all of our friends and family are there. You know, it'll be perfect." He smiled infectiously.

Alex smiled with him, then mentally chided herself. She had allowed her thoughts to wander while he had been rambling on about his plans. What was nagging at the back of her mind?

Then she realized with a start that she had been unconsciously searching the crowd for Ian. She hadn't seen him yet, but she knew that he would be present. It piqued her to admit to herself that the thought of seeing him was, after all, the real reason she had come tonight.

Tom's voice suddenly dimmed as Alex's heart sped up, causing a loud pulsing in her ears that drowned out most of the sounds around her. She had spotted Ian.

He was even more attractive than she had remembered, if that was possible. He was lounging against the opposite wall, his tall frame managing to look both relaxed and tensed for action at the same time. One ankle was crossed casually over the other, and his arms were folded across his broad chest. His thick hair appeared to have been brushed to a shine. He wore tailored beige slacks that hugged his long legs and narrow hips in all the right places. His pale blue polo shirt was open at the neck, exposing a provocative patch of curly chest hair. A chocolate-brown, suede sport jacket and a pair of brown loafers completed his outfit. Very town-and-country, Alex observed to herself. It was one of her favorite looks on a man.

Even from across the room, she could read the expression in his eyes. She had the distinct impression that he'd been there for some time, watching her as she talked with Tom. The idea both intrigued and nettled her. His blue eyes were hooded, the lids drooping languidly. His unwavering gaze smoldered across at her and made her catch her breath. The classic planes of his face were arranged in a quirky half smile, his lips held loosely together. He seemed to be willing her to get up and cross the room to him.

She clutched the edge of the table and almost spilled her wine. Please don't walk over here, she silently implored.

"Is something wrong?" Tom asked. He was looking at her curiously.

"Oh, no," she managed to get out. "I—I'm just fine."

She turned away so she wasn't facing Ian, but she fancied she could feel those penetrating eyes boring into the back of her head. Her face began to feel hot, and her breath came out in ragged little gasps.

She felt, rather than heard, his approach.

"Hello, Alex," his smooth, deep voice said from right behind her. "Tom, I wonder if I may steal Alex away from you for a moment. I'd like to speak with her."

Tom was instantly on his feet. "Why, sure, that's fine, Mr. McLeod. You two go right ahead." He turned back toward Alex and said, "Be on the dock around seven in the morning. We're getting kind of a late start because of the dance."

"Thanks, I'll be there," she replied through lips that were trembling nervously.

Tom headed off toward the food counter. Alex stood up and faced Ian.

"And what if I don't want you to 'steal me away,' as you call it?" she asked testily.

"Now let's not have a scene, Alex," he said in a silken tone. He waved away the stinging retort that sprang to her lips. One eyebrow rose as he asked, "What's this about meeting Tom in the morning?"

She was in no mood to cooperate with him, so she snapped, "That doesn't concern you."

"Everything at this cannery concerns me, lady," he said in a soft voice that held an unmistakable warning. The tone told her he would not be put off so easily. He repeated his request. "I want to know why you're meeting Tom in the morning. Isn't he a little young for you? I think you should stick to your birds and leave the fishermen who work for me alone."

She gasped. "Are you assuming that I was making some kind of play for him?"

Ian raised his chin a fraction and looked down at her with eyes that insinuated just that. "Come on, Alex, I saw how you hung on his every word. Don't try to kid me. You were playing the old flatter-him-by-being-very-interested game. It's been used on me a few times." He suddenly smiled roguishly. "It worked, too."

Alex felt anger bubbling inside her, but she forced herself to smile, however thinly. She thrust her own chin up as she replied, "Tom is engaged, Ian."

"Yes, I know," he said. His eyes briefly scanned the length of her, searing her with his appreciative gaze. "All the more reason for you not to tempt him with your...obvious charms."

Alex felt her cheeks color under his wanton appraisal. "We were having a very innocent conversation," she insisted. "He was telling me about how homesick he is. And he told me all about Susie, the young woman he's engaged to." She forced her voice to sound cool, as if she'd scored a point. "Now, don't you feel just the tiniest bit silly for having misjudged what you saw? By the way, do you always lurk around keeping tabs on your employees?"

That one hit home, she could tell, because she saw a small twitch flicker at his jawline. His eyes narrowed slightly as he continued to look at her.

"Unless I'm sadly mistaken about the definition of the word 'lurk,' I'd say that what I was doing was standing around making sure that my employees are having a good time. And if I was wrong about you and Tom—" he dipped his head "—please excuse me. But you still haven't told me why you're meeting him in the morning."

"You never give up, do you?" she demanded.

"Not when it's something I really want," he replied smoothly.

He reached up with one hand and brushed a lock of hair from her cheek. In doing so, his warm fingers lightly grazed her skin, leaving a searing trail in their wake. Alex caught her breath.

"Tell me, Alex."

There was no way she could resist that quietly insistent tone of voice, that magnetic gaze. There was also no way she was going to let him know how he affected her.

"Oh, for heaven's sake," she fumed. "He suggested I go out on the boat he works on—"

"The *Stephanie Lara*?" he interrupted.

"That's right," she said impatiently. "I told him about my project, and he said I could get some good pictures out on the water." She paused. "And that's all there is to it. Now, if you'll excuse me..." She moved as if to leave.

He stepped in front of her and blocked her way. "Just a minute," he said. "I want to talk to you."

She folded her arms in front of her. "Fine, so talk."

She knew he wouldn't let her go until he'd had his say. She just hoped it would be short and sweet; being near him was too disturbing.

"Not in here," he said.

He took her by the arm and steered her toward some double doors that stood open to the night. Before she could protest, they were leaving the warmly glowing room and stepping out onto the wide porch that flanked the entire length of the mess hall.

As they crossed the threshold, Alex caught a glimpse of Hazel, the woman from the store. She was a mass of lime-green chiffon from throat to waist. A shapeless black skirt and some large rhinestone earrings completed the picture. Was it just Alex's imagination, or did she really see a frown cross Hazel's face as she watched them leave?

Her apparent disapproval rankled Alex. After all, Alex had as much right as anyone else to talk to Ian. Besides, she had every intention of holding her emotions very much in check with him. Never fear, she wanted to call out to Hazel, your little Sylvia's claim on Ian McLeod's heart is safe and secure with me.

A few moments later, she wasn't quite so sure about that. The night was made for romantic trysts in shadowed doorways. How would she resist if Ian tried to draw her close? She steeled herself to avoid another close encounter with him. She would not allow him to make her feel the fool again.

It was a glorious, star-spangled night. The black sky was pricked with a million glittering gems. Lights twinkled on the many boats that floated at anchor in the bay. The air was soft and balmy, the breeze light and playful as it lifted Alex's hair from her warm neck. Some night birds called softly, plaintively, from the beach. Their cries mingled with the rhythmic sound of waves lapping up on the gravel.

Ian still held her arm firmly in his hand. His lean fingers seemed to caress her bare skin, causing her pulse to leap with anticipation. She told herself to calm down and took several deep breaths to relax her jittery nerves. It aggravated her to think that he always had such a powerful effect on her.

He led her down toward the beach. Strains of music trailed after them. Someone had put on a waltz. Its tender melody, played by a string orchestra, wafted to them as Ian pointed to a driftwood log.

"This may be the best seat in the house," he said. "Would you like to sit on my jacket?"

He began to take it off, but Alex held up a hand to stop him.

"I see you've put on your best party manners," she commented dryly. "Keep your jacket on, thanks. I can manage."

His eyes gleamed at her for an instant and his mouth hardened into a line. She was instantly sorry for having unintentionally rebuked him.

"I'm sorry," she said. "That wasn't very gracious of me."

He shrugged. "Forget it." He sat down and patted the spot beside him. "Have a seat."

"No, thanks," she said. "I really don't think I should even be out here with you. Please tell me what it is you wanted to say."

His soft chuckle drifted to her on the breeze. "I'm not going to bite you, Alex, although I'd very much like to." He added softly, "But only in a way you'd enjoy."

Her heart thumped as she heard the words. No other man had ever been able to produce such vivid mental images of sensual abandon with so few well-chosen phrases. She knew she should walk away from him this instant, but her feet stayed firmly planted in the sand near him.

He reached up, grasped her by the wrist and gently pulled her down to sit beside him on the log.

"Relax, Alex," he said.

"I really should go," she said. "Please say whatever it is so I can leave."

"Don't be in such a rush. The fireworks display will be starting in a few minutes, and like I said, this may be the best seat in the house." He looked out over the water. "I'm glad there's no moon. The display shows up better that way."

"It's a good thing it isn't raining," she said, trying to relax and sound natural. Her feelings battled within her. She was very curious to learn what it was he had to say, but another part of her itched to get away from him. She simply didn't trust the emotions this man stirred in her.

"Yes," he said. "It rained last year and nearly ruined the display. Ray—my foreman—was so disappointed. This is his baby."

The log was a small one so they were forced to sit with their shoulders and thighs touching as they looked out toward the bay. Alex's skin, even through the layers of clothing separating them, could feel the brand of his. The clean, faint scent wafting to her was that same spicy fragrance she'd come to associate with him. It teased at her nostrils, making her remember the exquisite things he'd done to her before.

She felt the touch of his firm mouth as it placed a kiss on her bare shoulder. In spite of the warm air, a shiver passed through her.

"Why have you been avoiding me, Alex?" he asked. His voice was as smooth as satin. "You don't really believe, do you, that I have some kind of sinister ulterior motive for wanting to make love to you?"

At that moment, she really wasn't sure about anything except that she wanted him to hold and kiss her. She fought the impulse to turn and look at him, knowing how close that would put her face to his. She stalled for time.

"It may look as if I've been avoiding you, Ian," she said, "but I've just been very busy."

His breath was warm on her skin. "You're lying to me, witch," he murmured. "I can tell."

"Well, okay, maybe I have been staying out of sight lately," she confessed, "but I honestly feel it's for the best."

His breath teased on her skin. "You think it's best for two people who are as attracted to each other as we are to stay apart? Now, what kind of logic is that from such a highly educated person?"

"Don't, Ian," she said. She drew away slightly as his mouth placed another burning kiss on her shoulder. "You're a terrible distraction." She bit her lip; she had revealed more than she'd meant to.

"The feeling is mutual, I can assure you," he growled close to her ear. "You're beautiful with starlight gleaming on your hair, you know. The night becomes you."

Her mind was swimming. His words spun fantasies of delight for her. Why was it that whenever she was with him, his charm and his silky ways seemed to take over, causing her to cast her good sense to the four winds?

"Ian, I really don't think we should pursue this," she said, trying to retain the last shreds of her dignity and her self-control. "We have a very basic philosophical difference. We are, in fact, adversaries."

She thought her words would anger him, cause him to draw away from her and retort with his usual arrogance when speaking of his determination to build the crab plant.

Instead, he murmured, "Give it up, Alex, at least for tonight. Let's agree that we don't agree, shall we? Join me in a truce, sweetheart. We're wasting the evening."

One arm went around her then, supporting her back firmly as his other hand gently curved around her cheek and pulled her lips toward his waiting ones. There was just enough light from the mess hall and the stars for her to see the expression in his eyes. She saw a deep desire there, a hunger that matched her own, and her firm resolve fled, scattering into the night like the fragments of a shooting star. Nothing in the world existed for her except the two of them, clinging to each other beneath a canopy of shimmering lights.

His mouth hovered just above hers. She moaned softly, willing his lips to descend upon hers. But he teased her, kissing the curve of her chin, the hollow of her cheek, her earlobes.

"Oh, Alex, darling Alex," he whispered, "you intoxicate me."

His tongue caressed the sensitive spot just behind her ear, and she caught her breath. Her hands slipped up to encircle his neck. Clinging to his lean frame, she wondered how she could bear letting him go.

His right hand fondled the tender place at the small of her back, gently kneading, drawing her around to face him. With his other hand, he grasped a mass of her hair and carried it to his face. He inhaled and a low moan sounded from deep in his throat.

Alex was almost weeping with desire. Her mouth was so ready for him. She sighed, turning her face toward his lips, which were pressing searing kisses on her cheeks, her temple—everywhere they touched. At long last, his mouth found hers. He brushed his firm lips across her parted ones, teasing, taunting, fanning the fires that leapt in her veins.

"How I want you, Alex," he breathed warmly into her eager mouth. "My dearest, I've wanted you ever since I first saw you."

With the tip of his silky tongue he touched the corner of her mouth, then slowly, sensually, dipped within to probe the sensitive skin behind her lips. Her own tongue mingled with his in intimate response.

Their bodies twined together feverishly. His arms tightened around her as he suddenly thrust his tongue deeper into her mouth. Her fingers clung to him convulsively, and bursts of light seemed to explode in her head.

"Take it off me," he panted against her hungry mouth. She didn't know what he meant at first. "My jacket. Take off my jacket, Alex."

"Yes," she whispered hoarsely.

Her hands dragged themselves away from his broad back and across his shoulders. As if he couldn't bear to be torn from her mouth for even an instant, Ian kept his lips on hers while, with his help, she wrestled the garment off him.

In one smooth movement, he spread the jacket on the soft sand behind the log and drew her down onto it to lie beside him. Her head lay cradled in his firm arm, his warm body pressed against hers. He had kicked off his loafers and one foot crept between her ankles, forcing her legs to part slightly. She could feel the pleasant weight of one of his long legs on her.

Alex felt her skin come explosively alive wherever his hands touched. He caressed her bare shoulders and the base of her neck as his mouth moved roughly over her lips. The clean taste and smell of him mingled with the freshness of the warm breeze. Her senses were tuned to fever pitch. His hand possessively cupped one of her breasts. She let out a small gasp of pure delight.

"Please touch me," she said, sighing up at him. "I want you to touch me." Eagerly she twined her fingers in the triangle of chest hair at the neck of his shirt. It felt soft and silky. She bent to kiss him there. He groaned.

Her dress was the kind that buttoned up the front. With fingers that were steady and sure, Ian unfastened her bodice and slipped the straps off her shoulders. Alex felt a weakness in her knees, a hot throbbing at the heart of her womanhood.

Intense waves of pleasure washed over her as his mouth kissed the upper swelling of her breast. His fingers undid the front clasp of her bra. He gazed down with a look of hunger and keen anticipation as he parted the lacy garment and her breasts broke free.

"Lovely," he said huskily. "So lovely. Oh, Alex, you're so very lovely."

He dipped his head and took her nipple into his mouth. She watched him, discovering that the sight of his lips caressing her firm, ripe breast further aroused her, adding a fine edge to her pleasure. She breathed raggedly through her mouth and plunged her fingers into his thick hair.

This is madness, a little voice said inside her. Then she banished all thought and gave herself up to the sensations that were pulsing within her.

She urged him on by drawing his head down even harder onto her eager breast. He cupped it with one hand, kneading it gently so that it stood up to meet his aggressive mouth. The sensitive bud hardened as he swirled his moist tongue around and around. He caught the tip in his teeth and gently nipped at it, causing her to cry out with the keenest of pleasure.

As his mouth moved back to hers, he caught the aroused peak between his thumb and forefinger. He kissed her deeply, penetrating her mouth quickly with his tongue, while stroking his thumb back and forth across the damp nipple. Waves of heat throbbed from her breast, spreading throughout her chest and down to her hips and legs.

Ian again dipped his head, this time kissing and teasing her other breast until that nipple, too, stood erect and pulsating.

"We're going to miss the fireworks," she laughed softly.

"We *are* the fireworks, lady," was his growled response against her breast. "You're so wonderfully responsive, so exciting. What a woman!"

He took her hand and brought it to the front of his shirt, indicating that she should pull the garment off him. She did so and reveled in the firm expanse of chest that met her eagerly exploring hands. His skin was smooth and hard and warm, the hair across his flat male breasts soft and springy.

He rolled over onto his back, carrying her with him until she was lying on top of him, their legs entwined. Grasping her shoulders, he moved her slowly from side to side, brushing the sensitive tips of her breasts against his chest hair. The sensations this motion created in her sent icy-hot shivers throughout her body. A moan escaped her lips, then another. She buried her head on his chest and caught one of his nipples in her mouth, nipping and teasing until he also cried out.

His hands swept down to her bottom, gently but urgently squeezing the globes until her loins were tightly pressed against him. She could feel the flaring tautness of his desire. His hand crept beneath her skirt, lifting the fabric until it was above her knees. With tender but insistent movements, his fingers caressed the sensitive skin of her bare inner thigh. Little tremors shook her body.

"I want you," he said, the tone in his voice somewhere between pain and pleasure. "I want you, sweetheart."

There was a loud explosion behind and above them, and the night sky suddenly lit up. Alex cried out with surprise, for she had momentarily forgotten about the fireworks display.

As three more rockets burst in the sky over Chulinka Bay, she lifted her head to look up toward the mess hall. She was suddenly afraid that people would see her and Ian lying sprawled together on the sand in sensual disarray.

It looked to her as if everyone from the dance had come out to watch the fireworks, for the porch was crowded with fishermen and cannery workers. She could tell that from where they stood they couldn't see hers and Ian's prone bodies. She was relieved to know that tales of their lusty romp in the sand would not be circulating around the compound the next day.

Several rockets exploded in the sky at one time, sending elaborate sprays of fire—rose, green, blue, silver—in every direction. The waters of the bay reflected the trails of sparkling colors. Collective "ohs" and "ahs" sounded from the porch, and some of the onlookers clapped and cheered.

In the next burst of light, Alex caught a glimpse of Hazel. She was standing off to one side. She seemed to be staring down toward the beach, not up at the sky as the others were doing. Was she looking at the reflections of the exploding rockets in mirrorlike Chulinka Bay? Or was she trying to penetrate the shadows to see what Ian and Alex were up to?

Sylvia! Alex jerked away from Ian. She had forgotten all about Sylvia! She began to struggle in his arms.

"Hold still, sweetheart," he said. "I'm sure no one can see us."

"You don't understand," she said. "I'm afraid I've let myself get a little carried away."

"It's just what we need. Lie down, Alex, and relax."

"I can't. I should never have come out here with you."

"What's the matter?" he wanted to know. "Why are you so upset?" He sat up. His hair was disheveled, and his eyes questioned her.

"I'm upset," she said, her anger beginning to rise, "because of Sylvia." She fumbled with her clothes.

There was a heavy pause. Was he collecting his thoughts, quickly making up a plausible story? She didn't especially want to hear what he would say to her.

"You mean Hazel's daughter?" he asked in a puzzled tone of voice. "What does she have to do with us? Why, she's not even up here. I don't get it."

"Your future mother-in-law filled me in on some rather interesting details at the store today," she said as she scrambled to her feet. She smoothed the skirt of her dress.

Suddenly Ian was also on his feet, towering above her, a look of disbelief on his face.

"My what?" he exclaimed. "Why are you calling Hazel my future mother-in-law? You'd better explain right now, Alex."

He caught her by the wrist, but she wrenched out of his grasp. She hated herself for having allowed her feelings to run away with her. Once again, Ian MacLeod had cast his spell over her and she had surrendered. But not for long!

"She told me that you and Sylvia are practically engaged," she almost spat out at him. "I kind of forgot about that, in the...heat of the moment, shall we say? I think it's awfully peculiar that a man who's going to marry one woman is making love to another one. I hope Sylvia knows what she's getting into."

A howl of laughter came from him. Alex was thankful that the sound of it was covered up by the exploding rockets behind her. She cast a nervous glance at the crowd on the porch. No one appeared to have heard him. Hazel was now looking up at the sky like everyone else.

"What's so damned funny?" she asked tartly.

"The thought of marrying Sylvia, that's what," he said, reaching out to touch her. "Why, she's just a kid."

"I don't understand," said Alex, a note of confusion entering her voice. Hazel had sounded so sure, so confident, as if the wedding invitations had practically already been sent out.

"Look," he said, "I'm sure Hazel would like to see me marry her daughter, but I'm not even remotely interested. Sylvia's more like a little sister to me." There was a tension-filled pause. "All right," he said. His voice had taken on a dangerous edge. His anger was rising, Alex could tell, and she knew he would not let her go until he'd spoken his mind.

He stood with his legs apart, staring at her. "Listen up," he said as he pointed one finger at her. "I want to say this once, and once only."

She folded her arms across her chest, as if to comfort herself, and stood still in the sand. Bursts of light and strings of explosions over the bay punctuated his words.

He told her that Hazel's husband had been a longtime employee of the company. Several years ago, he died on the job, leaving behind a widow and a little daughter—Sylvia. As partial compensation for this tragedy, Ian's father gave Hazel employment with the company. He promised her that she could have her job for as long as she wanted it, and that she would also receive a generous retirement pension. In addition, Sylvia's education would be paid for by McLeod's Seafoods.

"Sylvia has spent every summer since then right here at this cannery," he said. "I've watched her grow up. Sure, I've taken her to a few special events in Seattle, to places like the Opera House, for example. But it was only in the role of uncle or big brother. At no time has our relationship been anything more than that."

"That's not what her mother thinks."

"Damn it, Alex!" His voice rose. "Will you forget about what Hazel thinks! What do *you* think?"

She wanted to believe him, of that she was certain. He sounded sincere and honest, and his story made sense. She suddenly felt very weary, as if her emotions had been wrung out of her. Maybe Sylvia was no more than a kid sister to him. The fact remained, however, that she and Ian were at odds over the ultimate destiny of the seabird colony. That was a problem that hadn't changed. She sighed deeply.

"I believe you," she said softly. "Look, I'm going to call it a night. I'm really tired. I enjoyed our truce, while it lasted," she said ruefully, "but I believe I need time to think about...everything."

"Fine, take all the time you want!" Ian exclaimed, impatiently throwing up his hands. He jammed his feet into his shoes and yanked on his shirt, not bothering to tuck it in. He snatched up his jacket.

His words and his tone stung Alex, and she felt tears welling up in her eyes. She was confused and hurt, and her stomach suddenly felt as if it were tied up in knots.

Ian waved his arm. "You just go out there with your birds and think all summer, for all I care. If you come up with any intelligent conclusions, you know where to find me."

With that he turned away from her and stalked off into the shadows.

Chapter Six

The next morning, Alex had to drag herself from her warm bed when the insistent clamor of her alarm clock startled her out of a restless sleep. It was the first time she had arisen with a feeling of sluggishness. She sat for many moments on the edge of her narrow bed. The cold of the room crept through her nightgown and chilled her bed-warm body.

She pulled the covers around her shoulders and slumped there, recalling the events of the previous evening. Her mind still felt numb with pain and confusion. After Ian's final words to her, she had turned and run down the beach into the welcoming darkness. Knowing she wouldn't have been able to sleep with her mind and feelings in such turmoil, she had walked along the shore for more than an hour, trying to sort out her emotions. She'd taken off her shoes and waded through the incoming waves. The coldness of the water had felt refreshing on her feet; it's chilly bite bracing to her still-inflamed skin. She'd hoped that it would cool her emotions, as well.

At last, she'd returned to her dark and empty cabin and had fallen into bed, where she'd passed the hours in fitful tossing. Every time she'd managed to sink into sleep, her dreams had been troubled, taking the form of vivid replays of Ian's stinging rebukes.

She pulled the blankets closer around her and noticed that her hands were shaking. His last words echoed in her mind, bringing tears to her eyes. She wiped them away with the crumpled hanky she had tucked beneath her pillow during the night. What pained her most was the possibility that she had unintentionally hurt Ian by jumping to the wrong conclusions about his relationship with Sylvia.

Her mind turned to another deeply troubling thought. What about their original conflict? She didn't see how that was ever going to be resolved. Ian hadn't given the slightest indication that he would change his mind about building his crab plant. And she certainly wasn't about to drop her project and let a natural area be destroyed without a battle. She wondered how it would all turn out. Would she find herself in court one day, defending the cause of saving the seabird colony? She could imagine him sitting across the courtroom from her. He would smile smugly as the judge proclaimed that, because the development was of economic importance, McLeod's Seafoods would be allowed to build the plant, in spite of the nearness of a large seabird rookery. Once again, the value of turning a profit would outweigh the cause of wildlife. She could see that she and Ian would always be in opposing camps.

Her head ached and her stomach churned. Getting to her feet, she did a few yoga stretches, then padded to the little kitchen and drew a glass of water. After she had gulped down a couple of aspirins, she wiped away the last of her tears and decided to pull herself together. The whole day lay before her and she intended to make the most of it. She would not let worries about Ian McLeod and his ambitions ruin it for her.

Fog engulfed the island as Alex walked briskly along the dock toward the *Stephanie Lara*, which was tied up at the end. Unlike the relative heat wave of the previous few days, this morning had dawned chilly and overcast. The fog masked the outer reaches of Chulinka Bay. Alex could see several fishing boats disappearing into the gray-white bank of swirling mist on their way to the salmon grounds. Terns and kittiwakes glided in and out of the mist, materializing then vanishing like phantoms. The air was cold and damp on her skin, and she was glad she had worn several layers of warm clothing.

The cannery had already started up for the day. It's now-familiar hum vibrated in the air and through the timbers of the old dock. Bleary-eyed workers straggled along the pier, headed for their posts at clanking machines and endlessly moving conveyer belts. Alex felt sorry for them. They had no doubt been up late last night at the dance, and would have preferred sleeping in this morning. She hoped that their workday would be a short one.

The dock was a hubbub of activity. Several other boats were tied up there, besides the *Stephanie Lara*. Engines were being gunned; puffs of diesel smoke belched up from the stacks. Crew members busied themselves with ropes, piles of net and armfuls of gear. There was much shouting and jesting from boat to boat. Alex could tell from the comments that there was a friendly rivalry among the crews to see which boat would catch the most fish that day.

"Do you fish in this kind of weather?" Alex asked Tom. She was now leaning over the dock to talk down to him on the *Stephanie Lara*.

Tom grinned up at her. "Oh, this will probably burn off before noon," he said. "Come on down." He pointed to a wooden ladder that was nailed to one of the pilings supporting the dock.

Alex threw her legs over the railing and descended to the boat. The first thing she was aware of was that, unlike the steadiness of the pier, the deck beneath her feet moved constantly. She reached for the handrail.

"Feel free to go wherever you want to on the boat and enjoy yourself," Tom said. "I have things to do, but I'll check back with you from time to time. Let me know if you need anything."

"Thanks, I'll try to keep out of your way when things get busy."

Before moving away to continue his chores, Tom quickly introduced her to the other two crew members, Hank Bonnell and Louise Adamson. Hank was about forty and built like a bull. He was of medium height, with a thick neck and barrel chest. His face bristled with a coarse, black beard and mustache. He shook Alex's hand in a meaty grip, the thick calluses telling her of many hours of hard work.

Louise was a college student. She was an engaging, freckle-faced young woman who wore a University of Washington sweatshirt over old jeans and a red bandanna covering her wheat-colored hair. Alex noticed that her hands, too, were deeply tanned and calloused from the weeks she had already spent on the boat.

As the crew prepared for departure, Alex realized that she felt much better than when she had first awakened. The pain of last night had subsided to a dull ache somewhere in her chest. She felt certain that a day spent out on the open water, away from Ian, was just what she needed.

Suddenly, the engine was revved and the boat began to pull away from the dock. Louise handed Alex a cup of hot coffee, which Alex accepted gratefully, smiling her thanks. She encircled the warm mug with both hands, dipping her face closer to the fragrant steam.

Within minutes, the boat had chugged its way to the narrow channel that was the only exit from Chulinka Bay. The cannery compound had long since disappeared behind them in the fog. Mist swirled around the seiner hiding everything from view, except for an occasional glimpse of rocky beach or jutting mountain slope. The cool, damp breeze felt bracing on Alex's cheeks. She pulled her wool hat down more firmly around her ears and sipped her coffee.

Alex spent the next hour chatting with the crew, exploring the deck area and photographing the pelagic birds that were everywhere on the water and in the air. The fog thinned and finally vanished altogether, so that the surroundings were visible in every direction.

"Is this where you're going to fish?" she asked Tom as the boat began to slow down.

"Yes," he said. "This is London's Bay. Named after Jack London, I think. I've heard he visited the Chain a time or two."

Alex looked around. The *Stephanie Lara* rocked in a wide natural harbor with islands on three sides. They looked much like Anfesia: soft green treeless slopes rose from beaches where driftwood and boulders lay in tumbled masses. Here and there she could see the bright orange or pink of a large crab-pot float.

Louise and Hank were readying a skiff behind the fantail.

"Have you been inside the wheelhouse yet, Alex?" asked Tom.

"No," she said as she watched him pull on rubber hip boots.

"I have a feeling the skipper would like some company. Why don't you go on in?"

Alex found her way to the enclosed area where the skipper was steering the boat. The windows were smudged. She rapped on the door, then slid it open and poked her head inside. On her lips was a thank you for letting her come out on his boat.

"Hello, there," said a very familiar voice. "How did you sleep last night? Better than I did, I'll bet."

"Ian!" she exclaimed. She had managed to put him out of her mind and now, here he was. "I—I'm so surprised to see you. What are you doing here?"

"Steering the boat, of course," he laughed as he indicated the wheel.

"No, I mean, *why* are you here?"

"The skipper had some urgent business in Kodiak, so he flew out very early this morning. I told him I'd take over for him for the day."

"I'd forgotten you knew how to do this," she said.

"Yeah, spent one whole summer playing skipper of a boat," he said. "Like I told you, my dad wanted me to know the business from every angle. And this is no hardship, believe me. I love being out here." He motioned to her. "Come in and close the door. You're letting out all of my warm air."

She stepped across the raised threshold and slid the door shut behind her. Ian was watching the proceedings with the skiff, turning the wheel slightly in order to steady the boat. He was dressed in faded blue jeans, scuffed deck shoes and a black turtleneck beneath a gray wool shirt. Her pulse quickened at being in this small space with the man who had played havoc with her emotions on the beach just the night before. Memories of the wondrous sensuality he had awakened in her came to mind in vivid flashes.

"Maybe you should've left that door open, after all," he said.

The corners of his blue eyes were creased with mockery, she thought as he looked at her. His dark hair peeked out from under his watch cap, and his wide mouth was quirked into a tilted half smile.

"Why do you say that?" she asked.

"Well," he drawled, "you look plenty warm to me. In fact, I'd say you look overheated."

She touched her cheek. It was hot. She realized that a flush had given her away again. He was mocking her; she was sure of it. She refused to give him the satisfaction of knowing what effect he had on her.

"It's just because I've come in from the cold," she lied.

She grabbed off her hat and stuffed it into one of her anorak pockets. Her hair fanned out around her face. She brushed it back with hands that were suddenly, maddeningly shaky.

"Oh," he said softly, "and I thought it might be because you're happy to see me. You know, flushed with joy."

His tone was hard to read. Was this a friendly tease, or was he baiting her? She couldn't be sure, but she thought she could see an ironic glint in his eyes.

"How *did* you sleep, Alex?"

"Not very well, I'm afraid," she admitted.

"Serves you right." One eyebrow rose. He shot her a frosty glance.

She turned to leave before they quarrelled again. She could feel that her stomach had already begun to flutter nervously in anticipation of another unpleasant scene.

With silent ease, he reached around her and grabbed the door handle.

"Take it easy, Alex," he said. "I'm just expressing my bruised ego. Don't leave." His tone had softened.

"Look, about last night..." she started as she turned to face him.

"Why don't we forget about last night," he said. He moved back to the wheel and glanced down toward the activity on the deck. "While I was thrashing around in bed, I realized you're probably right about us."

"What—what do you mean?" Her voice was almost a whisper. A dull ache of apprehension began to form in her stomach.

"We're adversaries, you and I," he said. "No matter what kind of attraction I may feel toward you, that fact remains. One of us is going to lose on this crab plant issue, and it isn't going to be me." His eyes took on a glittering hardness as he spoke to her. "Your instinct is to pull away from me, for in the end, that's the way it must be anyway. Am I right?"

"Yes," she murmured, "that's the only way I see for this thing to turn out. But," she added in a firmer voice, "don't be so sure about the crab plant. I'll fight you every inch of the way, you know."

"I do know that. But you'll only end up regretting you expended so much time and emotion for nothing."

His attitude rankled Alex. "You are the most arrogant, stubborn…"

He caught her by the wrist and leaned close to her face. "Look who's talking stubborn. Can't we table this stimulating conversation for now? I have work to do."

She closed her mouth in a tight line, then relaxed somewhat, for she had caught the smallest flicker of desire—or was it sadness—in his eyes. There was an awkward little silence in the small enclosure.

"All right," she finally said. "Another truce."

"And," he said as he turned back to the wheel, "I won't bother you again. It's best we nip this thing off now before we both get hurt."

These words cut into Alex sharply, even though she knew he was right.

"You might want to put your hat back on," he said. "I've got to get topside. Come with me to watch as we set the net."

"Fine," she said and pulled on her hat. She was determined to put her hurt feelings aside and concentrate on the new things she was seeing.

Throughout the entire operation, Alex took many photographs, finding the purse-seining method of fishing a fascinating spectacle. A large flock of seabirds was attracted by the activity, gathering from unknown distances to congregate where there might be food for them to snatch and gobble down. As soon as the crew had stored the salmon in the hold, the boat was again on the move.

The sky suddenly clouded over and some rain fell. Alex gathered the lapels of her jacket closer around her neck and fastened the top snap of the anorak against the slight lowering of the temperature. She stayed in the wheel-house, venturing out once with her hood up against the short squall.

Very few words were exchanged between her and Ian during the move to the next fishing spot. She found herself mulling over Ian's stand regarding the crab plant. She forced herself to mentally step back and try to be objective. Was it possible that Ian's determination to see his project completed was based on something besides a personal aggrandizement? She knew that he had a commitment to his workers and to this area. A new crab plant would help a great many people—not just Ian. Maybe a plant near the rookery wouldn't wreak havoc on the bird life, as she was convinced it would. Provided certain precautions were taken, of course. She seriously doubted it, because all evidence was to the contrary, but she would give it some thought. She didn't like to admit it, but Ian was right about one thing: he wasn't the only stubborn one.

Ian also seemed to be deep in thought each time she cast him a secret, sidelong glance. His chin was firmly set, his eyes gazing straight ahead into the rain. Every now and then he referred to the radar and to some intricate nautical charts that were spread out before him. Then he adjusted the wheel as he changed course, presumably choosing the deepest, safest channels.

Alex wondered where his thoughts were. It couldn't be easy being the head of such a big business, and he was still new at it. She imagined that the responsibilities of looking out for the local economy and all those workers must weigh heavily on him at times. Still, he mustn't be allowed to sacrifice an important natural area, even if his intentions were of the very highest. She gazed silently out the window, fretting over her thoughts.

By the time the crew was again making another set with the net, the rain had stopped. The sun came out, warming the water that had accumulated on the deck and turning it to steam. Alex undid her anorak and took off her hat, jamming it into one of her pockets. She joined Tom on deck.

"Crazy weather," she commented to him as he closely watched the length of net he was feeding out.

"Typical Aleutian summer, I've been told." He grinned back at her. "That hot spell we had was just a fluke."

"That's what I've heard, too," she said. "Where are we, by the way?"

"Oh," he said, "you're going to love the name of this place. It's called Peregrine Harbor. That's some kind of bird, isn't it?"

"Yes, it is."

She looked around. This body of water had land on two sides—islands that curved in toward each other, forming a large, natural harbor. Both islands had cliffs of gray stone flecked here and there with patches of grass and small willows that clung precariously.

"Funny, I thought there were only seabirds and eagles up here," he commented. "A peregrine is some kind of hawk, isn't it?" He shaded his eyes as he watched the skiff dragging the net out in a big arc. "What would a hawk be doing in the Aleutians?"

"Actually, it's a type of falcon," she said. "See those cliffs over there?" She pointed and he nodded. "Those would be very attractive to a peregrine for building an aerie—a nest."

"What kind of fish do they eat?"

"Oh, they eat mostly birds. They stoop—dive—from the air at unbelievable speeds. They capture birds either by grabbing them on the ground with their talons, or by knocking them from the air and catching them before they land."

"Whew! That must be something to see." He sounded impressed.

Gazing through her binoculars, she said, "Yes, it is. I've only seen it a couple of times myself, and it took my breath away." She swung her field glasses slowly along the tall cliffs as she looked for a likely ledge for the regal falcon. "If you see anything that remotely resembles one, let me know, will you? I'd love to get some pictures of a peregrine up here."

"Will do," Tom agreed.

The first two sets in Peregrine Harbor yielded several hundred fish each. Alex stayed on deck and chatted with Tom, for she sensed that Ian wanted to be alone with his thoughts. She looked up at him on the bridge a couple of times, but he seemed not to notice and didn't acknowledge her glances.

Ian didn't strike Alex as a man who would withdraw like this very often. And on those rare occasions when he did, she suspected his reasons were sound. Perhaps he was thinking about their conflict over the crab plant or maybe his abrupt announcement that their relationship should cool off. Was he regretting his decision as having been too hasty? Was he wondering if he could keep such resolve?

As a third net load of wriggling, flapping fish was swung aboard, there was a loud shout from the bridge.

"Open the net!" Ian yelled down to Tom. "There's a seal caught inside it. Louise, come up here and take the wheel!"

Suddenly, there was a lot of activity. Alex jumped to one side as Louise ran to the bridge. Then, Ian rushed past her to help Tom with the sagging net. Ian hurriedly opened it and the boat became awash in flopping salmon. Their slippery bodies slid every which way, some thudding against Alex's ankles, others escaping back into the sea. Ian made no attempt to stop the avalanche of fish as he grappled with the webbing. At last a tiny seal pup, bawling loudly, emerged from the pile of jumping salmon. It looked around, peering up at the humans with large, brown eyes. It had stiff whiskers on either side of its mouth, and its head moved gently from side to side as it gazed about at its alien surroundings.

"What a beautiful little animal," breathed Alex as she bent closer to look at the perfectly formed seal.

Its coat was slick with seawater, its eyes liquid with curiosity. It took a couple of steps forward, lunging on its flippers and belly. It bawled again, and this time it was answered by a sharp bark that came from the water near the skiff.

"Look, Alex," Ian said, pointing to a large seal head that was poking up from the waves. "There's its mom. I'll just check out her youngster before we hand him back."

He knelt beside the little pup, gently feeling its pudgy body and carefully examining its flippers. At last he got up and said, "No damage done, thank goodness."

"Do seiners capture many seals?" Alex wanted to know.

"Oh, a few," he said. "Especially pups, who don't know any better. I'm glad this one, at least, didn't get hurt in the process. Maybe now it'll stay clear of boats."

"Wait a minute," she said, looking intently at him, "don't fishermen hate seals? Seals eat the fish the boats are trying to catch, right?"

He wiped his hands on his jeans and looked over at her. "Yes, there are those fishermen who don't like seals."

"So why are you saving this one?" Her voice was quiet.

He smiled ironically at her. "I know you believe I'm a cold, bloodthirsty capitalist, but I'm not as insensitive as you seem to think. Sure, seals eat some of the salmon. But the way I look at it, there are more than enough fish to go around, as long as people don't get too greedy. The fishermen who work for us make their living by catching salmon, not by killing every seal they come across. Besides," he continued, "harming a sea mammal is against the law. You're not suggesting I'd break the law, are you?" He glanced at her sharply.

"No, I'm not," she said. "I guess I'm just surprised to see you acting on the part of wildlife for once. It's a pleasant change," she said a trifle more caustically than she'd intended.

"You have a lot to learn about me, Alex," was his retort. His eyes narrowed, but whether it was from the sun's glare or emotion, she couldn't tell. "I believe we humans share this planet, we don't own it. And if we use the natural resources properly, there should not only be enough salmon for us and for the seals, but for the generations of seals and humans coming up. That's why there are such strict rules about fishing these waters, or haven't you noticed that the boats don't go out every day?" His voice carried an argumentative tone of challenge.

Alex refused to get caught up in another battle with him. She turned back toward the seal. "Yes, I've noticed that, and I knew it was because Fish and Game had closed some of the days to fishing." She put out her hand

and touched the little creature. "Don't you think we should reunite these two?"

She looked up at him. He was standing with his legs slightly apart. His hands were on his hips in that familiar pose, the one he tended to assume, she'd noticed, when he was behaving as her adversary. In the struggle with the net, his hair had fallen forward; a shock of it lay mussed on his tanned forehead. His cap had come off and lay somewhere in the mass of fish bodies. His mouth was set in a firm, determined line, and his blue eyes, the color intense and startling in the sunlight, were staring unflinchingly at her. She could see that she had offended him and it made her sorry.

"I think the mother's getting upset," Hank shouted from the skiff. He pointed to the mother seal which was swimming back and forth beside the *Stephanie Lara*. She was keeping her distance yet demonstrating that she was unwilling to leave without her pup. Hank steered the skiff farther away from the animal, leaving a wide trail of foam and roiling water in its wake.

"Right," Ian yelled back to him, waving as he did so. Then he said to Alex, "I'll let you do it. Go ahead, help this little one jump overboard."

Alex stepped through the fish that littered the deck and approached the pup, which had moved away and was again calling loudly to its mother. She gently lifted it over the side. The baby lunged forward and dived into the water. It swam to its mother, which nuzzled it in greeting, then led it away through the swells. Both dived and were gone.

Ian threw a pair of gloves at Alex. "Help us get these fish into the hold."

"Sure thing, Skipper," she said. She didn't at all mind being asked to take an active part in the cleanup. Within a few minutes, they had recaptured the salmon, except for a few that slipped back into the sea.

Ian replaced the hatch cover. "That's it for the day. Let's head for the tender," he said. "Bring it on in, Hank," he shouted to the bearded man who was standing in the stern of the skiff, waiting for instructions. Hank waved and guided the smaller boat over to the *Stephanie Lara*.

By now it was late afternoon, and Alex had assumed that the boat would soon be heading back to Chulinka Bay. She had shared a light lunch with the crew some hours before, and now her stomach rumbled as she thought about the lonely dinner she would make for herself. Somehow the solitary aspect of the meal didn't appeal to her in the least.

"What's this about a tender? I thought we'd be going back to the cannery about this time," she said to Ian.

"Normally, we would," he said, "but today is kind of special. The crew made plans to meet the *Nancy Pat* and the *Carolynda* for a crab feed. Instead of taking our fish back to the cannery ourselves, we'll transfer them to the tender, then go meet the other boats." There was a tentative look on his face as he added, "Of course, you can get on the tender and head back, if you'd rather, but you're welcome to stay with us."

Was it just her imagination, or did he really sound as if he wanted her to come along with the crew? Careful, she told herself, don't read more into this than there appears to be. He's probably just being courteous. She again pictured herself eating alone in her cabin. That image settled the matter for her. She forced aside her misgivings.

"Do you really think I'd pass up the chance to go to a real Aleutian crab feed?" she asked, laughing up at him. "Of course, I'd love to join the crew."

Ian seemed to be trying to mask his emotions. It was almost as if he didn't want her to think that her answer mattered to him one way or the other. He said, "Fine, then. We'll get under way and be at the tender soon."

He and Alex returned to the wheelhouse, and shortly thereafter the boat was chugging out of Peregrine Harbor. Ian guided the *Stephanie Lara* through a maze of sea stacks where gulls and kittiwakes swirled overhead. Alex remained pressed close to a window, deep in thought. She noticed that the shadows in the canyons between the stacks were lengthening with the oncoming end of the day. As it sometimes did, the approach of twilight created in her mind a wistfulness. Usually the sensation was fleeting, but now it lingered. She searched her mind for the cause of this emotion.

Something about the seal pup. Ian and the seal pup. She recalled this afternoon's scene in vivid detail: the pup entangled in the net, Ian rushing to its aid, his careful inspection to make sure the animal had not been injured. And then his words. What were they? "We humans share the planet, we don't own it." And he'd referred to the necessity for people not to be too greedy, and to protect marine resources with strict fishing laws.

Alex stole a glance at Ian, who was checking one of the charts. Suddenly her mood lifted as an idea occurred to her. She and Ian had been at loggerheads over the issue of his crab plant. Her insight today into his views on protecting the environment just may have given her the key she needed to dissuade him from his plan. She hadn't thought it possible before, but now she did—maybe he was open to compromise, after all. She took a deep breath and forged ahead.

"Ian?"

He looked at her. "You've been quiet, Alex. What's on your mind?"

So he'd been observing her, too, even though it had appeared that he'd forgotten she was even in the wheelhouse with him. Yes, she definitely had a lot to learn about him.

"As a matter of fact, Ian, I was rather deep in thought." She paused, momentarily unsure of how to broach the subject.

"Go on," he encouraged softly.

"Well, I...I was thinking about that little seal you rescued today."

Ian chuckled as he gazed out the window at the waves crashing against the tall stacks. "Set your mind at ease, Alex. It's just like you to be worried about it, but I'm sure that pup was none the worse for wear." He smiled over at her.

Alex shook her head. "No, actually, I wasn't worried about the pup. I think it'll be okay. What I was really thinking about was what you said while we were freeing it. You know, about humans sharing this planet with other species, and about the need to protect the environment and its resources."

"I see."

Alex noticed that Ian's expression immediately became guarded at this reference to environmental issues. She forged ahead before he could become defensive and try to cut her off.

"What I was thinking was that I've gained an important insight into how you look at things." She laughed at her own embarrassment. "In fact, if you want to know the truth, I've thought of you as being pretty unreasonable, but now I see there may be hope for you, after all." She purposely ended her admission on a note of humor as a way of trying to hide her discomfort.

"Gee, thanks." He quirked an eyebrow at her, and his tone reassured her that he'd accepted the humor and was touched by her candor. "Go on."

"I have a plan. Would you be willing to consider a compromise of some kind on the issue of your crab plant?"

He shook his head gently. "I guess my first reaction is that I don't see how there could be a compromise. I mean, to build it or not to build it seems like a black-and-white issue to me. Where are the areas of gray?"

Alex's feeling of hopefulness blossomed even as she listened to Ian's objection. His tone of voice told her that he would hear her out. She hastened to explain her plan more fully.

"Look, I'll admit that I've been pretty stubborn about this disagreement of ours."

"No kidding," he replied dryly, but his half smile softened what could have been a stinging remark.

Alex continued. "I've been unable to see areas of gray myself, but maybe they are there. Here's what I've been thinking. Would you be willing to read some materials I sent for? I contacted Dr. Harper and had her send up some seabird studies I know about. Perhaps if you read about other rookeries that have been threatened by development, you'd see that..."

He broke in. "I doubt that they'd change my mind, Alex."

"But won't you at least look at them and consider their findings before you go ahead with your plan? Please, Ian?"

"Alex, I'm sure you can pull out reams of evidence for your cause. But I'm telling you that the rookery won't be affected in the first place."

"And I think it will," she said softly.

There was a tension-filled silence in the little wheelhouse. Alex held her breath as she waited anxiously for a hint from Ian that he would yield even slightly on this important issue. She watched as his facial expression turned stony. His hands tightened on the wheel, and a muscle twitched at his jawline.

Finally, he let out a sigh and said in a low voice, "Okay, Alex, I'll read your case histories, and I'll think about a compromise." He dipped his gaze toward her and added in a warming tone of voice, "Just don't get your hopes up too high. I really doubt that there's a thing you or anyone else can do or say to make me change my mind about this."

Alex bit her bottom lip to keep from smiling broadly, and let out her breath with relief. In spite of his reservations, this tiny concession felt like a major victory. Hope was soaring in her breast, but she fought to keep her response in perspective.

Lightly she said, "That's just great, Ian. Thank you."

She turned to gaze out the window, already making a mental list of the reports and journal articles she would give him to read. This new tack of hers might fall flat, but it was definitely worth a try.

An hour later, the boat was tied up to the tender, a bargelike vessel into which the crew off-loaded their catch. Soon the two vessels were under way again, the tender heading back toward Chulinka Bay and the *Stephanie Lara* chugging toward its rendezvous with the other two boats.

Alex joined Ian in the wheelhouse. His expression was noncommittal as he glanced in her direction.

"So, have you enjoyed your first day on a purse seiner?" he asked her.

She leaned against the instrument panel and sighed deeply. "Yes," she said, "I really have. It's so interesting to be out here and see how this is done. I think I'll remember this day every time I open a can of salmon."

He smiled, but she could tell he was keeping a certain reserve with her. He was apparently determined to stick to his promise to keep their relationship on a friendly, platonic level. Why did an unbidden pang of wistfulness pass through her when she thought about that, Alex wondered. She knew it was really for the best, and all things considered, she thought they had both been very civil and adult the entire day. There had been many times when they'd been alone. He could have taken advantage of those moments of privacy to press an embrace upon her. But he hadn't; he'd kept his distance.

"Don't the boats sometimes fish much longer days?" she asked, trying to keep the conversation impersonal.

"You bet," he said. "There are times when the fish are running heavily and a crew might work sixteen hours or more a day for several days in a row. That is, if Fish and Games says so." He changed the subject. "The other boats beat us to the tender. There should be a nice fire going by the time we get there."

"Fire?" she asked. "For some reason I didn't realize we were going to be on land."

"We're headed for Beatrix Cove, right here," he said, pointing to a speck on the map. "We're going to go ashore at a little sandy beach on the south side and feast on Dungeness crabs. Ever had one of those?"

"In Iowa?" she said, laughing. "Have you ever tried to get fresh crab, even fresh-frozen crab, in the Midwest? If you can find it, it costs a small fortune."

"No, I guess I haven't," he answered. "Well, you're in for a real treat, then. Tonight you can eat as many Dungeness crabs as you can hold."

He smiled at her and suddenly the air was electric with unspoken feelings that crossed the small cabin, from his eyes to hers and back again. There was an awkward pause as both of them seemed to be holding their breaths, simply looking into each other's eyes. Alex felt a shiver go through her in spite of the warm, almost close, atmosphere in the little room.

The sound of Hank's voice broke the spell. "Smoke ahead," he yelled.

Alex wiped the steam from the window in front of her and peered out. Sure enough an island had materialized in the pale light of dusk. She could just make out a curl of gray smoke rising from a tiny beach.

"We're there," Ian's soft voice said just behind her.

He stopped the *Stephanie Lara* near the other two boats and ordered the anchor dropped. Then the five of them got into the skiff and made their way toward the beach and the crowd that was already gathered around a bonfire.

Alex looked around wide-eyed at the beauty of the Aleutians. Two other small islands lay to the west, their darkened outlines a sharp contrast against a florid sky. The sun was putting on its usual dramatic final act of the day, sending bands of vermilion, rose and orange fingering across the heavens. An early star winked on, then another. The sky was quickly turning from pale blue to deep violet. A few wispy clouds clung to the southern horizon.

Ian leapt from the boat and sloshed to shore. Hank helped him pull the craft partly up onto the beach. They tied the rope to a large rock as the others clambered out of the skiff and onto the shore. Some gulls and terns announced their arrival.

"Ahoy, the *Stephanie Lara*," someone from the crowd at the fire called out in greeting.

Ian walked with Alex toward the group, taking her elbow as he did so. Suddenly she felt foolishly proud and almost giddy at being seen with the handsome cannery owner. Calm down, she scolded herself, this doesn't mean a thing. After all, it was quite by chance that she and Ian had been thrown in each other's company today. And besides that, he'd promised there would be nothing more between them. She put a smile of greeting on her face as they approached the group on the beach.

There were about thirty people gathered around the bonfire talking and laughing. Some cannery workers had joined the festivities, too. Several driftwood logs had been claimed for seats. Some people were sitting on the sand, gazing into the flames. Alex caught Velma's eye, and waved to her. The redhead was sitting on a blanket with several other cannery workers. After returning Alex's wave, Velma poked at the fire with a stick and gave Alex and Ian a long, thoughtful look. Her gaze made Alex feel shy and flustered and she turned away and sat quickly on a small log. It was obvious that at least one person here tonight could sense her mixed emotions, Alex mused to herself.

A huge pot of water was already steaming on the coals toward the edge of the fire. Several large buckets of crabs had been carried to the fire's edge. Once the crabs were cooked, everyone began eating, the sound of cracking crab shells filling the evening air. The talk died down as the hungry crowd devoured the mounds of hot crab.

Ian had shown her how to suck the tender delicacy away from the shells and dip the succulent meat into the melted butter that had been provided by one of the crew. Tom had produced some loaves of crisp French bread, which he'd purchased from the tender. The air carried a pleasing mixture of odors: pungent wood smoke, sweet cooked crab and melted butter, and the salty tang of the sea that lapped behind them.

The piles of succulent meat never seemed to diminish. Every time Alex looked up, more cooked crabs were being placed on the handy weathered planks that had been salvaged from among the banks of driftwood. Steam rose from them on the cooling air. The fragrance drifted to Alex and made her mouth water for more, even though she had already eaten several.

Alex suddenly felt that all was right with the world. She cracked open one more claw section with a rock, pulled the crab meat out with her fingers and popped the morsel into her mouth. Finally satisfied, she leaned back on her elbows in the soft sand and sighed languidly. Someone was strumming a guitar on the other side of the fire. The mellow strains played upon her senses, causing her to smile lazily.

"You look awfully pleased with yourself," commented Ian, who had also put aside the remains of his own feast. "May I interpret the heartfelt sigh to mean that you enjoyed your first Dungeness crabs?"

She nodded toward the sizable mound of empty shells that lay to one side of her. "I think that's a pretty safe guess. That was fantastic, Ian. Food for the gods."

He leaned closer to her in the sand. "You're very beautiful." He said it so softly, she was sure no one had overheard him.

His comment sent pleasant shivers through her, but a warning siren sounded in her brain. She sat up. "Now don't start that kind of talk, or I won't believe you meant what you said this morning."

He smiled devilishly at her. "There's something about firelight and shadows and being near you that makes me forget every bit of my firm resolve." He grabbed her hand and pulled her to her feet. "Come on, I think I hear some sea otters."

She held back, wanting very much to vanish into the dark with him, yet feeling sure that she shouldn't give in to her impulses. They always seemed to get her into difficulties. She glanced around nervously. How would it appear to the others if she followed Ian out of the circle of light cast by the bonfire? But no one was looking their way; they were too interested in trying to sing along with the fisherman and his guitar. A glance at Ian told her that he didn't seem to care whether or not anyone saw them. She pulled her hand from his.

"Sea otters?" she asked. "Do you really hear some, or is this just a ploy?"

"Both!" He grinned, snatching up her hand again. "I really do hear some, and it's just the ploy I need to lure a scientist out into the dark."

So saying, he led her along the sand until they were behind an outcropping of boulders that concealed them from the others.

"Relax, Alex," he whispered close to her ear. His warm breath stirred her hair.

"What about our agreement not to get involved?" she asked.

He turned her toward him, refusing to let go of her. "Alex, Alex," he murmured, "I think both of us knew we'd never be able to keep such an agreement."

He cut off her protests by pressing his mouth against hers suddenly, forcefully, bringing to her mind a wash of heated memories of them sprawled together in sensual abandon the night before. His lips were firm, their demand easily read. His hands moved hungrily down her back and along her hips, as if renewing their acquaintance with her body.

Alex felt immediately aroused by his nearness and his intimate caresses. She had wanted all day to be held in his strong arms and pressed against that broad, firm chest; she had longed to taste his mouth on hers. His clean scent intoxicated her. Her lips tingled as he teased them apart to permit the kind of sweet intimacies that left her breathless and giddy.

"Wait," she panted. She pushed herself away from him, making one last attempt to keep their mutual resolve not to become romantically involved with each other. "Why don't you show me those otters. I really would like to see them, you know."

He sighed, then chuckled in a low voice that vibrated pleasantly on the night air. "Okay, I'll show you the otters."

The stars winked above them in an ebony sky. A pale sliver of a new moon had risen, casting a thin illumination over the bay. Ian took her by the hand and led her down to the water's edge.

"Do you hear them?" he asked her.

"I'm not sure." She strained to sort out the various night sounds around them. "Is it that high twittering?"

"That's it. Now look out there." He pointed. "Do you see that bump on the water? And that bump over there? Those are sea otter heads."

"I do see them!" she exclaimed.

As she spoke, the otters swam a few feet. The edges of their V-shaped wakes captured the faint moonlight, making the watery trails glitter on the black sea.

"Oh, I hope I get to see some in the daylight," she said.

"You might, although in this part of the Chain they're pretty rare. These creatures were almost hunted to extinction. They have rich fur coats, to keep them warm and dry in this cold water. Their fine pelts were almost their undoing."

"How many of them are there now, do you know?" asked Alex as she peered hard, trying to see the otters better.

"All told, there are about twenty thousand, I've heard," he said. "Of course, they're fully protected now, as they should be."

She turned to gaze up at him. "You're glad they weren't wiped out, aren't you?"

"What a crazy question, lady," he said laughing softly. "Of course, I'm glad. What's the expression? 'Extinct is forever.' Who in his right mind would want to be responsible for causing the extinction of another species?"

"I just don't understand you," she said, feeling some exasperation.

"What do you mean?"

"On the one hand, you talk very reasonably, just like an environmentalist..."

"Careful, your bias is showing," he interrupted to chide her.

"And on the other hand," she continued, "you act as if you couldn't care less about destroying the seabird rookery."

"Now wait just a minute," he said, holding up his hand. "You make me sound brutish. The argument you and I have about those birds isn't whether or not I care about them, it's whether or not they'll be affected by my building the plant nearby."

"You know that developing there will affect those birds!" she said heatedly.

He quickly moved toward her, saying in a mollifying tone, "Sweet Alex, I love your concern. But isn't there something better we could be doing with this romantic night?" He chuckled deep in his throat. "Besides, about two hours ago you worked your powers of persuasion on me and actually got me to consider—mind you, I said, consider—a compromise. Have you forgotten that already? I'll read the material you sent for, but I can't very well do it right now, can I, sweet Alex?" He paused and his voice became mellow, silken. "Now, where were we? Ah, yes, we were thinking of better ways to use this romantic night, weren't we?"

Once again, he'd sidestepped the issue, using his smooth voice and his virile appeal to draw her away from their dispute. He was infuriating, she thought to herself. He was right, though. She had gained some ground today, and she would be wise to drop the subject for the time being.

He was right about something else, too—the night was romantic. A galaxy of stars twinkled above them. The moon-sliver seemed magically suspended in the inky blackness and the lapping waves were gently erasing her objections.

He drew her up the beach, back to the sheltering boulders. Before she knew what was happening, he had pulled her down to lie beside him in the still-warm sand, cradling her body against his. He covered her eager mouth with his hot one, teasing her lips apart, thrusting his tongue inside to taste the sweetness he sought. A searing heat began building in her loins, spreading in waves to her limbs and out to her fingers and toes.

"Well, Alex, so much for firm resolve," he whispered raggedly in her ear. "I can't keep my hands off you."

He cupped one of her breasts in his hand, teasing the nipple, gently kneading it until she felt it grow hard and uptilted. He caressed her slowly, causing her to bend into him, pressing her body to meet his. She was burning with desire, wanting to give in to the sensations that were scorching a trail through her entire body. Her hands clasped his back. She felt the taut lines, the rippling muscles, as his hands continued their ceaseless exploration of her body.

She reached up to caress his face and felt the light stubble of a beard. Then her fingers wandered to their mouths. She gently explored with her fingertips, touching the outer edges of their joined lips. He broke away from their kiss and caught two of her fingers. She gasped as he drew them deeply into his mouth, capturing them in a wet embrace that made her throb with an almost painful ache. As she moaned softly, he showed her with his tongue on her fingers what nuances of pleasure awaited her if she abandoned herself to the urges that were leaving her breathless and wanting more. Her sob of desire was cut short by his mouth as it returned to her lips.

"How I want you, Alex," he murmured against her cheek. "How very much I want you."

He pressed one leg between hers, causing her to spread her limbs in the sand. Then he rolled partially over on top of her, bringing their hips and thighs together in a way that left no doubt in her mind about the urgency of his need.

With one hand, he reached under her sweater and pulled it up until her thin cotton blouse and her bra were the only barriers between her breasts and his hungry, seeking mouth. With a tenderness that brought a catch to Alex's throat, Ian cupped her breast and brought his lips down to capture the nipple. Even through the fabric, she knew the heat of his mouth, could feel the teasing sweep of his tongue as he aroused the bud to a taut peak. He began undoing the buttons on her blouse as she urged him on. Never before had she felt such an overwhelming desire for a man.

Suddenly he jerked his head up and seemed to be listening.

"Damn!" he swore softly, looking back down at her. "Someone just started up one of the skiffs. The crab feed's over, sweetheart. Much as I hate to stop here, I'm afraid we'll have to continue this later...unless you want to spend the night on this island." He nuzzled her neck, planting several warm kisses there. "Come to think of it, that might not be such a bad idea," he growled against her heated skin.

Alex, however, felt a twinge of panic. She struggled to rise, pulling her sweater down as she did so. "Oh, no, we can't do that, Ian. Come on, let's go."

She stood up, wobbling a little on unsteady legs, then laughed shakily, leaning against Ian in the dark. What a powerful effect his lovemaking had on her!

During the short trip back to Chulinka Bay, they were never alone in the wheelhouse. Crew members kept coming and going on errands or to chat, and several cannery workers had hitched a ride on the boat. It was impossible to exchange private words. Alex knew, however, by the unspoken messages that Ian sent to her with his adoring eyes, that she would be spending the night with him in his cabin. The thought both thrilled and frightened her. She wanted nothing so much as to throw herself into the passionate flow of intense feelings that had been kindled between them.

On the other hand, she knew in her heart that there would be a price to pay for her sensual abandon. How would this change things between them regarding their conflict over the rookery? Would he use her emotional involvement with him as a lever to wear down her resistance over the issue? Or would the increased intimacy ease their relationship in this area? Would they find a compromise, after all? She fervently hoped so.

These questions were still whirling in her mind when the boat docked at the cannery. The long pier was dark except for one large light that shone down from one of the warehouses, casting a pool of illumination onto the timbers. Alex, Ian and the crew and cannery workers disembarked into the pale light. Suddenly there was the sound of running feet on the dock. Alex looked up in time to see a young woman throw herself into Ian's arms. Instinctively she stepped back into the shadows and stared in surprise.

The woman appeared to be about nineteen. She was of medium height and had short, curly, nut-brown hair. Designer jeans and a dance leotard made of shiny fabric showed off her centerfold figure to perfection.

"Oh, Ian," the pert young woman exclaimed, "I was beginning to wonder if you'd *ever* get back. Mama said you were out on one of the boats, and I've been waiting and waiting for you. I just can't tell you how glad I am to see you."

"Sylvia," exclaimed Ian, "what are *you* doing here?" He removed her arms from around his neck, and looked down at her upturned face.

"I knew you'd be surprised, Ian," she laughed. "Aren't you glad to see me?" She pouted up at him.

"Well, yes—yes, of course, I'm glad, Sylvia," he said. A slight note of annoyance crept into his voice. "I just wish your mother had thought to mention that you were coming up, that's all." He looked around. "Alex, I'd like you to meet Sylvia."

Alex stepped out of the shadows and into the pool of light. Sylvia's sudden appearance had made her feel flustered and like an intruder. She tried to shake the reaction, but the feeling persisted. After all, Ian and Sylvia had known each other for many years.

Sylvia's familiar greeting had definitely put Alex off. The romantic mood of the evening had been shattered by the sight of the young woman bounding into Ian's arms. However, not wanting to seem rude, Alex smiled at the new arrival.

"Hello, Sylvia," she said. "I'm pleased to meet you."

Sylvia looked at Alex with an expression of surprise on her pretty face. "Oh, I didn't see you there. Hello." Then she turned back toward Ian. "Mama says to tell you she's prepared a special snack for you, Ian. She knows how hungry you get out on the water. She told me I was to bring you right up for it as soon as you got back." Sylvia's tone of voice conveyed how pleased she was to be springing this second little surprise on him.

"Uh, well actually, Sylvia," Ian began, glancing over his shoulder at Alex, "I had a big dinner. I'm not ready to eat again. And besides..."

Sylvia followed his glance and suddenly seemed to remember her manners. She was not quite able, however, to keep the note of reluctance from creeping into her voice as she said, "Oh, excuse me, Lynn..."

"Alex," Ian corrected softly.

Slyvia was a little taken aback by the correction, but she quickly regained control of the situation. "Oh, I mean Alex. Would you like to join us?"

Alex shook her head. "No, really, I can't. It's been a very long day, and I'm tired. And I ate a big dinner, too." She was already backing away, feeling an urgent need to escape. "Thank you, though, for wanting to include me."

"Alex, wait," Ian said. He sounded as if he wanted to escape with her.

"I really must go, Ian. Thank you for a very pleasant day. It was so interesting seeing how salmon are caught. Good night, now."

In his sigh, Alex could hear both exasperation and resignation. Perhaps he, too, felt that the romantic mood had fled.

"All right. Good night, Alex," he said.

She turned and walked away into the shadows, moving quickly to put a distance between them. The last thing she heard was Sylvia's voice saying something about chocolate-chip cookies.

Near her cabin, Alex relaxed her pace and expelled her own sigh—of relief. Unwittingly, Sylvia had provided her with an excuse to extricate herself from the situation that had been causing her such painfully conflicting emotions. Even though she had believed Ian when he'd said he wasn't interested in Sylvia, it was obvious to Alex that Sylvia was very much interested in him. The young woman's sudden arrival had snapped Alex back to reality, and she was relieved to have made her escape.

Suddenly she laughed, her mirth tinged with irony. She pictured Ian sitting with Sylvia and her mother, eating chocolate-chip cookies. If there was any way the scheming Hazel could figure out how to get her hands on a love potion, those cookies would carry quite a jolt.

Chapter Seven

The next few days dragged by for Alex, even though she immersed herself in fieldwork, trying to blot out her memories of being held in Ian's arms. Once he came by and asked her to walk with him along the beach so that they could talk. He'd read the articles and reports that she'd dropped off at his empty office the morning after the crab feed. The look in his eyes told Alex all she needed to know, and his words confirmed her fears.

"I've read these, Alex," he began. He indicated the bundle of journals that he held in one hand. "Look, I'm afraid there's nothing here that convinces me that my plan shouldn't go forward on schedule."

He handed her the journals, and she began searching through the bundle. She extracted the issue she was looking for, then held it up and showed it to Ian.

"Not even in this one?" she asked. "I can't believe this one about the gannet colony in Scotland didn't prove something to you."

He shook his head, "I'm afraid it didn't, Alex. That was a completely different kind of case. It was a different species of seabird, and the threat to the colony there was by an industry that's not even remotely connected to fisheries."

Alex hugged the other journals to her chest, and quickly leafed through the issue containing the gannet article. She wasn't about to concede the argument just yet.

"Wait," she said, "let me find it." She located the right page and quickly skimmed it, looking for a particular passage. "Here it is," she said and looked up at him. "Okay, listen to this."

"Alex, I've already read all of those, and I—"

"Please, Ian," she broke in, "just let me go over this one part with you. It sums up all that I've been trying to tell you about the rookery here."

She read the passage aloud, emphasizing certain key words and phrases, looking up as she read to check his reactions. His face registered barely disguised impatience. Clearly she'd about run out of options with him. She finished the paragraph and closed the journal.

"Well, what do you think?" she asked, and held her breath.

"Look," he said, hands on his hips, "like I said, I've read it all, and my decision is the same." He paused. "I think I've met you more than halfway on this, Alex. I've considered a number of possible compromises, and I'm sure none of them would work. Besides, I'm certain that the new processing plant will have minimal impact, if any, on the rookery."

Alex bit her bottom lip and tried to suppress any outward display of the extreme frustration she was feeling at his inability to grasp the basics of her argument. It was clear to her that he was trying to break the news to her as gently as possible, but it still hurt.

"I'm sorry, Alex. I did try to prepare you for this. That day on the boat, I said you shouldn't get your hopes up too high."

She gazed out at the water where the swells reflected swatches of bright sunlight. A couple of fishing boats bobbed at anchor, and the green mountains provided the usual serene backdrop. How ironic, she thought, to be embroiled in such an unsettling situation yet be surrounded by utter peace. What a contrast. She suddenly felt as if she was single-handedly fighting a secret war. Her hopes for a compromise had been dashed and she and Ian were right back where they'd started—at a stalemate. *Damn*!

She looked up at Ian, and she knew her firmly set jaw and snapping eyes were conveying a clear message to him. He spoke, his tone thoughtful.

"I can almost see the wheels turning in that pretty head of yours. You're not going to give up the battle, are you?"

"Of course not," she tossed back, holding her head higher.

He chuckled, shaking his head. When he looked back at her, he quirked a half smile in her direction.

"That's no surprise to me. You're one determined lady. I have to say, you have earned my respect."

In spite of her letdown feeling, Alex was warmed by Ian's words. The expression in his eyes told her he was sincere.

"Thank you," she murmured.

He changed the subject. "I, uh, was pretty disappointed the other night when you practically ran away from me on the dock. I was really looking forward to..." He paused and looked at her with an intensity of unspoken desire that brought a feeling of warmth to her cheeks. He went on, "To spending more time with you that night. Sylvia's a good kid, but she thinks of herself as the center of things." He smiled indulgently. "I'm sure she'll outgrow it. Her arrival was pretty untimely." Again he paused and took Alex's arm. "May I see you later tonight, Alex? We need to talk some more. About us."

She firmly pulled free from his grasp. "I don't think so, Ian. We can't very well pretend that the rookery issue doesn't exist." She sighed. "At least, I can't. I don't see any point in discussing our very brief relationship. I suppose we should have kept our agreement to halt our involvement with each other." It pained her to say this to him; she wished it didn't have to be this way.

She saw a hurt expression come into his eyes. Without another word, he turned and walked away, leaving a terrible silence in his wake.

From that day on, he'd left her alone. It was as if she didn't even exist, she thought to herself. The cannery became very busy as the salmon season reached a peak. When she did see Ian, it was always at a distance, and he was either deep in conversation with an engineer or consulting with one of the skippers. If he happened to glance in her direction, he didn't even acknowledge that she was there, but looked away without nodding or smiling.

She noticed, too, that Sylvia was frequently with him. Once the young woman reached up to brush a lock of hair from his forehead. Alex wondered if Sylvia's little grooming gesture, and Ian's apparent acceptance of it, bespoke of even greater intimacies that passed between them in private. Even though he had not been romantically interested in Sylvia in the past, perhaps he was now, she thought, and it hurt. Alex tried to avoid running into the two of them, finding it painful to see the man who had awakened such desire and longing in her. She renewed her efforts to push thoughts of him from her mind and concentrate on her work.

One day she sat for at least an hour on a heather-covered bank overlooking a stream. A pair of dippers busily came and went, gathering food for unseen nestlings. Alex watched carefully, noting their behavior.

At last she looked up from the fascinating scene. Someone was waving at her from a nearby bluff that overlooked the ocean. She waved back. It was Velma. Even at this distance, the older woman's flaming red hair stood out vividly against the green and brown landscape. Since their first meeting, she and Alex had gotten to know each other rather well. Alex had found Velma to be just what Ian had told her she was—a wonderful storehouse of amusing tales from her years in show business. Even better, Alex had found in Velma the friendship she'd been lonely for. The older woman was as sensitive and caring as she was entertaining. Alex hadn't yet broached the subject of Velma's art; today might present a chance.

She gathered up her materials and stowed them in her knapsack. She needed a break from her work and would join the other woman for some conversation. As much as she enjoyed spending long hours alone in the field, lately she'd been feeling the need for some company. She looked up at Velma and wondered what had brought her out here, so far from the comforts of the compound.

Her question was answered when she reached the other woman and saw what she was doing.

"Velma," she exclaimed, "Ian told me you painted, but I didn't think you'd come all the way out here to do it."

The fiery-haired artist greeted Alex with a broad smile. "Honey, there's a whole lot you don't know about me," she said, "and some things I'll never tell." She winked and chuckled to herself, as if at some secret and probably risqué memory. "Take a load off your feet, Alex, honey, and talk with me awhile."

Alex complied gratefully, slipping her pack to the ground and sinking down onto the spongy heather. The day, which had started out cloudy with a threat of rain, had turned sunny and rather warm with a stiff wind on the water. She could see whitecaps on the blue-green sea far below, but the breeze on the bluff was of a milder sort. Gulls were ivory specks on the waves and against the lighter blue of the sky. She leaned back on her elbows and closed her eyes for a moment, savoring the quiet. Then she looked up at Velma's painting, which was held in place on a small portable easel. Velma sat on a tiny folding stool, her paint box open on her lap.

A thought suddenly occurred to Alex. Her derisive snort caused Velma to pause in her work and look down at the younger woman with an expression of surprise and mock hurt feelings.

"Well, my goodness," she commented dryly. "I've had a lot of reactions to my paintings, but never one quite like that." She bobbed her head toward her half-finished seascape. "You think I ought to trash this one, is that it?" Humor twinkled in her eyes.

Alex laughed and sat up, brushing off her hands. "Oh, no, Velma. I'm sorry. Your picture's beautiful and so professional looking." She sighed. "I wasn't thinking about your painting when I made that sound."

Velma returned to her work, adding some daubs of color to one corner. "Well, that's reassuring." She paused. "But something tells me that you're not trying to learn birdcalls, sweetie. Come on, you can tell your old pal, Velma. That was a noise of scorn if ever I've heard one. So who's the unlucky person—anyone I know?"

Alex smiled at her friend's jocular probing. It was always so easy to talk with Velma.

"I was thinking about Ian and the big lecture he gave me when I first got here. He tried to scare me right out of my hiking boots with tales of how dangerous it was to wander around alone on Anfesia. He said none of his workers ever left the cannery compound by themselves. Oh no, they always went in groups." She paused and waved her hand for emphasis. "Yet here you are, far from the cannery. And, unless you have a chipmunk in your pocket, you were definitely alone until I joined you."

Alex realized that her diatribe against Ian had taken on a decidedly bitter ring toward the end. She ducked her head and bit down on a blade of grass she'd yanked out of the ground.

"Well," said Velma, "it's true he doesn't like us to go off by ourselves, but some of us do from time to time. Ian's pretty protective toward his workers, in case you hadn't noticed."

"Oh, I'd noticed, all right." Alex's voice carried a sarcastic edge.

"Besides," Velma continued, "I'm just too independent to be kept in one little spot, and Ian knows that. And to tell you the truth, he probably thinks I'm too tough of an old nut to get into trouble out here." She laughed good-naturedly, and Alex joined in. A thoughtful note entered Velma's voice. "I think that Ian, being the kind of man he is, would be particularly nervous about a young thing like you—new to the island and all—getting herself into difficulties. He'd take it personally if you got hurt while on 'his' island, if you know what I mean." She went on after glancing at Alex. "Something tells me that's not the only thing that bugs you about Ian McLeod."

"You can say that again," said Alex. "The main thing is his awful stubbornness, especially about that blasted crab plant of his." She pulled little tufts of grass out of the ground and flung them away in exasperation.

Velma stopped painting and stared down at Alex. "Do we know each other well enough, honey, for some straight talk?"

"Sure, Velma. You know I trust you. Go ahead."

Velma took a deep breath and resumed painting. "You and Ian remind me of Driscoll's coin."

Alex was puzzled. "Driscoll's coin? What's that?"

"Driscoll was an old buddy of mine in the theater. He always played the same trick on newcomers to the show. He'd offer to flip a coin three times, and he'd bet that it would always come up heads. He never failed to get the new sucker to lay down a dollar bet against him, and Driscoll always won. Why? Because his coin had heads on both sides, that's why." Velma shook her head and laughed. "Oh, he'd give their money back afterward, then everyone who'd been watching would laugh. That's how newcomers were sort of initiated into the troupe. You just were not the part of the 'family' until you'd fallen for Driscoll's coin trick."

"Okay, so how are Ian and I like Driscoll's coin?"

"Now comes the straight talk. You and Ian, in some very important and basic ways, are as identical as the two heads on that coin. I'm talking, Alex, about stubbornness. Now, that's not always bad, mind you. Stubbornness can mean determination, that you stick to things until they get done. But it can also mean holding on to an idea long past its usefulness."

Alex felt herself smarting a bit from Velma's words. It wasn't that her friend was being unkind, it was that her words carried more than a little truth in them.

"Have you, for example," Velma continued, "tried to work out a compromise about this project of his?"

"We came close, or so it seemed at the time," Alex responded. "I actually got him to agree to read some reports about some other seabird rookeries that had been threatened by development. He read them, but nothing changed. He said there's no way I can compare what happened at a rookery off Scotland, for example, to what's going on here. He absolutely refused to see the parallels. I had even stayed up half the night making notes in the margins and highlighting passages in yellow, so he'd see my point of view. But oh no, he's set on his plan, and nothing in the world is going to stop him from his grand march toward so-called progress. Honestly, he is the most arrogant man I've ever met!"

In her frustration, Alex stared at the ground as she bit off these last words. The two women sat for a while without talking. From far below came the gentle sound of waves breaking on the shore. Finally Velma broke the silence. At first Alex thought her friend had steered the conversation rather abruptly away from Ian.

"Have you ever thought about getting married, Alex?" asked the older woman.

The question was so unexpected that Alex was caught off guard.

"Well, I...I guess I'll get married someday. I'm not really looking for a husband, if that's what you mean."

Velma looked down at the young woman with a shrewd expression. Alex suddenly felt transparent under Velma's very perceptive scrutiny. She squirmed under her friend's gaze.

"All right," said Velma, "if you're not looking for a husband, are you at least open to the idea?"

Alex shrugged, at a loss to know where this conversational gambit was leading.

"Sure," she said. "I guess so."

"And you're not keeping yourself so busy and so preoccupied with your project that you'd miss a good husband prospect, even if he were right under your nose? Hmm, Alex?"

Now Alex really squirmed, for she sensed that the "husband prospect" Velma was hinting at was Ian. The idea left her feeling flustered and embarrassed. She sought an escape.

"I...I don't know what you mean," she stammered.

"Just keep your eyes and ears open, sweetie, and don't miss the forest for the trees, if you follow my drift."

Alex wasn't sure she did, but she certainly felt the need to steer Velma away from this topic. She quickly analyzed her reaction, and had to admit that her friend had no doubt sensed the romantic involvement that had been brewing between her and Ian. Suddenly this conversation had become too hot for Alex. She changed the subject.

"Do...do you work mainly in watercolors?" Alex asked, gazing up at the unfinished picture.

"That's right," Velma said as she added a wash of pale blue to the paper. She paused and looked into Alex's eyes. Her expression seemed to say that she would respect her young friend's privacy and go along willingly with this obvious shift to another topic.

She turned back to her painting. "Thank goodness we have a half day off. I'm so sick of feeding can lids into that noisy machine, I could just about scream." Instead of screaming, however, the good-natured woman simply laughed. "I've been dying to get out here to paint this scene, and it's tough to find the time. Not to mention that the weather has a way of not cooperating." After looking around she added, "Today is the perfect combination."

Alex sat up and looked more closely at the picture. "Velma," she began, "I'm no art critic, but I think that's very good."

"Why, thanks, Alex, honey," the older woman beamed as she reached for another smaller brush. "I just love painting, it relaxes me, you know what I mean? Way I figure it, everyone needs a hobby of some kind." She dug into one of the large pockets of the loose work shirt she wore over her sweater and slacks and withdrew a rag that was speckled with countless paint daubs in all colors.

"Have you, uh, ever considered turning your hobby into cash, Velma? I think you may be able to sell your work."

Velma laughed. "Oh, goodness no, I've never given it a thought. I just do this because it feels so good, know what I mean?"

Alex persisted. "Do you have any other pictures with you?"

"Sure, honey, right there in that case. Help yourself." She chuckled quietly to herself as she tossed the rag beside her and began mixing water with pigment.

Alex opened the battered wooden case and pulled out a pile of watercolors. She looked through the stack, then turned to Velma excitedly.

"These are very good. Why, you've got landscapes here that really capture the spirit of this rawboned land. And you've painted some absolutely lovely miniatures of the wildflowers. How many pictures do you think you have, altogether?"

Velma paused and looked down at her, her gray eyes twinkling. "Dozens and dozens and dozens. Don't forget, I've been coming up here for the salmon season for a good many years. And I always bring my paints along."

"And you've never tried to sell any of these?"

"Oh, who'd want to buy my little pictures?" Velma chuckled again as she patted her bouffant hairdo.

"People who visit my sister's art gallery, that's who," said Alex. She rushed ahead before the other woman could express her surprise. "My sister, Monica, owns a gallery in Des Moines, Iowa, and she's always looking for new talent. Just the other day, in fact, I got a letter from her. She asked me to be on the lookout for any art I find up here that might sell in her gallery."

"Well, I don't know..."

"No, wait, let me finish before you object," said Alex, holding up a hand. "She said that people in the Midwest would be fascinated by Alaskan art, especially paintings—you know, scenes from 'the last frontier.' I think your paintings would do very well. Not just because they're out of the ordinary compared with what's available back home, but because they're also genuinely good.

What do you say, Velma, may I send some of your work to my sister and see what she thinks?''

Alex waited for what seemed a long time, mentally crossing her fingers in the hopes that the artist would at least let her try to sell some of her work. She knew that Velma was struggling to help put her two children through college and could certainly use the extra money. If Alex's guess was right, the redhead stood to make a tidy sum off her art.

Velma had put down her brush and was looking out at the water, her hands still in her lap. At last she spoke.

"This has come right out of the blue, sweetie. I hardly know what to say."

"Say yes," prompted Alex.

"You honestly think that my little pictures are good enough that people would pay money for them? Cash?"

"There's only one way to find out, isn't there?"

Velma shook her head, causing her gold-hoop earrings to sway crazily. "Imagine that." She laughed. "Me in the art world. Why, it'd be a little like being on the stage, wouldn't it?"

Her eyes gleamed with fond memories and Alex realized how much the flamboyant former entertainer missed being in the limelight. She pressed her point.

"I guess it would be. You'd certainly have an audience."

"This is really nice of you, Alex. Are you sure your sister wouldn't mind?"

Alex smiled. "Mind? She loves showing new artists." She paused, warm feelings of affection for both Monica and Velma welling up in her. "And, Velma, I'd take it as a real privilege to be able to get you two together."

Before Velma could waver, Alex rose to her feet and brushed off her pants. She picked up her pack and said,

"What do you say? Will you do it? I don't think you'd ever regret giving it a try."

"You bet I'll do it, honey!" the older woman said with spirit. "How do I get in touch with your sister?"

Excitement gleamed in her eyes, causing Alex to feel a wave of joy for her. She could imagine all sorts of good things happening to Velma in the future if she took this first, and very important, step. And she knew her sister would adore the woman's theatrical ways. It was one of the reasons Monica was so successful in her dealings with people. She accepted, and even encouraged, any interesting eccentricities they happened to have.

"I'll send Monica a message today," Alex said as she adjusted her pack and hung her binoculars around her neck. "I'll tell her that some of your work is on the way. Would it be convenient for me to drop by your room later to help you pack some of your paintings? You could pick out some of your best things, and I'll try to find a good box and some packing material. I think I have just what we need among the crates the university sent up with me."

"Today will be just fine," said the redhead, her eyes shining. She reached out a paint-smeared hand adorned with several flashy rings. "Thanks, Alex honey," she said in a quiet voice. "You know, things haven't been too easy since my husband died. I want you to know that I appreciate what you're trying to do for me."

"I hate to see talent going to waste," Alex replied, feeling warmed by the woman's response. "Believe me, it's my pleasure. I'll see you later."

She spent the next hour at the seabird rookery, but found it hard to keep her mind on the birds' activity. She was so excited about Velma's venture into the art world that she could hardly contain herself. Finally she gave up trying, packed up her gear and returned to the compound early.

Back at her cabin, she found a packing crate that would be perfect for shipping paintings. On her way to Velma's, she stopped off at the radio shack and sent a message to Monica, telling her she'd be sending some art. After exchanging a few words with Dan, who hadn't seen her in some time, she walked to Velma's room.

The older woman lived in one of the bunkhouses that had been provided for the cannery workers. As Alex headed for the two-story, weather-beaten structure, a spot of color caught her eye. Sylvia, in a very revealing hot-pink bikini, was lying on a beach towel spread on the sand. It was unusual to see the young woman alone, Alex thought to herself as a pang of sadness and annoyance whipped through her. Where was her mascot, Ian?

Setting her chin against the emotions that had suddenly made her lower lip tremble, she tried to slip by the sunbather unnoticed, but Sylvia must have heard the sound of her footsteps on the path. She raised her head and spoke.

"Is that you, Ian? Where have you been? Come on down here and rub some of this lotion on my back." Then she looked at Alex and saw her mistake. "Oh, sorry," she said. "I thought it was someone else."

She sat up and tucked shapely legs beneath her. The tops of her full breasts were gleaming half-moons above the flimsy little strip of cloth that passed for a bikini bra. Her flat belly glowed slickly with oil. Her skin was golden, and her mop of curly hair was becomingly tipped with blond highlights from the sun.

"You haven't seen Ian, have you?" she asked Alex.

"No," Alex said, "I haven't." She tried to move on, but Sylvia held her back with another question.

"Are you still counting birds? My mother told me what you're doing up here."

Alex didn't particularly want to talk with the young woman, but she would never be intentionally rude to her. She pasted a smile on her face and said, "Yes, that's right."

Sylvia picked up a pair of sunglasses from among a pile of fashion magazines. Her mouth formed a moue. "No offense, but looking at birds sure isn't my idea of a good time." She put on the glasses and stared out at the blue-green water, which was studded with gulls. "I mean, I don't see what there is to look at. You've seen one bird, you've pretty much seen them all, right?" She glanced back at Alex as if she expected her to agree, then continued without giving the scientist a chance to respond. "It's so *boring* on this dull, little island. I just don't know how I'd be able to stand it if Ian weren't here. I mean—" she sighed, waving her hand to indicate her surroundings "—what's there to do out here in the middle of nowhere?"

Alex was stunned by the young woman's words. How anyone could be bored on this fascinating wilderness island was utterly beyond her. Never in her life had she seen such stark, magnificent beauty, and she knew she would never get her fill of it. She thought of the sturdy Aleutian plants that maintained a toehold under some of the harshest conditions in the world. And she thought about the seabirds that nested here and of the other creatures that had carved out a niche for themselves in this wind-swept archipelago. Why, it would take several lifetimes to discover all there was to know about these enchanting islands. The Aleutians, she realized, had worked their subtle magic on her. Whatever the outcome of her work on Anfesia, Alex knew that she would be back to explore further this remote string of pearls called the Aleutian Islands.

Boring? She was suddenly filled with pity for Sylvia, who was now thumbing idly through one of the magazines, a vapid look on her pretty face.

"Hello, Alex," a deep voice rumbled from behind her.

Startled out of her musings, she whirled around to see Ian standing on the path. Her heart seemed to skip a beat, and she felt a flush of warmth stain her cheeks. He looked wonderful. He wore his usual snug, fitted jeans and open-necked shirt. A lock of dark hair fell forward onto his tanned brow. Flashes of sensual hunger stabbed through her entire body, leaving her weak-kneed.

"Hello," she said, feeling uncomfortable. Not knowing quite what to say, she continued. "Sylvia and I were just talking about the island and what there is to do here."

"That's right, Ian," Sylvia said, leaping to her feet and scampering over to him. She leaned her nearly nude body toward him and placed her hand on his arm. "I was just saying how much I *adore* being here to keep you company." She took him by the hand and started tugging him toward her beach towel. "Come and rub some lotion on me, Ian. There are some spots I just can't reach." She smiled brightly, flirtatiously, as she coaxed him to follow her.

During this display, Ian's eyes never left Alex's. Even as his feet took a couple of steps toward the beach towel, he continued to gaze at her with an expression that was as intense as it was unfathomable. Briefly, so briefly that Alex assumed she had imagined it, a flicker of sadness and hunger seemed to seep through the blue eyes that bored into her. She flinched without meaning to. Instantly his expression once again became veiled and unreadable. Sylvia looked at both of them in turn, then shrugged and walked back to her towel.

"How's your work going?" he asked in an impersonal tone of voice.

"Just fine," Alex replied, forcing her own voice to be cool and steady. She lifted her chin a trifle. "In fact, I'll be leaving soon."

"Oh?" One dark eyebrow rose slightly. Again that unguarded look tugged at the corners of his eyes and was gone. An immense sadness, reminding her of wind on a lonely beach, blew through Alex's mind and heart.

"Ian," Sylvia called, "I'm ready."

"Sylvia," he said over his shoulder, "I'm busy right now." His voice had a studiedly patient tone, almost like that of a father pointing something out to a child.

"Oh, you're always busy," Sylvia complained. "You never have any time for fun." A magazine hit the pile with a slap.

Still his eyes held Alex's. It was as if he was waiting for a sign from her.

"I have to go," she said and took an unsteady step backward.

"Yeah, well, I'll see you," he said coolly, abruptly breaking the lock his eyes had been holding on hers.

He turned and sauntered toward the towel. "All right, Sylvia," he said. "I can spare a minute or two." He picked up the bottle of lotion and knelt behind her as she dropped the straps of her bikini bra off her shoulders. "Do you remember that talk we had yesterday, Sylvia?" Again that patient tone of voice. He began rubbing lotion on her back.

There was a pause, then Sylvia answered, sounding petulant. "I suppose you meant that lecture you gave me."

"Advice, not lecture," Ian corrected her. "Stop depending on me to keep you amused up here, Sylvia, and meet some other people. Have you done that? That young Sam off the *Toni Bea*, for example, is dying to get to know you."

"Oh, I'm having dinner aboard his boat tonight," admitted Sylvia.

"Now that's more like it," said Ian.

Suddenly feeling like an eavesdropper, Alex briskly left the scene. She struggled to pull herself together before she knocked on Velma's door. She couldn't quite put her finger on what had bothered her so much back there. Ian's odd behavior left her with many questions. But there was probably no point in trying to decipher vague looks and fleeting impressions, she told herself. She sighed and tapped lightly on Velma's door.

"Come on in," the redhead's cheery voice came through to her. "It's unlocked."

Alex had liked Velma's little room at first sight and had told her so. The older woman, because she was a regular at the cannery, was assigned the same room season after season. Over the years she'd added many small touches that made the space homey and attractive. One wall was covered with a length of weathered fish net she'd found on the beach. Attached to it were dried starfish, some small glass fishing floats and several bleached crab shells. On the other walls hung several of her delicate watercolors. Great bouquets of wildflowers arranged in vases and empty jars sat on nearly every surface. Brightly colored rag rugs were on the floor, and her bedspread was a rainbow of multihued granny squares. On the windowsill was a collection of colored glass from the beach, each piece worn smooth by the waves. A decorative tin held a handful of fluffy cotton grass. The overall effect was cheerful and reassuring. It was just the kind of room Alex needed to be in at the moment.

"Want some tea, honey?" Velma asked. "I've got the only can of Earl Grey on the entire island. You look like you could use a cup."

Alex set her box on the floor. "Sounds great," she said.

"Have a seat at the table while I put on the pot." Velma turned on a hot plate and placed a teakettle on it to boil, then reached for some cups and saucers. "You know, I think there's just nothing that quite hits the spot this time of day like a nice, hot cup of good ol' Earl Grey tea. My mother—rest her dear soul—used to tell me…" She broke off suddenly and rushed to Alex's side. "Why, Alex, honey, you're crying. Whatever's the matter?"

"I…I'm just tired, I guess," she said, sniffing loudly as she accepted the tissue Velma pressed into her hand.

She knew she should pull herself together, but part of her wanted desperately to let go. She needed to release the pain and loneliness she'd been suppressing in the past few days. Velma put an arm around her shoulders. This gesture of wordless comfort burst a dam of feeling within Alex, and she sobbed for several minutes before either of them spoke again.

"It's Ian McLeod, isn't it?" Velma finally said.

Alex looked at her through a blur of tears. The older woman's words stunned her; they were so unexpected. "What?" she said. "I don't know what you mean." She dabbed at her eyes and wiped her cheeks.

The kettle whistled shrilly. Velma walked over and poured the water into a large teapot that was encrusted with a raised design of dragons and golden pagodas. She set the steaming pot on the table and sat down across from Alex, handing her several more tissues.

"I didn't just fall off a turnip wagon, you know," she said to Alex. "And I'm not blind, either. I've seen how you act around each other. When I saw Ian whisk you out the door at the dance, I figured there was something in the air between you two. Then when you disappeared with him the night of the crab feed, I was sure of it. And I was tickled about it, too, do you know that? I've been coming up here for years, and I've wondered for a long time just when that gem of a man would be swept off his feet." She patted her teased red hair and smiled at Alex with a wicked grin. "Would've gone after him myself if I'd been a few years younger." Her face got serious again. "You're in love with him, aren't you?"

"No!" Alex almost shouted. "In love with that impossible man? Never!" She clenched her jaw and spoke through gritted teeth. "If he were the last man on the face of the earth, I wouldn't give him two minutes of my time!"

Velma leaned back and seemed unimpressed by this outburst. She poured two cups of tea.

"Sugar?"

Alex shook her head and took the cup in trembling hands.

"If you're not in love with him, why all this emotion? Did you two nice people have some kind of disagreement?"

With a deep sense of relief, Alex unburdened herself to Velma. She told her of the many times she and Ian had quarrelled over the future of the seabird colony, but didn't talk about the romantic moments they'd shared.

"So you see," she said, "neither of us is going to give in on that subject. We'll end up in facing each other in court, I suppose." Her heart felt heavy as she thought about the ugly legal fight that could ensue between her side and his.

"You know he'll get his way, don't you, honey?" Velma's voice was quiet in the little room. "That's a man who doesn't quit, no matter what. He'll have his new crab plant. And you'll end up wishing you'd gone home—like he tried to make you do—before you got so involved."

"Well, I'm a *woman* who doesn't quit," Alex said vehemently.

Velma sighed. "It's just too bad you and Ian have locked horns over this, because if ever I saw two people who were meant for each other, it's you and he. Well," she said and sipped her tea, "I suppose it'll be settled in court, then."

Alex barely heard her comment, for her mind had shifted back to the scene on the beach. She could hear peals of Sylvia's laughter drifting through the open window. In her mind's eye she could picture Ian's strong, tanned hands as they caressed the oil into Sylvia's smooth skin. Her vivid imaginings so distressed Alex that she gave a little choked sound and grasped her cup so tightly her knuckles turned white.

"Say," said Velma, glancing over at the window, then back at Alex, "isn't that Sylvia's voice I hear?" A sage look appeared on her face. "Well, I can add two and two and come up with four." She leaned toward Alex and said, "You're fretting because of the way Sylvia acts around Ian—like she has some kind of hold on him—am I right?"

Alex nodded her head vigorously from side to side, denying it even as she admitted in her heart that it was at least partly true. Judging from the conversation she'd overheard, Ian had apparently made clear to Sylvia his lack of romantic interest in her. But with persistence, perhaps Sylvia would capture his heart, after all.... The thought pained Alex, and she sniffed loudly into her tissue.

"Why," Velma snorted, "that little girl doesn't mean a thing to that man. You just dry those eyes, Alex, and listen to me. That mother of hers has been egging her on, all right, but I'm telling you, a man like Ian would never fall in love with someone like Sylvia." She wagged her finger. "Honey, she's not his type at all—anyone can see that." She paused. "Except you, I guess."

Alex dried her eyes, then blew her nose loudly. She felt much better now that she'd gotten her worries off her chest. Nothing had been solved, but some pressure had been released. She looked over at the redhead, who still wore a concerned look on her face.

"Thanks, Velma. It was good of you to listen to my tale of woe." She got up and reached for the box. "Let's start packing your pictures, shall we? I'm anxious to see which ones you've picked out to send to my sister."

Velma gave her one more reassuring hug, then they began their project. Within a couple of hours, two dozen of her best watercolors had been carefully crated, with the address of Monica's art gallery crayoned on the outside of the box. Velma said she'd send it out on the morning plane.

As Alex was leaving, the older woman again thanked her profusely for being the catalyst in launching this venture. Her eyes were shining brightly with emotion as she grasped Alex's hand, and the young woman again felt glad that she had stepped in to help the artist.

Several days sped by. Alex spent every daylight hour out in the field, mostly at the seabird colony. By now she had covered every inch of the island several times over, and felt she'd done justice to the task that had been given to her. The species she'd observed had been cataloged and counted; she'd accumulated thousands of photographs; and she was almost finished with her preliminary report on the rookery.

After a quick dinner each night, she sat at her typewriter for several hours, organizing her notes and presenting her findings in a clear and persuasive manner. She felt it was the most important thing she'd ever done in her life, preparing that report. She labored over its wording, writing draft after draft of some pages, until she felt satisfied with the results. No less than her very best effort would do in her attempt to save the wild spot she'd come to love. There were some nights when she forgot about the time and fell asleep slumped over her machine.

One day while she was sitting in her blind at the rookery, she realized that she felt an ever-increasing sadness as her departure day drew nearer. She knew that some of her sadness was caused by the fact that she couldn't remain on Anfesia Island. The small island had worked its Aleutian magic into her very soul. She felt torn up inside whenever she thought about leaving its pristine wilderness.

The day had dawned cool and misty. A few drops of rain had fallen as Alex had trudged along the familiar trail to the rookery. Now she pulled her anorak more closely around her as she gazed through her scope at some preening kittiwakes. She made some notes in the little pad she held on her lap, then looked through the spotting scope again.

Her mind began to wander. For the hundredth time since her last talk with Velma, she thought about what the older woman had said about Ian. Was the artist uncannily perceptive? Was Alex in love with him? Again she banished the thought. True, she was powerfully attracted to him and had been from the start, but animal magnetism wasn't a very solid base for a long-term relationship, she told herself.

There seemed to be more to it than that, however. She felt a sharp yearning, a longing for something she couldn't name. Part of her distress at leaving the island was connected with that yearning, she knew. Well, she thought with a sigh, if she was falling in love with Ian McLeod, she was out of luck. Their differences were too pronounced, and she must thrust such notions from her mind right now, she told herself sternly. There's no point at all in mooning over what you can't have.

"Alex?" a deep voice sounded from right outside the blind. "May I come in?"

Ian's approach had been silent and unnoticed by Alex. She jumped at hearing his voice and dropped her notepad and pencil.

"Sure." She made her voice sound light and natural. "The flap's in back."

For a moment, the dimly lit canvas blind was more brightly illuminated as Ian opened the flap and slipped his bulk into the already crowded space. Alex moved over to give him room, then closed the opening behind him. She looked at him, sitting so close to her in the pale, filtered light.

"How did you know I was out here?" she asked. She was curious and wary about his motives.

He smiled at her. "I watched you leave this morning. I figured you'd be coming here when I saw you take the trail." He looked around. "Cozy, isn't it?"

"So now I'm under surveillance," she remarked.

His eyes locked with hers in the dusky light. His voice was calm, reasonable. "Alex, you know you're not under surveillance. The only reason I watched you was because I wanted to grab some time alone with you. Calm down, okay?"

She thought she heard a pleading note in his voice, so she took a deep breath and decided to hear him out.

He reached into a bag he'd brought into the blind with him. "First things first." He grinned. "Food." He handed her a sandwich wrapped in waxed paper. "I figured you'd want some lunch out here and something hot to drink, this being your average Aleutian summer day."

Alex could see the mist swirling right outside the blind. She hadn't realized how chilled she'd become, sitting still for so many hours. He poured two mugs of steaming coffee. She took one mug gratefully, dipping her face close to catch the heat. The tantalizing fragrance wafted up to her.

The sandwich turned out to be slabs of juicy turkey on thick slices of freshly baked French bread. The latter was from the cannery's bakery, she knew. The food was delicious. She was touched by his thoughtfulness in bringing her this treat. Suddenly it was the best meal she had ever eaten.

Feeling unaccountably shy, she said to him, "Thanks for the lunch. This sandwich is great. Did you make it?"

"Sure did," he smiled.

I love his face, she found herself thinking. I love the way his blue eyes crinkle at the corners when he smiles. I love his expressive dark eyebrows and the clean blade of his nose. Strong chin, firm lips—she drank it all in until she realized she was staring and turned back to her sandwich. A wave of self-consciousness swept over her.

Ian acted as if he hadn't noticed her looking at him with such intensity. He had already started on a second sandwich and was taking sips of coffee between bites.

He was wearing a wool watch cap over his thick, dark hair. To keep out today's chill, he had donned a navy-blue jacket. Alex could see the moisture droplets on the dense wool. She loved the way his turned-up collar stroked his cheek each time he dipped his head for another bite of food. Realizing that she was again staring shamelessly at him, she looked away and fumbled with her mug.

"More coffee?" he asked, reaching for the thermos.

"Yes, thanks," she answered. "This is really very nice of you."

"My pleasure." He smiled, and she could see that it was.

He looked out at the cliffs and the blizzard of birds that wheeled above them. "This is kind of a solitary life, Alex," he said. "Don't you ever get the urge to settle down with someone?"

His question was so unexpected she almost choked on a bite of food. She caught herself just in time. Lately she had been feeling a little bit lonely, and she couldn't lie to him.

"I—I guess 'settle down' isn't the way I'd put it," she said. "Getting married is something I might do someday, but I'll never give up my career."

He was looking at her thoughtfully. "Then you haven't ruled it out all together?" he pursued.

She wondered where this line of questioning was leading.

"No, I guess I don't rule out anything when I think about the future. I'm just so happy with my work, I don't worry about tomorrow."

She wasn't being entirely truthful with him, and she disliked herself for it. She *had* been thinking about tomorrow the past few days, wondering if her career would give her enough emotional satisfaction. It had, until she'd met him and had other possibilities suggested to her. She hurriedly pushed such thoughts from her mind. Don't wish for the moon.

"Well," she rushed on, changing the subject, "I can't believe you came all the way out here to discuss my life goals." She paused. "Why did you come?"

She dreaded hearing his answer, but she had to know. Suddenly the atmosphere in the small canvas cubicle was awkward and tense. He cleared his throat and looked down at his mug. It was the first indication she'd had that he, too, was nervous.

"I thought I'd try one last time to talk some sense into you, Alex," he said as he looked over at her. She felt herself stiffen with resentment.

"You're the one who needs sense talked into him," was her tight-lipped response. "Thanks for the lunch. I think you'd better leave now," she said in dismissal, turning back toward her scope.

She could see from the corner of her eye that he had again turned to look out the blind at the seabird cliffs. The sound of the crashing surf mingled with the calls of thousands of screaming birds that filled the sky.

"I'm not leaving until we settle this," he said in a very quiet voice. "I know you'll probably be flying out of here in a few days, and I can't let you go without giving it one more try." He placed a firm hand on her arm, forcing her to look at him. "Hear me out, Alex." His eyes held hers and she steadied herself. "That crab plant is going to be built right here where I've planned for it to be. You know, you haven't even considered the fact that it will create new jobs for the Aleuts who live near Anfesia."

"Don't make it sound as if I'm against creating jobs for people," she said. "The point is that you could expand your present plant to handle crab processing, and you know it. You don't have to build here."

"You're an outsider, Alex," he flared. His words stung her, for she had come to feel as if she belonged there. "You have some nerve coming up here, where you weren't welcome in the first place, and trying to tell me how to run my business. I've planned for the new operation to be built in this location, and I intend to carry out the plan. Period." His harsh words rang in her ears.

"Well, I'll see you in court, then," she said levelly. "You and your kind have to be shown, as often as it takes, that you can't be allowed to spoil every remaining wild place on the planet just because you have a blood lust for money."

"And I'm telling you that if you pursue this, you'll be wasting your time. That rookery out there will be totally unaffected by the development. You know my aim is not to destroy it."

"We've already been through all this before," she snapped back. "We don't agree. The material I've collected supports my opinion that if you build near this rookery, it will eventually be destroyed." She jerked her arm out of his grasp. "Why did you even bother coming out here? You're wasting my valuable time!"

There was an awkward and painful silence. The air inside the blind crackled with emotion.

The unexpected touch of his hand on her cheek made her catch her breath. The little sound was clearly audible in the small enclosure. His fingers felt slightly rough on the smoothness of her skin. They were warm and sure as they stroked her flesh with indescribable tenderness.

"I came because I care about you, Alex. Let me care about you."

His voice was low, deep, husky with emotion. She felt a throbbing in her heart and an intense longing to surrender her entire being to this man. He was the very first to arouse such feelings in her. Yield, her emotions told her, give in, surrender.

Even she was surprised when instead she flung out at him, "No, Ian. What you care about is making money."

Her voice carried more of an edge than she had intended, and she watched with dismay the effect it had on him. His face, which had softened with longing, instantly hardened and became the guarded mask she had seen that day on the beach with Sylvia. His lips tightened into a white line, and he withdrew his hand as if she had struck at it.

"Well," he said, a sardonic smile pulling at the outer corners of his mouth, "I won't take up any more of your..." he paused, then continued in a tone that dripped with sarcasm "...valuable time. And I won't waste my time explaining again my plan to improve the economy of this island. You've had your mind made up about me and 'my kind,' as you call us, from the very beginning, haven't you? You're foolish and stubborn, and you've managed to tear up my life in more ways than you'll ever know. The sooner you get off this island, the better I'll like it." He turned to leave. "Now, I have a cannery to run. As you say, Alex, I'll see you in court."

She waited as long as she could, holding back the sobs until she was sure he was far enough away so that he wouldn't hear her. Then the small enclosure rocked with the sound of her crying. She drew her knees up and hugged her folded legs tightly against her chest in a gesture of futile self-comfort. Sobs racked her chest, their hoarse sound filling the blind with pain. It felt good to let go, but the agony of facing up to her bitter unhappiness was almost more than she could bear.

She cried for a long time, hugging her legs, letting the tears run down her cheeks in a steady stream. At last it was over. Once again, the only sounds on the windswept cliff were those of the pounding waves and the shrill calls of the milling seabirds. The latter sounded to Alex like the keening of a thousand mourners.

Chapter Eight

Several days later the pain of her last encounter with Ian was still fresh in her memory as Alex listlessly packed some of her gear into the crates that would be shipped back to the university. She had made an important decision: she would try one more time to persuade him to drop his plans for the new development. Before she left the island, she would give him a copy of her preliminary report. Perhaps if he saw in writing what her findings had been, and read about the diversity of species she had discovered on Anfesia, he would appreciate the importance of disrupting the chain of life that existed there. She was forced to admit that she didn't hold out much hope that he would change his mind, but she had to try.

The sound of loud, impatient rapping broke into her thoughts. When she opened the door, bright sunshine poured into the room.

"Velma," she said. "What a nice surprise. Please come in."

She was very happy to see the artist. Not only was she fond of her, but she knew that a few minutes spent in her company would almost certainly lift her spirits.

"Got a minute, Alex, honey?" Velma asked excitedly as she came in. She was waving a piece of paper in one hand. "There's something I've just got to share with you."

Alex closed the door. "Of course I have time. What's up?"

"Dan found me and gave me this cable from your sister." Her eyes were shining brightly with happy agitation. A few flame-colored strands of hair had strayed out of place in her beehive hairdo. Her hoop earrings bobbed as she spoke.

"And?" prompted Alex.

"She likes my paintings," exclaimed Velma, waving the letter. The bangles on her wrist jingled.

"That's wonderful. I had a hunch she would."

"Not only that," the older woman paused dramatically, "but she's already sold one of them. Can you believe it? And she's going to send me a check. I've made some money off my art."

"Sold one? Why, someone must have snapped it up practically the minute your work went on display."

"That's what Monica says. She thinks there's a nice little market back there for my kind of work. Oh, Alex, I'm so doggone thrilled I can hardly stand it." Velma beamed at her.

"I'm so pleased for you."

"Listen, honey, I've really got to run. I'm on my coffee break, and I have to get back to that lid machine." She opened the door, then turned back to face Alex. "I just had to let you know before anyone else, sweetie. I can't thank you enough for what you've done for me."

"Oh, that's fine, Velma. Believe me, it was my pleasure."

"Well, got to run. During lunch and after work today, I'm going to sort through my other paintings. Your sister wants me to send a few more. Then there're all those scenes I've already painted at home, like the ones from the Pike Street Market in Seattle. Suddenly I'm a very busy person, and I love it. See you later, sweetie."

Alex watched the exuberant redhead walk quickly down the path toward the dock. Then she closed the door and returned to her packing. The day had started poorly, her mind preoccupied with worries. Now she felt better, she noticed. Sharing Velma's happy news had lifted her spirits. Maybe it wouldn't be such a bad day, after all.

She spent the next two hours sorting and packing her gear. Every time her mind strayed to thoughts of Ian, she forced herself to think about other things. The only matters that should be on her mind now, she told herself, were getting ready to leave and putting the finishing touches on her report.

After lunch she hiked out to the seabird rookery to disassemble her blind. She was determined to keep her emotions in check when she did so. But when it came time to walk back, the strong feelings she'd been suppressing washed over her. Tears sprang to her eyes.

She had folded the blind and stuffed it into her pack. Before she hoisted the bundle onto her back for the return trek, she paused to look around one last time. Would she ever return to the Aleutian Islands or to this particular spot that she'd come to love?

It was a particularly warm day. She shaded her teary eyes to look up at the myriad seabirds that wheeled above her. Their grace and their piercing calls filled her with the pathos of parting. The warm breeze carried spindrift up from the crashing waves below. It dampened her skin with a fine dew that mingled with her tears.

Almost angrily she wiped her eyes and cheeks and set her jaw with determination. She lifted the pack onto her back, swearing to herself that if there was anything on earth she could do to protect this area, she would do it. Ian McLeod hadn't won yet!

She stopped to rest several times on her way back to the cannery. The lush greenery was alive with birds today. Perhaps the warm sunshine had coaxed them out of hiding from among the rye grass and cow parsnip. It felt to Alex as if all the species of Anfesia Island were showing up to wish her goodbye.

As she was nearing the compound, Tom came running up the path toward her. "Alex, I've been looking all over for you!" He stopped in front of her, his earnest countenance animated with excitement.

"Hi, Tom," she said. "I was out taking down my blind." She eased her pack to the ground.

"Oh, yeah? That must mean you're getting ready to leave."

"That's right."

"Say," he said, "everyone's going to miss you."

"I can think of at least one person who won't," she said ruefully as the image of Ian's face flashed through her mind. "But never mind that," she hastened on. "Why did you want to see me?"

"I found a peregrine falcon's nest!" he exclaimed. "Remember how you told me—that day when you came out on the boat—that I should tell you if I saw a hawk-like bird flying really fast? Well, I saw one yesterday. I watched where it went, and I found the nest."

His news excited her. She would love to see the magnificent raptor. She knew that she'd never witness a sight more dramatic or awe-inspiring than that of a peregrine falcon—monarch of the air—in a full stoop with the wild Aleutians as its backdrop.

She clutched his arm. "Where?" she demanded.

He grinned. "I thought you might be interested, so I brought a map along to show you."

He knelt down and she followed suit. He spread the map in front of her, smoothing it out on the path.

"Okay, here we are at Chulinka Bay." He pointed. "Now, do you see Sumiak Island, this one northeast of Anfesia?" He indicated a dot on the map. More dots fanned out north of it into the Bering Sea.

"Yes," she said, "I do—just barely."

"Well, you're right, it's not a big place. But it has great cliffs on the west side, and that's where I saw the peregrine." He paused. "I'd offer to run you out there, but I'll be stuck here for a few days, working on our engine. Maybe someone else could take you to Sumiak, though."

Alex sighed as she looked down at the map. "Thanks, Tom. It was nice of you to tell me about this, but I think I'm going to have to pass. There are so many things I need to do before I leave. I don't think I'll have the time for a trip like this."

"You're leaving that soon?"

She looked up at him. "In a day or two."

He began rolling up the map. "Oh, I see what you mean." He smiled. "Well, look at it this way, Alex—now you'll have to return to the Aleutians to see that peregrine."

Being reminded of a return that might be years away put a painful edge on Alex's feelings. She struggled to present a brave front for the cheerful Tom.

"Yes," she replied. "Now, I'll have to come back to see the peregrine."

Both of them got up. Alex dusted off her knees as Tom finished rolling up his map. He glanced at his watch. "Hey, I've got to get back to the boat. Sorry to run." He held out his hand and Alex clasped it. "Take it easy, Alex. It's been great getting to know you."

"Thanks, Tom. Same here. Oh, and have a terrific wedding when you get back to Colorado."

"Thanks." He grinned. "I can't wait."

Alex watched his jaunty figure trot back down the path, then she hoisted her pack and resumed her slow descent to the cannery. Suddenly she realized that she was tired and quite hot. She shifted the bulky pack on her back and wiped the perspiration from her brow. There was no breeze at all, and her clothes were sticking to her in sweaty patches. A nice cool dip would be wonderful, she thought to herself. But swimming in the bay was out of the question because of the extreme coldness of the water, even on a hot day like this.

Then she remembered the tiny hidden lake that was behind and up the hill from the cannery. She had no swimsuit with her, but the lake was sheltered from the compound. No one would ever see her if she stripped down to her bra and panties and took a quick dip. The thought of the cool water sliding down over her heated, naked limbs put haste in her footsteps. She walked faster until she came to the fork in the trail.

In minutes she was standing beside the lake. Gratefully she dropped the heavy pack to the ground, then sat down to pull off her dusty hiking boots and wool socks.

She looked around with pleasure. About an acre of co-
balt-blue water gleamed at her from a cleft between two
green hills. Even though it was less than a quarter of a
mile from the cannery, it was perfectly concealed by the
configuration of the land. She would spend an hour or so
there, taking a much-needed rest break, then return to her
cabin to finish her report.

She peeled off her jeans, then unbuttoned her shirt,
tossing it down beside the discarded pants. Then, in her
bikini panties and soft lacy bra, she dived off the heathery bank into the still pool. She swam underwater for
several yards, then broke the surface, gasping. The top
layer of the water was quite warm from the sun, but below that, where her legs and feet were, the lake was chilly
and bracing. Her body had been so overheated from her
hike that the plunge into the lake was a bit of a shock.
But she soon adjusted to the temperature, luxuriating in
the silky feel of the water sluicing over her bare skin.

She swam out to the middle, playing like a seal, then
tread water as she felt the bottom of the pond fall beneath her feet. She flipped over onto her back and floated
there for many minutes, waving her arms languidly at her
sides. The feel of the cool-warm water rushing over her,
sliding along her thighs and swirling around her waist and
breasts, was just the tonic she needed. She half closed her
eyes in utter contentment as she stared up at the flawless
blue sky. This, she knew, would be another pleasant
memory she would add to the countless ones she was already taking home with her. Aleutian magic, she whispered to herself.

"How's the water?"

At first Alex was unsure if she had even heard the deep,
masculine voice, because her ears were just below the
surface of the lake.

"Hey, out there!"

This time there was no doubt in her mind. A man was calling to her. Damn! She had been so sure no one would bother her here. Who could it be?

She dropped her legs and paddled around to face the shore where she'd left her clothes. Ian was hunkered down on the heather, watching her intently. She was so surprised to see him, she forgot to kick her feet. Sinking below the surface for a moment, her open mouth filled with water. She rose again, sputtering and gasping, the water streaming down her head and face.

"Hey, be careful out there, or I'll have to jump in and save you," he taunted.

"How did you know I was up here?" she was finally able to ask.

"Would an ornithologist believe me if I said that a little bird told me?" He smiled ingenuously, his eyebrows raised in mock innocence.

She rolled her eyes, then answered. "No, she wouldn't. Come on, did you follow me or what?"

"I ran into Tom," he said. "He told me he'd just been with you on the path to the rookery. When I didn't find you on the trail, I figured you must have come here."

"I thought you'd see me in court," said Alex.

"Oh, I'm sure I will," replied Ian ruefully. Then he smiled. "But I much prefer seeing you in this setting. Besides, you must know by now that I'm incapable of staying angry with you."

"Well, maybe you should turn around and go right back to the cannery," Alex said. "I really don't think there's any point in our being together. We have nothing to say that hasn't already been said. I think we proved that the last time we talked."

She was sorry to utter these words because part of her really was glad to see him. But she knew she must harden her heart and try to get this disturbing man out of her system. She had come so close to losing her head over him. Now that she was about to drop out of his life forever, she was in no mood to torment herself with his presence. Besides, their last encounter had been so painful, she feared being drawn into another one. He, on the other hand, seemed to have determinedly put that incident out of his memory.

"Please leave," she repeated. "I'd like to get out of this water and put my clothes on. It's starting to feel a little chilly in here."

Instead of leaving, however, Ian sat down on the heather and continued observing her. A languid smile spread across his handsome face.

"Please don't let me stop you," he said. "Come on out. I'll even dry you off."

Her clothes were right beside him so she couldn't slip out of the water and get dressed without him seeing her in her transparently wet panties and bra. She decided to bluff.

"Fine," she said in the lightest tone she could manage, "I'll just tread water until you leave. Wait there all day, if you want to."

She stayed out in the deep water, away from shore, keeping as low as she could so he wouldn't see her nearly nude body.

"Sounds like a good idea," he said, leaning back on the bank with his hands behind his head. "I'll just do that while you enjoy your little swim."

He closed his eyes as if getting ready to take a nap, and Alex felt her irritation rise. She'd been a fool to try to bluff him. It hadn't worked before, and it obviously wasn't going to work now. Her feet were beginning to feel positively numb from the chill of the water. Shivers passed through her body. In another few minutes her teeth would be chattering. She was about to hurl some very uncomplimentary remarks his way when she saw that a third person had arrived at the lake. Some private swim!

It was Sylvia. She was dressed in shorts and a stretchy tube top. She was out of breath from climbing up the hill, and she stumbled a little as she approached the water. Alex wondered how the young woman had ever negotiated the rough trail in the strappy sandals she wore.

Sylvia stopped and took in the scene before her, her chest heaving as she tried to catch her breath. She peered out at Alex. From where she stood, it must have looked to her as if Alex was swimming in the nude. Well, so be it, Alex shrugged mentally. Maybe the young woman would get Ian to leave.

"Ian," Sylvia fretted, "I had a *terrible* time getting up that awful hill. Why in the world are you up here, anyway?"

Ian sat up and looked at her. His voice was calm and level as he ignored her question and asked one of his own. "What do you want, Sylvia?"

"Mama made me find you. I want to go back to Seattle because I can't stand another minute on this island. Sam said I could ride to Kodiak on his boat, then catch the plane home with him from there." She made a little moue of impatience. "Mama said I couldn't go with him unless I checked with you first. Honestly, you two treat me like I'm a baby or something."

"It's fine with me, Sylvia. Tell your mom I said that."

Sylvia smiled. "Oh, thank you, Ian. I knew you wouldn't mind. Well, I'd better pack. They're leaving right away. Goodbye, Ian.'' She tossed a wave in Alex's direction. "'Bye.'' Then she was gone.

Ian had removed his shoes and socks as Sylvia talked to him. Now he got to his feet with masculine grace and quickly pulled off his shirt and jeans, tossing them in a heap beside Alex's clothes. There was complete silence. Alex stared at him poised at the water's edge. His broad, muscular chest with its feathering of soft hair was splendid in the sun. A trail of the curly mat descended his flat stomach and disappeared beneath the waistband of his briefs. His thighs were well formed columns above athletic calves. In spite of the chill Alex was experiencing, her cheeks suddenly felt hot as she realized where her eyes had strayed. Her curious gaze left no doubt in her mind about the splendid masculine strength of the man before her.

He took two quick steps and plunged into the lake, slicing neatly and expertly into the water. Before Alex could gather her wits, he swam over to her and captured her in his arms. She would have cried out in surprise, but he covered her mouth with his in a passionate kiss that effectively stifled her exclamation. Their two bodies sank until their mouths were beneath the surface. She broke free and gulped for air.

"What do you think you're doing?" she sputtered.

He grasped her more tightly and said close to her face, "I'm getting to live one of my favorite fantasies at last—swimming with a beautiful mermaid."

His mouth once again claimed hers. Alex began to feel a drunken lethargy creep down her arms and legs. Her lightly clad breasts floated weightlessly in the water. They swayed repeatedly against his chest until the nipples were stiff and erect. Ian held her up in the water as he continued to grasp her by the shoulders and cover her mouth with his. His firm lips were wonderfully warm and inviting.

"Woman, you feel so good," he growled against her neck. "Your skin's like satin. I want to touch every delicious inch of you."

He wrapped her more completely in his strong arms, bringing his chest into firm contact with her aroused breasts. He kissed her again, this time teasing her lips apart to taste the sweetness within. Alex's mind whirled with conflicting emotions. As if sensing her confusion, Ian reassured her.

"Just follow my lead, sweetheart," he said softly and kissed her again. Then he leaned back a bit to gaze deeply into her eyes. Water droplets glittered like crystal beads on his brows and eyelashes. His bronzed skin was a sheen of wetness, and his hair framed his face in a shiny mass of damp waves.

"Hang on to me," he said.

He reached behind her and wrapped her legs around his sturdy waist, treading water for both of them. The movement threw her off balance and she was forced to put her arms around his neck.

"That's right, honey, just hang on to me."

He smiled roguishly as he looked down at her breasts, which buoyantly rose and fell near him. Their crimson tips were clearly visible through the flimsy bra. She felt naked all of a sudden, and wondered if she should try to swim for her clothes. Something—curiosity, she told herself—kept her right where she was, however. Her feet were locked together behind his back, and she was beginning to notice a delicious warmth where her thighs were pressed against his middle. She could feel the muscles beneath his smooth skin working to keep them afloat.

His lips nuzzled against her neck, and she suddenly felt dizzy and tingly all over. One of his hands slipped beneath her scantily clad bottom and pressed her closer to him. Flashes of heat exploded from her center to her extremities.

Alex's voice trembled as she asked, "Do you really think we should be..." Her voice trailed off, for her objections suddenly seemed irrelevant.

His words were muffled against her skin. "Oh, yes, Alex, I certainly do." Then he made swimming motions toward the shore. "Come on, sweetheart, let's get you out of this cold water. You're starting to shiver."

She had begun to tremble, but it was far more from the potent emotions that were coursing through her body than from the chilly water. Together they swam to the heathery bank. When their feet touched the bottom, they rose, rivulets of water streaming down their sleek bodies. Alex felt a wave of shyness pass through her as she glanced down at her scantily clad form. The lacy little scraps of fabric that were her panties and bra were plastered against her skin. Her full breasts and the mound of her womanhood were revealed through the transparent cloth.

She tried to cover the dark triangle that showed so clearly but Ian caught her hand.

"Let me look at you, Alex. You're so very lovely."

It seemed to Alex that the two of them, their damp bodies glistening in the sun, stood on the bank for many long moments while Ian openly admired her, clearly hungering for her. His eager gaze swept the length of her, pausing often to appreciate particular aspects of her form.

Then, in silent accord, they walked the short distance to a grassy spot, Ian gently leading her by the hand. He dropped to his knees before her and pressed his face to her flat belly. His feathery kisses sent molten shocks throughout her body. He murmured endearments against her still-damp skin, and his hands clasped her from behind, where they touched the upper slope of her bottom.

With her hands on his shoulders, Alex let her head fall back in sudden ecstasy. His hands and his lips were erasing the sadness that had held her heart since their last encounter. The hurtful words that had passed between them at the rookery now had no meaning for her. Within his eager embrace there was only today—this moment. All past events, all pain, had vanished as completely as a whisper on a windy cliff.

Renewed trembling coursed through her as Ian's head dipped lower and he kissed the top of her thighs. His lips were warm and searching. A little moan of pleasure escaped her throat. She had never before experienced such aching desire. As if he was aware of the ache she felt for him, his embrace became more tantalizing. His lips teased feather light on her skin as his hands explored the smoothness of the backs of her legs. His mouth brushed against her inner thigh and she moaned with a hunger she had never known before.

She knew that on this sun-drenched bed of moss and sweet grass she would give herself to him without reservation. Her heart reached out to him. She wanted to know him in all ways, for in the very core of her being, she knew that she loved him. She couldn't deny the messages that her heart and mind had been sending for so many days. Come what may, she admitted to herself that this man had captured her heart. She wanted nothing so much as to give herself to him completely and to know the sweetness their two bodies could create.

In one fluid motion they sank to the ground, legs and arms entwined on the soft green mat. Alex could feel the heat of his body warming her where his skin touched hers. His hands never stopped their exploring, their eager searching. His caresses kindled a fire in her that spread throughout her body. She heard him laugh softly with pleasure as he rolled with her on the spongy bed. Her body felt as light as thistledown as he masterfully tumbled with her in sensual play. Her mind whirled, fountains of color exploding in her brain, as she silently repeated over and over: *I love you, I love you.* It was such a tremendous relief to finally admit it, to give herself up to the feelings that had been with her for so long. She loved this man, and nothing would ever change that.

He laid her on her back and she looked up at him. His face was slightly flushed. Passion blazed in his eyes. One hand caressed the smoothness of her belly, then roamed upward to lightly touch the under curve of one breast. She caught her breath in sweet anticipation of what he could do to her body, and found herself gazing deeply into his adoring eyes.

"Alex," he murmured in a husky voice that left her gasping. "What a hot-blooded woman you are."

She trailed her fingers down his cheek. He caught her hand in his and pressed it to his mouth, closing his eyes as he did so. Flames licked through her as he kissed her sensitive palm, then her fingertips. Her mouth ached to feel the touch of his lips on hers, and she knew he was tantalizing her, making her wait for his kiss until she cried out for it. She curved her body against his, silently begging, imploring. At last, after a long pause, during which he simply looked deeply into her eyes, he slowly lowered his mouth to hers. For a fraction of a moment they were so close Alex could feel the soft tickle of his warm breath

on her eagerly parted lips. A low moan of desire escaped
her throat. She didn't know if she could stand another
second of the sweet agony he was causing her.

"Kiss me, Ian," she groaned. "Please kiss me."

"Oh, yes," he chuckled throatily, "I'll kiss you, Alex.
I'll kiss you as much as you like."

With that, he ground his mouth onto hers. Her hands
flexed with the keenest pleasure she had ever known. She
clutched in ecstasy at the muscled ridges of his back as he
slipped partway onto her. The hair on his thigh felt deli-
ciously ticklish on her smooth, bare skin. His knee
worked its way between her legs, parting them slightly.

His lips moved on hers, pressing firmly into the sweet
recesses of her mouth. She eagerly parted her lips and felt
his tongue slip inside to taste her honey and warmth.
With sensual abandon, she thrust her tongue into his
mouth and was delighted to hear a low, erotic moan issue from deep within his throat. Her skin, now dry from
the sun's warmth, was beginning to heat up, so intense
was the fire that he was stoking within her.

With one eager hand he cupped her breast. She felt it
swell and strain upward at his touch. He gently fondled
it, brushing his thumb over and around her sensitive
nipple. Vivid memories of the night they had lain on the
beach swept through her like a hot wind. Every sensation he'd aroused in her then was being repeated now
with even greater intensity. Seeing him make tender love
to her in broad daylight, with the vast blue sky as their
backdrop, put a keener edge on the pleasure.

Her nipple stood up stiff and erect, teased into intense
arousal by his thumb and forefinger. She guided his hand
to the front catch of her bra, encouraging him to explore
further. In a moment he had freed her breasts. Swollen
erotically, they were proud and eager in the balmy air. He

sighed raggedly and caught the tip of one breast between his lips. The sensation of his warm mouth on her cool nipple shattered Alex's already tingling nerves, and she writhed involuntarily. Her head fell back and her eyes closed as he worked his sensual magic on her. He flicked the nipple with his tongue and swirled around the dusky bud until it was throbbing with feverish agitation. He nipped and bit, causing ripples of excitement to flow through her. She felt the warm, hidden place of her womanhood pulse with eager anticipation. She was keenly aware of his stunning virility as his thighs pressed closer, brushing slowly and erotically against her. He was awakening sensations in her that she'd never known existed, fanning flames of passion that were beyond her wildest imaginings. With her whole being she longed, ached for him.

As his mouth returned to hers with an insistence that left her mind reeling, his hand trailed down her body. His slightly roughened palm caressed the satin of her narrow waist and the smoothness of her thigh. His fingers brushed the band of her bikini panties, then slipped beneath it. In a slow, deliberate motion, he smoothed and stroked the curve of her hip, all the while pressing ever closer to her. Alex was keenly aware of his strength as he ignited more and more sensations within her, urging her to respond to his driving need. She knew that in a moment the words that had been uppermost in her mind would spill from her lips. There would be nothing she could do to stop from telling him how much she loved him. She arched her body against his, eagerly meeting the sensual challenge of his hands and mouth and letting the unleashed passion that was sweeping through her claim her entire being.

The high wail of a siren cut through the air.

For a few seconds, Alex was sure that the loud insistent howl came from within her own brain. But when Ian jerked his head up, an alert look on his flushed face, she knew that the sound that rent the air was coming not from her own inflamed imagination, but from the cannery.

He quickly got up. "My God, Alex, there's some kind of emergency. I have to go!" He shook his head and tried to smile at her. "Terrible timing!"

He reached down and helped her to her feet, then ran the few steps to his pile of clothes.

The siren continued its mournful cry, shattering the serene, golden afternoon. Alex felt stunned, startled. Her nerve ends jangled at being snapped away so abruptly from the warm cocoon of lovemaking and into a maelstrom of hideous noise.

The sound conjured up frightening images in her mind. As she reached for her clothes, she wondered just what had happened. Had one of the machines broken down? No, that couldn't be. The engineers could handle that. This had to be something else, something much more serious. She knew, just from the haste with which Ian was pulling on his clothes, that this was a human emergency. Someone at the cannery was injured, perhaps even dying.

Chapter Nine

Ian was almost completely dressed. Alex was still fumbling with her jeans.

"I'm sorry to dash off," he said, looking over at her as he pulled on shoes and socks. He stood up. "This could be serious. I think someone's been hurt. That's the only reason that siren would blow, unless it's a fire, and I don't see any smoke." He glanced in the direction of the cannery.

"That's all right," she said. "I'll manage. You go on and see to whatever it is. There's no reason to wait for me."

"Will I see you later, Alex?" He was poised to leave. A question mingled with the concerned look on his face.

"Yes," she said, "you'll see me later."

He took one or two quick steps, then suddenly turned back and spoke to her. "Look, there's something I want to tell you."

"Yes, what is it, Ian?"

A knot of fear suddenly lodged in her stomach. Why did the expression on his face, the tone of his voice, make her feel panicky? Somehow she knew he was about to say something awful.

The siren clamored in the background, its wail a dirge on the still air.

He seemed to be wrestling with his thoughts. Then he looked at her and said, "No, not now, Alex. This would be a terrible time. Look, I'll tell you when I see you tonight, okay?" He smiled as if to reassure her that all would be well, and her fears vanished.

"All right, Ian," she said.

She watched him as he ran down the hill. Then she finished dressing, hurriedly buttoning her shirt and jamming her feet into her socks and boots. She wondered what he had to tell her. Could he have come up with a plan for a compromise about the rookery? No, that seemed unlikely, somehow. What, then—that he loved her? If that was it, he surely would have said so a few minutes ago as they lay together, wouldn't he?

She shrugged her shoulders. She'd find out tonight why he'd been so mysterious, but for now, there was the emergency at the cannery to think about. Hoisting her pack, she started down the trail.

When she arrived at the dock, she lowered her burden to the ground and walked out onto the pier. The cannery area was a scene of chaos. The siren had, by this time, stopped its dreadful wail. In its place was the shouting of many voices. Several people rushed past, their feet pounding on the heavy timbers. It looked to Alex as if everyone from the cannery had stepped out onto the dock. They stood around talking in anxious groups. Each little knot of people was a tableau of shock and surprise.

Many shook their heads, their hands to their mouths. Conversation was hushed and an air of dismay blanketed the dock. The cannery still hummed at its regular pace, as if in heartless counterpoint to the disruption Alex read in the scene.

She hurried over to Velma. "What's happened?" she asked. "Has someone been hurt?"

Velma turned toward her. Alex could see that her face was ashen, her mouth curved downward. The outer corners of her eyes were creased with worry.

"Something terrible, Alex, honey," Velma responded, "just terrible. Bennie, who works in the fish house, accidentally stuck his hand into the machinery. We think he lost some fingers."

Alex gasped, one hand going to her mouth in shock. How awful! That poor man.

"You don't know for sure how badly he was hurt?" she asked.

The older woman shook her head. "No," she said, "none of us saw it happen. But one of the other guys from the fish house told us there was a whole lot of blood. Bennie just sort of keeled over, holding his hand kind of funny."

"What will happen? I mean, surely he'll be flown out to Kodiak."

"Oh, yes. In fact, there's a plane on its way right now. It won't be long before he can be taken out of here. It's just terrible." Velma shook her head and bit her bottom lip.

"Here they come," someone said.

Alex looked in the direction the worker was pointing. She saw a group of people emerging from the fish house. Ian was among them. He was walking beside the stretcher that bore the injured man. All talking ceased as the party headed up the dock.

When the stretcher was in front of her, Alex recognized the man from her tour of the cannery. He was still dressed in his protective rubber clothing, but one sleeve, as well as the sleeve of his work shirt, had been cut away. The hand on that arm was concealed inside a mound of cloth and bandages. Blood stained the bundle in brilliant red patches. The man's face was white and drawn. His eyes looked up imploringly at Ian. Ian placed one hand on the man's shoulder and leaned over to speak to him. His voice was so soft and low Alex didn't catch the words he uttered, but it was obvious that he was comforting the injured man.

Ian glanced up and looked directly into her eyes. She saw a flicker of friendly recognition cross his face before he returned his full attention to Bennie. She watched as the group hustled down the dock and around the corner.

Feeling at loose ends, Alex wandered back to her cabin and sat down at her typewriter to try to finish her report. She found it difficult to concentrate on the page before her, however, because vivid images of the day's events kept racing through her mind.

She recalled the intense waves of emotion that had swept through her as she and Ian lay entwined, surrounded by sun-drenched heather. The exquisite feel and taste of him teased at her memory, and she closed her eyes to bring the images closer. She recalled, too, the scene on the dock, the sound of hurrying feet, the echo of the siren. Ian's face had been a mask of concern, his body tense, his stride purposeful.

As these thoughts churned in her mind, she heard the seaplane arrive, then leave shortly thereafter. It must have been the plane summoned to bring Bennie to the hospital in Kodiak. She knew that Ian wouldn't leave Bennie's side until he was sure his employee was all right. Considering how responsible Ian felt toward his workers, she knew that such a vigil could carry him to Kodiak with Bennie.

Sighing, Alex rolled the paper from her typewriter and set it on a stack of finished pages. This could wait, she decided, as she brushed one hand across her forehead.

The cabin suddenly seemed too small, and Alex realized that she was restless. Grabbing a sweater, she left the cabin and strode quickly toward the store. She'd pick up a few items for supper and see if any new magazines had arrived.

After her first meeting with Hazel, Alex had shared few words with her since it was usually Jennie, the young Aleut woman, who waited on customers. Often Alex caught a glimpse of Hazel in the back office hunched over her ledgers and stabbing at a calculator. Alex saw her out front only rarely. Today, however, Jennie was not in the store, and Hazel was behind the counter again. She wore a black smock over tan slacks, and her wiry hair bristled around her face in static disarray. Alex could see that Hazel was feeling even more harried than usual.

Alex set her purchases down on the counter for Hazel to ring up. They were alone in the store. The older woman weighed two tomatoes for the young scientist.

"Hello, Hazel," Alex said.

Hazel glanced up and appeared to force a quick, tight smile.

"Hello, Alex," she responded. She tapped some keys on the cash register and darted Alex a guarded look. "Well, I guess you've heard the news."

"You mean about Bennie? Yes, it's a real shame. I hope he'll be okay."

"Oh, that," replied Hazel. "Yes, yes, I hope so, too. He's such a nice man, always so polite." She paused and placed a green pepper in the bag with the tomatoes. "Actually, I meant about Sylvia. She's gone, you know."

She looked up into Alex's eyes with such a beseeching expression on her face that Alex felt a stab of pity for the woman. She recalled their first meeting when Hazel had revealed the supposed wedding plans to her, plans for Ian and Sylvia that existed nowhere but in Hazel's own wishful imagination.

"Well," said Alex, "perhaps it's for the best. I think Sylvia was sort of unhappy up here. I mean, don't you think she was, well...bored?"

Hazel set down the bag and rapped the counter with a small can of mushrooms. With rhythmic taps, she emphasized her words. She leaned forward and said to Alex, "That girl should *not* have been bored. How could she be bored with the handsomest, most wonderful—and certainly most eligible—man in the Western Hemisphere right here under her nose! She could have snapped him up. So who does she hook up with, instead? Who, I ask you?" Hazel sputtered as she appeared to search her memory. "What's his name?" She paused. "Sam." She rolled her eyes in a broad parody of disgust and waved the mushrooms. "Sam! A boy hardly older than she is. A young pup who hasn't a bean. A fisherman! But Sylvia seems to think they're falling in love with each other. My goodness, it's enough to break a mother's heart."

So saying, Hazel closed her eyes and pressed her hand—still clutching the can of mushrooms—against her breast.

Alex wasn't sure how to repsond to Hazel's tirade, and as it turned out, she didn't have to. The familiar voice of a third woman suddenly came from behind her.

"Oh, for heaven's sake, Hazel, get ahold of yourself!"

Alex turned to look at Velma, who had entered the store silently. Velma had apparently caught Hazel's little monologue of self-pity and was obviously not impressed.

Velma continued. "And please put down that can, will you? In your present state of mind, it's a lethal weapon."

Alex could tell by her friend's tone of voice that, in her no-nonsense but kindly way, Velma was trying to coax Hazel out of her doldrums.

Hazel opened her eyes, set down the mushrooms and looked at Velma, an exaggerated hangdog look on her face. She said, "Easy for you to tell me to get ahold of myself, Velma. You haven't just watched your only daughter throw away the chance of a lifetime."

Velma now stood at the counter beside Alex. She quirked an eyebrow at the younger woman, then leveled her gaze at Hazel. Velma spoke slowly and with emphasis.

"You can't throw away something you never had, Hazel."

Hazel stood up straighter and stuck out her chin. "What do you mean, never had?" She gestured with her hands, opening one palm up and tapping it with the fingers of her other hand. "Right here in the palm of her hand. She could have married Ian, and instead she throws him over for a young pup of a fisherman."

Velma put one hand on her hip, her rings clicking together and flashing fire. Her silver-hoop earrings bobbed as she talked to Hazel.

"Hazel, I've known you for several years, and you and I both know you're inclined to exaggerate."

Hazel reacted with a look of surprise: eyebrows up, mouth open in an O, one hand at the collar of her smock.

"Velma, dear, I'm not exaggerating. If that girl of mine had taken my advice—done what I'd told her—she could have snapped him up. They had dates. *Dates*, Velma, in Seattle."

Velma snorted impatiently and shook her head. "Those weren't dates in the true sense of the word, Hazel. Ian wasn't courting your daughter. He was just doing what he's always done—playing big brother to your little Sylvia. Sylvia told me about those so-called dates, Hazel, and even she didn't interpret them the way you do. So just stop reading things into them, will you?"

Hazel pulled a hankie from her pocket and dabbed at her eyes. She blew her nose loudly, then put the hankie away.

She looked at Alex and said, "I suppose you agree with Velma. No one seems to see things my way."

Alex felt trapped between a desire not to cause the woman further discomfort and her belief in candor. She hesitated, then responded in a firm but kindly manner.

"Hazel, I do believe Ian and Sylvia were never romantically involved. Sylvia is much too young for Ian, for one thing, and he seems simply protective toward her. I'm sure they have a certain affection for each other, since Sylvia did, after all, spend her summers here, the same as Ian. But in love with each other?" She shook her head. "No, I don't see that as ever having been a possibility for those two." She sighed ruefully. "At least, now I don't." She glanced meaningfully at Velma, who returned her look. Alex was remembering their chat in Velma's room when Alex had broken down and cried, and Velma had explained Ian and Sylvia's relationship to her.

Hazel said, "But if they'd just given it a little time…" Her voice trailed off. When she spoke again, her voice took on a wistful tone. "All I wanted was the best for my little girl. She's all I've got, and I wanted her to set out in life in style."

Velma reached across the counter and laid a comforting hand on Hazel's shoulder.

"Hazel, honey, style has nothing whatsoever to do with how much money you've got. Style is something you develop over time. Don't you worry about Sylvia. She just needs a few years of living so she can grow up and figure out for herself what she wants out of life."

Velma took her hand from Hazel's shoulder and patted her red bouffant hairdo. Her eyes twinkled as she continued. "And even if she marries Sam, who's a very nice young man, by the way," she added pointedly, "it won't be the first time a woman lost her head over a sea-going man. My first husband—may he rest in peace—was in the merchant marine. Didn't have a dime when we got married, but my oh my, were we ever the happy pair. Now, there was a person with style." She looked at the ceiling for a moment and hummed a snatch of a tune Alex didn't recognize. Perhaps it had been "their song."

Velma looked back at Hazel and said, "So set your mind at ease, Hazel. Your daughter will be just fine."

Hazel's face creased into a worried frown. "But she's on a boat right now, headed for Kodiak. What if there's a storm? What if they hit some rocks? Or what if Sylvia falls overboard? Oh, I shouldn't have said she could go, I should've—"

Her voice had risen until it was shrill with worry. Velma cut her off. "Take a few deep breaths, Hazel, and calm yourself. Sylvia will be just fine. That crew she's with knows what to do out on the water. It's their job. Nothing's going to happen to her.''

Hazel closed her eyes, and as Velma had instructed, breathed deeply. It seemed to help, too. When she opened her eyes again, she was no longer on the edge of hysteria. Alex could see that the day's events had nearly undone the poor woman.

Hazel said, "You're right, Velma. You're absolutely right. Sylvia will probably be fine, and I should stop worrying about her. It's just such a habit."

Hoping to change the subject and steer Hazel away from this disturbing topic, Alex asked in a conversational tone, "Where's Jennie today?"

She was immediately sorry she had brought up what had seemed to be an innocent subject, for Hazel reacted with irritation. The older woman's eyes snapped, and her unruly hair appeared to bush out even further, as if the wiry strands were electrified with pique.

"That's another thing!" Hazel exploded.

She launched herself into a second tirade, and Alex was suddenly relieved that the three of them were still alone in the little store.

Hazel gestured wildly and spoke with the intensity of rising emotion. "I don't blame Jennie, mind you. The timing's just bad, that's all. Her mother's sick, so Jennie went to her home village to see her. She'll be gone at least four or five days, maybe more. I was counting on Sylvia to help out in the store. But no—" she rolled her eyes in disgust "—*she* has to follow this young pup of a Sam and go traipsing off into the sunset with him!" She paused and looked first at Alex, then Velma. "Which means I now have to wait on customers while my desk work stacks up. Just look back there."

She pointed an ink-stained hand at her desk. Alex could see that, indeed, it was piled high with receipts, bulging manila file folders and ledgers with green covers.

Alex offered a suggestion. "Maybe you can catch up a little at night when the store's closed."

"Pah!" Hazel responded. "I'm already working at night because of all the salmon processing right now. You wouldn't believe the paperwork!" She shook her head. "You haven't even heard the worst part yet."

Alex and Velma exchanged bemused glances. There was something else? And it was the worst part? Oh, dear.

Both women looked back at Hazel, who said, "The worst part is this."

She drew a letter out of her pocket and waved it in the air. Then she used the business-sized envelope to tick off items on the fingers of her other hand.

"It's not enough that Jennie leaves me high and dry, or that my only daughter goes off with a fisherman. Oh, no." Her eyes sparked fire. "To top things off, this morning Mr. McLeod brings me this letter from his tax man in Seattle, and tells me to run up some figures for him. You know that crab plant he's been planning to put in on the other side of the island? Well, now he's changed his mind about it."

Alex had been only half-listening to Hazel's ranting. In her mind she had been forming a plan for making an exit from the store without appearing to be uncaring. She was sorry that Hazel's emotions were in such turmoil right now, but her instincts told her that once Hazel had vented her feelings, the older woman would probably cope pretty well. Hazel's last words rang in her ears, however, and she was suddenly alert and very interested.

She felt light-headed and a little breathless as she asked Hazel a question.

"You mean, he's not going to build it, after all?"

A flower of hope and joy blossomed in her breast. So that was what Ian had been alluding to up at the lake. He had been about to tell her, as he was hastening to respond to the emergency siren, that he wasn't going to build the plant, after all. Alex's spirits took flight. How wonderful! How absolutely wonderful!

Her embullience was quickly deflated, however, as she listened to Hazel's response. The bookkeeper looked at her, an expression of disbelief on her face. "Not build it? Of course, he's going to build it. What a question." Hazel looked at Velma as if asking for help in explaining the simplest of ideas to a witless person.

Alex's voice sounded chill and small. "What, then? I...I don't understand. How has he changed his mind?" Her disappointment was keen.

Hazel said, "Ian had been planning to start construction on the plant next year."

"Yes, I know that," Alex interjected with some impatience.

"Well, according to his tax man, it would be better to start the project this year. Ian has never been one to let grass grow under his feet. So this morning he gives me this letter and tells me he'll start building the new plant next week. Now I have to come up with some figures he needs fast, and clear off that mess—" she waved toward her desk "—and run the store, and..."

The rest of Hazel's words were lost to Alex as the awful truth sank in. Ian hadn't been going to tell her good news at the lake, but the worst possible news. It had never occurred to Alex that Ian might step up the construction schedule. Her ears rang and her vision blurred as she realized the full significance of this latest twist. Now Ian could neatly sidestep any legal challenge she and Dr. Harper could mount to prevent his project. By the time the courts could assess the situation, it would be too late, and the crab plant would probably be close to completion.

Without fully realizing what she was doing, Alex made a fist and softly pounded the counter. Silently she swore to herself. Damn him, damn him, damn him. Even as they had made love at the lake, he had known. He had already changed his mind, and with that secret knowledge he had kissed her and touched her and...

Alex shook her head to clear it of the painful images. She felt a reassuring hand on her arm. Velma was near and must have sensed her young friend's anguish.

Velma said, "Alex, honey, are you about ready to go?" Her caring tone of voice prodded Alex into action.

A fisherman had entered the store and was waiting for service behind Alex and Velma. Wordlessly Alex paid Hazel and picked up her bag of groceries. Soon she and Velma were outside and walking toward Alex's cabin. En route, Velma said, "I think I know how you feel, honey. Let's go inside your place and we'll talk." Alex nodded her assent, still too stunned and angry to speak.

A few minutes later, Alex and Velma were sitting at the table where Alex had been working earlier. Velma looked at the stack of typed pages beside the typewriter and said, "This is your report on the rookery, I'll bet."

"That's right," replied Alex, finding her voice at last, a voice that sounded subdued. "A lot of good it will do now." She sighed with frustration. "How could he do this? How could he just...just go ahead as if there was nothing in the world more important than building that damned crab plant of his?'' She shook her head, once again amazed at the wide disparity of their views.

"Honey," said Velma, "I just wish you weren't so emotionally involved in this issue. I could see that you were when we talked about it before." Velma's face wore an expression of concern. Alex could tell that her friend was very sorry to see her so disappointed.

Velma continued. "You approach your work seriously, Alex, and that's good. But you've taken this project too much to heart." She shook her head slowly from side to side. "I had a terrible premonition that you'd get hurt in the end. Ian is determined to bring economic growth to the island, and I figured your chances of changing his mind about that plant were just about nil."

"What did I do wrong, Velma? Did I miss something?" Alex begged for enlightenment from her friend.

"It's nothing you did or didn't do, Alex," replied Velma. "I don't think anyone could have changed the course of events up here. Ian is a stubborn man once he gets an idea. Remember how we talked about that? And, sweetie, I did try to warn you about it, just so you wouldn't get your hopes up too high."

"I know," Alex admitted dully. She gritted her teeth. "It just seems so...so underhanded, somehow, for him to change the date for beginning the development. He knows he can't really be challenged now before he starts building."

Velma shook her head. "It's not underhanded, Alex, and surely you must see that. It's a cold, hard fact of business that you do things to make money. And if Ian can get a better tax break by starting the project now, I'm sure he'd take that into consideration."

Alex sighed deeply. She felt resigned and helpless. "You're right, I suppose. I just have trouble understanding the motives that drive the businessman in him."

There was a long pause as the two women sat without talking at the little table. Alex could hear the muffled hum of the cannery punctuated by the sharp cries of gulls. She realized that she had become so used to these sounds in the background that she would miss them after she left the island. The thought of leaving added a wistful edge to her sadness. She stared down at her hands and bit her bottom lip to keep from crying.

Velma broke into her thoughts. She said softly, "I really wish you two could have figured out a compromise, Alex. I'm very, very sorry it didn't work out."

Alex looked at her friend and managed a smile. "Thanks, Velma. I appreciate that. I guess it just wasn't meant to be. Like you said once, we're two sides of the same coin, Ian and I—both as stubborn as can be." She chuckled without mirth.

Velma glanced at her watch. "My time's about up, Alex. They made everyone leave the cannery because of Bennie's accident, and told us to be back about twenty minutes from now. I need to stop at my place and change clothes, so I think I'd better scoot."

She stood up and so did Alex. Velma took Alex's arm. "Are you going to be all right, honey?"

"Oh, sure," Alex responded quickly, trying to make her voice sound more cheerful and optimistic than she felt. "You go ahead, Velma, and thanks again for listening. You've been such a good friend to me."

"Honey, it's been mutual," Velma said warmly. "Chin up, Alex." She walked to the door and turned to look back. "You know, I do believe in miracles. Something could still happen to change this situation. You never know.''

Alex sighed. ''Well, it would certainly take a miracle. I can't imagine what it would be, but I'll keep my eyes and ears open, just in case.''

''That's the spirit!'' rejoined Velma. ''Well, I'm off. See you later.''

Alex closed the door behind her friend and leaned back against it. She suspected that Velma's optimistic parting words were more of an attempt to cheer her up than an expression of what Velma really believed was possible. How on earth could Alex change Ian's plan now?

She silently thanked Velma for tactfully not referring to the romantic involvement between her and Ian. How like the perceptive older woman to realize that, even more than the issue of the crab plant, this subject had wounded Alex profoundly. It would be a long time, Alex believed, before she could speak of this deep, personal disappointment with anyone.

The admission that she'd lost the fight to save the seabird colony lay like a heavy lump in her stomach. Her one big desire now was to get off the island and as far away from Ian as she could. She tried to think of some way to stop him, knowing that it was hopeless. The best thing for her to do was to crawl away and lick her wounds. There would be other battles to fight, other wild areas to cherish and preserve. And, given time, she might get over her feelings for Ian. She would somehow relegate him to the past, to her memories.

Feeling more dejected than she had ever felt in her life, she looked around her cabin. The floor was littered with boxes and crates she'd already packed for the return trip. With weary resignation, she sat down at her typewriter. The report was a good one—she knew that. Even though she was resigned to the fact that it would not now be used in an attempt to prevent Ian from building his crab plant, she still wanted it to be the very best she could produce, from beginning to end. There were only a few more pages to type; she would work into the night until the project was completed.

The next morning dawned chilly and overcast. A few drops of rain splattered against Alex's window, awakening her at an early hour. She sat for a moment on the edge of her bed, stretching and yawning, and thought about yesterday's events. She wondered about Bennie. She hoped that he was recovering from his injuries.

After Velma had left yesterday, Alex had continued working on her report, taking only one short break to prepare and eat a simple dinner. The original and one carbon copy now lay on her desk. Late last night, she had read over the report, slowly paging through it, and she had been satisfied that it was the best work she had ever turned out. She felt certain that Dr. Harper would have no reason to regret having allowed her to conduct the species census by herself.

She was aware of feeling strangely calm when her thoughts turned to Ian and his effective defeat of her efforts to preserve the rookery. She could not deny that she loved him, though she tried. Neither could she deny that their conflict over the seabird colony seemed to epitomize a basic difference between them that could never be resolved. She felt coolly philosophical in the gray light of the blustery day. It was her misfortune to have fallen in love with a man who was as ruthless as he was attractive. In time she might even be able to forget him. Even as she told herself this, a little voice at the back of her brain told her that she would never be able to erase from her mind the memory of his lips on hers, the touch of his hands—so gentle, yet insistent—or the look of desire in his expressive eyes.

Brushing these disturbing thoughts from her mind, she got dressed and fixed herself a light breakfast. Then she went down to the dock to take one more look at the barn swallows. The five babies that had been raised in the warehouse had fledged. Alex found them perched on some wires above the dock.

As she watched the young birds taking short practice flights, the weather changed. The sun came out and warmed the air, making steam rise from the moisture on the roofs and the dock. The clouds that had obscured the sky were blown away to the far horizon. Only a few wispy shreds were left scattered across the vast blue canopy.

Alex's next stop was the radio shack. Dan was pleased to see her. He swiveled in his chair, its squeak still loud and unoiled. He folded his hands across his ample stomach and peered at her over his glasses, which were balanced, as usual, on the end of his nose. The radio crackled behind him.

"Come on in, Alex." He smiled at her. "I've been expecting you."

"Oh?" she asked as she entered. She sat on the scarred wooden chair beside his desk.

"Well, I heard you'd be leaving us pretty soon, and I figured you'd be asking me to reserve you a seat on one of the planes."

"That's exactly why I'm here, Dan. When's the next one?"

"Let me see," he said. He swung around in his chair and located a paper in the clutter on his desk. "There's a plane tomorrow afternoon at three. Should I save you a place on it?"

She hesitated for a few seconds, then said, "Yes, I think you'd better. I'm finished with my project, and it's time to leave." She added ruefully, "Much as I hate to say goodbye."

"They kind of get into your blood, these islands, don't they?" he said, looking at her with a kindly expression on his face.

To her dismay, Alex felt a lump forming in her throat. She fought to suppress her emotions and said, "Yes, they sure do. I know I'll never be the same again." In more ways than one, she added silently. She hastened to change the subject. "How's Bennie? Do you have any news about him?"

"Oh, very good news, in fact," Dan answered. "Ian flew to Kodiak with him, and he radioed me just about an hour ago with a report. Turns out Bennie was very lucky. He could've lost a couple of fingers, the cut was so bad. But the doctors in Kodiak were able to save them. He's out of a cannery job for the rest of this summer, but there's a fair chance he'll be back next year, good as new."

"That's wonderful," Alex said. "I'm so happy to hear it."

So, Ian was in Kodiak. She was relieved that she would not have to risk bumping into him at the cannery, for she knew she could not trust herself to be civil to him. All things considered, it would be best for her to leave the island before he returned. Her heart, however, suddenly felt leaden as the reality of never seeing him again sank in.

As if to confirm her thoughts, Dan said, "Ian won't be back for a day or two. He wants to wait for Bennie's wife to fly up from Seattle. And he says he can attend to some other business, as long as he's kind of stuck there anyway." He paused. "Is there any message you'd like me to give him?"

Alex smiled ruefully as she considered having Dan tell Ian that he was rid of her at last. "No," she said, "no message."

After leaving the radio shack, Alex hastened back to her cabin. The remainder of her packing took less time than she'd anticipated. By early afternoon she had finished and had formed a plan for the rest of the day. She felt such a pull toward the rookery. She would roam the island one last time and visit the seabird colony. She welcomed this chance to fill her remaining hours in the Aleutians with action. Passively sitting around feeling sorry for herself was not the way she wanted to remember the end of her stay.

Hurrying now, she stuffed a jacket and some food into her pack. Then she grabbed her camera and some extra film, slung her binoculars around her neck, and she was ready.

As she was leaving, the report on her desk caught her eye. She paused. She'd meant to give Ian the extra copy to read. Should she still do it? She took a couple more steps. Why bother? He probably wouldn't even open it, let alone read it. Again she stopped. Even if there was only a slim chance that her findings could dissuade him from going ahead with his plan, she had to try. Believing that Ian would probably toss her unread report into the nearest trash can, she nevertheless picked up the extra copy and left her cabin.

A few minutes later she was standing in Ian's empty office. It was quiet except for the muffled hum of the cannery. She ran her hand over the smooth leather of one of his chairs, remembering the night she had sat here pinned by his cool appraisal. So much had happened since then. She had come here on a scientific errand, never suspecting that she'd end up losing her heart. As she had said to Ian that first day, life *was* full of surprises.

The faintest essence of him lingered in the small room—that fragrance of spice and maleness that had so many times filled her senses with a passionate longing. She shook herself angrily and pushed these distressing thoughts from her mind. There was no reason why she should stand here and torture herself over memories of Ian. Almost belligerently she tossed the report onto his desk, right in the middle, so that it would be the first thing he saw when he sat down.

"Take that, Mr. Ian McLeod!" she said, her voice ringing with defiance. Then she spun on her heel and was out the door.

As she passed the dock she saw two fishing boats, the *Cathy Deb* and the *Morganna Kaye*, nosing up to the offloading area. The seiners rode low in the water, an indication that their holds were full of salmon. The crews waved, and Alex returned their greeting. She had come to feel so much a part of all this that she knew it was going to be very difficult to get on that plane tomorrow, especially since she didn't know when she'd be coming back to these seductive islands.

She started hiking up the trail. The sun warmed her bare arms, and the air smelled of sweet flowers. How many times had she walked this path, Alex wondered to herself with a feeling of poignancy.

When she came to the branch that led to the lake, she paused. She would have liked to see the little hidden body of water again, and she took a couple steps toward it. Then she changed her mind and returned to the main trail. No, it was better not to see the spot where she and

Ian had last lain together. The grassy bank might yet carry the imprint of their entwined bodies—had it been only yesterday?—and Alex knew she could not bear to remember the sweet passion she would never again experience.

Further on, she left the path and struck out overland. Soon she stood on the bluff where she had found Velma painting. She dropped her pack to the ground, and, shading her eyes, looked out at the magnificent view that had so entranced her artist friend.

In all directions stretched seemingly endless expanses of white-tipped blue, dotted here and there with rugged-looking emerald islands. A few fluffy clouds slid by overhead, blown by sea breezes that fluttered the short-stemmed flowers all around her. Is this the way the world looked before humans came along, she wondered.

She sat down and pulled an apple out of her pack. Biting into the fruit, Alex thought about Velma. Later on this evening she would stop by the older woman's room to say goodbye. Alex didn't like the thought of leaving the warm comfort of Velma's companionship, but she knew they'd keep in touch with each other. This was especially true now that Monica was handling Velma's paintings.

As these thoughts were passing through her mind, she heard the sound of a seaplane. That's strange, she thought to herself. Dan had said the next plane wouldn't arrive until tomorrow. But from the sound of it, the plane was now coming in low for a landing at the cannery.

She shrugged. It wasn't the first time an unscheduled flight had arrived on Anfesia. She lay back in the grass, her eyes closed and her head resting on her pack. The sun's warmth felt so soothing. She knew she'd remember the many pleasant sensations she'd experienced on this island for the rest of her life. Soon she heard the seaplane again, this time as it took off and headed back to Kodiak. She sighed. Tomorrow she'd be on a plane— perhaps that very one—as she began the first leg of her journey home. Home. It's funny, she mused to herself, but this place feels like home to me now.

She lay there for another thirty minutes, just letting her mind drift. Then she stood up and lifted her pack. She realized that she had been unconsciously putting off the most important part of this venture. She felt strangely reluctant and eager at the same time. But there was no sense in further procrastination. It was time to pay her last call on the seabirds.

Chapter Ten

A cloud of seabirds rose into the air as Alex approached the rookery. The piercing calls of kittiwakes echoed in the deep canyons that had been carved by centuries of battering by the sea. The sound of the flapping of thousands of wings filled Alex's senses and brought a catch to her throat. How many similar concentrations of wildlife had been destroyed because of the thoughtless encroachment of human beings?

Even as this gloomy thought flashed through her mind, Alex's heart leapt in celebration of all the life around her. She sat on a rock and drank in the scene, trying to etch in her memory the myriad sights and sounds that were bombarding her senses.

What was left of the afternoon sped by as she sat there, lost in thought. Later she looked up and noticed that the shadows around her had lengthened, and that the sun had started its slide into the sea. She hated to leave; she decided to wait a while longer before she started back.

With approaching twilight the air became chilled. A few gray clouds scudded overhead, and Alex felt a drop or two of rain fall on her bare arms. She laughed softly as she pulled her jacket out of her pack and put it on. There was that unpredictable Aleutian weather again— from sunshine to rain in a matter of minutes.

As Alex stared into the darkening canyons, she pondered her situation. What weighed on her mind was the fact that she had failed to save the rookery and had lost her heart in the bargain. Velma's words returned to haunt her: she'd said that Alex and Ian were like two sides of a coin—both alike in their stubbornness. Once or twice it had seemed that there could have been a compromise, but Alex now knew that was impossible. The situation was beyond her control.

Stubbornness.... She should have seen it from the very beginning. When she'd arrived, Ian had insisted she leave, and she had been just as insistent that she would stay. That first clash of their strong wills should have shown her that there could be no compromise between two such determined individuals.

Or could there? Perhaps she had been too hasty in her conclusions about the threat to the rookery. Velma said she believed in miracles. Well, why not? Alex reluctantly admitted that she had not worked as hard as she could have for a compromise with Ian. She had gotten on her high horse and pretty much stayed there. Maybe she could bring about a miracle herself if she considered the issue one more time. It could be she'd overlooked some key factor, something that would open the door to a mutually beneficial solution. She could call Dr. Harper for advice as soon as she got to Kodiak tomorrow. It was worth a try.

She wanted to run and tell Ian about her plan. But then she remembered that he wasn't on the island. She sighed deeply. There was no point in going over the problem now. To do so would only torment her. Tomorrow she would leave the Aleutians and put this particular phase of her life behind her. In the meantime, there were these lovely seabirds to enjoy....

A few minutes later she heard the sound of heavy footsteps behind her. She turned and saw a tall man striding rapidly in her direction. She jumped to her feet.

"Ian!" Seeing him was the biggest surprise of her life. "What are you doing here?"

He closed the distance between them and gathered her in his arms. Her face was pressed against his rough wool jacket as he crushed her to him. His strong arms encircled her, and he murmured into her hair.

"Oh, Alex, Alex. How I've missed you. It feels so good to hold you in my arms."

Her senses were reeling. She could hardly believe that he was here. Wasn't he supposed to be in Kodiak? How did he know she was at the rookery? And why was he here? A dozen questions tumbled around in her mind.

His jacket felt cool and slightly damp from the light rain that had begun to fall. He smelled wonderfully of that faint spiciness she'd come to associate with him, of maleness and of clean, salty air. Her heart responded with joy to his unexpected presence. Never had she been so happy to see anyone, and she twined her arms around his neck and hung on. All of the hurts—the harsh words that had passed between them over the weeks—melted away in those brief moments as they clung together atop the sea cliffs. All Alex could think of was that the man she loved was here with her. Nothing else existed. He was holding her fast and whispering endearments to her. Dare she hope that he might love her, after all?

It was some minutes later when he at last drew away from her and looked deeply into her eyes. She dropped her hands to her sides, for she felt suddenly and unaccountably shy. He held her by the shoulders and kissed her tenderly on the forehead.

"How did you know where I was?" she asked. "Why are you here? Why aren't you in Kodiak?" The questions spilled out of her.

Instead of answering her, Ian said, "Alex, you're trembling all over. Here, take my jacket."

He removed the garment and placed it around her shoulders. His warmth, captured in the heavy wool jacket, enveloped Alex like a balm. Without noticing, she had become chilled as she'd sat and watched night fall at the rookery. However, her trembling was due more to Ian's unnerving presence than to the change in temperature.

"Thank you," she murmured. "Now please tell me why you're here instead of in Kodiak."

"I'll explain the whole story, sweetheart. But later. It's raining, and it's getting dark. How does a cup of good hot coffee sound to you? Come home with me, Alex."

Alex was so overcome with emotion, all she could say in response was a heartfelt, "Coffee sounds absolutely wonderful." And the part about coming home sounds even better, she added silently to herself.

Ian put his arm around her shoulders and led her away from the cliffs, toward the path back to the cannery. They walked quickly, trying to beat the nightfall, but were unsuccessful. By the time they stood in Ian's cabin, it was dark outside. Ian snapped on a small lamp, instantly transforming the atmosphere of the cabin to a glowing coziness. She shrugged off Ian's jacket, then took off her own. She moved instinctively toward the cold stone fireplace, warmed just by the thought of flames leaping there.

"Can you make a fire?" Ian called over his shoulder as he headed toward the kitchen.

"Sure."

"You do that while I get the coffee going."

"You're on."

She knelt on the thick, soft rug in front of the fireplace and took kindling and paper from a box at one side. Soon a little fire was crackling on the stone hearth, sending out a warmth that made Alex sigh with contentment. She kicked off her shoes and added some larger logs to the blaze. The welcome fragrance of freshly brewed coffee drifted to her from the kitchen, and she could hear the closing of a cupboard door and the clink of cutlery. She flexed her hands in front of the fire and listened to the soft breeze that was soughing around the corners of the cabin. The old timbers overhead creaked comfortingly, and reflections from the fire danced on the walls and ceiling.

"Say, you've made it nice and cozy in here," Ian said as he entered the room. He placed two steaming mugs of coffee in front of the fire. Then he snapped off the lamp so that the only illumination in the room came from the flames. He kicked off his shoes and sat down beside Alex.

"Try your coffee," he urged her.

Alex picked up the mug and took a sip. The rich brown liquid was strong and delicious. "It's wonderful," she said. "Just what I needed."

She looked at him. He wore jeans and a wool plaid shirt, opened to that provocative triangle of chest hair. Glancing up, her eyes caught Ian's. The intensity of his gaze made her pulse leap. She knew he wanted her to spend the night with him and she wasn't sure if she welcomed the prospect. How would she be able to resist if he tried to make love to her? Did she even want to resist him?

He took her hand and raised it to his lips, never taking his eyes from hers. Ever so gently he pressed fervent kisses on her palm and fingers. The touch of his warm lips sent shivers of delight through her entire body. She knew with certainty that only tonight existed for her, and that she would follow his lead, no matter what he asked of her. The thought was both stimulating and humbling.

She felt as if his gaze would melt her. There was something different about him, she thought, but she didn't know just what it was. Although his altered demeanor confused her, it made her heart flutter with hope and joy.

"Now will you tell me why you're here?" she begged, striving to maintain her sanity.

He added a couple of sticks to the fire. "First of all, yes, I was in Kodiak with Bennie. He'll be fine, by the way."

"I'm so glad," she breathed.

"Yeah, I was relieved. Bennie's been with us every summer for at least fifteen years and I feel very close to him and his family." He paused, then continued with his narrative. "Well, anyway, I had planned to take care of some business while I was waiting for Bennie's wife to arrive from Seattle. I hated to leave until I'd gotten the two of them together." He rubbed a thumb across his bottom lip.

"Yes," she said softly, "Dan told me you'd be gone for a day or two. That's why I was so surprised to see you turn up at the rookery, of all places."

"I got a pilot friend of mine to fly me back to the island after I radioed Dan a second time and found out you were leaving tomorrow."

"Oh, that explains the plane I heard a little after noon today."

"That's right." He continued. "When I talked to Dan, it didn't take me more than two seconds to realize I couldn't stand the idea of not seeing you again. I was pretty mystified about why you'd leave so suddenly without even saying goodbye."

A look of genuine hurt flickered across his face and Alex felt a pang of guilt to think that she could cause this reaction in him. Then he went on.

"When I got back to the cannery, I asked around and found out Hazel had told you I'd pushed up the building schedule for the crab plant." He whistled softly. "I began to put it together. I can just imagine how that news hit you. I tried to tell you about it myself at the lake, but the timing was off. There was just no gentle way I could have done it. That's why I got you to agree to see me later that night, remember?"

"Yes, I remember," Alex said softly.

"Of course, then I had to fly out with Bennie, and you heard the news from Hazel instead of from me." He shook his head and gazed into the flames, a thoughtful look on his face. "To be honest with you, Alex, I don't know if hearing about it from me would have been any better. I don't know how I could have told you so it wouldn't hurt. I just kept thinking that maybe you and I could still work something out, that maybe there was a chance you'd change your mind and see things my way.

I know it must seem crazy, Alex, but I still held out hope for us."

As if he suddenly felt self-conscious about this disclosure, his face reddened slightly. He changed the subject and began unbuttoning his shirt, "Mind if I take this off? It's pretty warm in here." He grinned at her wolfishly. "Don't hold back if you discover you can't keep your hands off me." There was a playful twinkle in his eyes. She watched him remove his shirt and toss it aside.

"You're awfully sure of yourself," she teased back, giving her hair a toss. "Now, please continue."

She didn't register his next few words. Teasing or not, his playful gibe held a grain of truth. She *did* feel as if she couldn't keep her hands off him. She actually clenched her hands into fists in an effort to keep from touching him. He was magnificient in the golden glow of the firelight. Patterns of dancing flames licked across his chest and his curly chest hair looked so springy and soft she longed to twine her fingers in it. The tanned, taut skin of his shoulders and arms gleamed in the amber light. He had drawn up his legs and was sitting with his arms resting on his knees, his strong hands clasped casually in front of him. His back was a supple curve, its musculature accentuated by the flickering shadows. The firm, lean line of his thighs made her heart beat faster. His potent animal magnetism filled the room. She caught her breath, intensely aware of her reaction to him. Never before had any man had such an impact on her.

"Alex? Are you listening?" He was looking at her curiously, his eyes reflecting the amber firelight.

"Y-yes," she said, "but I'm afraid I missed the last thing you said. Would you mind repeating it?"

A slow smile curled his handsome mouth as he sized her up. She could tell that he'd guessed just where her mind had been wandering, and she felt her cheeks grow warm. Once again she was reminded of his perceptiveness.

"No," he said, "I don't mind repating it. I said that when I went to my office, I found your report on my desk."

She stiffened a little as she recalled her mixed feelings about sharing the report with him. She opened her mouth to speak.

"Wait," he said, "let me finish. I wasn't going to read it at first. I figured, what's the point?" He sat gazing into the flickering fire for a moment, then turned to look at her. "But I did read it, Alex. Maybe I was curious. I don't know. Once I'd started the first page, I couldn't put it down. It didn't take long. It's very good—quite well written and very persuasive."

She glowed under his compliments, then said, "A lot of good it will do, now that you've decided to start building your new plant next week. I just don't see how—"

He interrupted her with an upraised hand. "Please," he said, "we can talk about that later. First let me finish telling you how I found you."

Alex was secretly relieved. Deep in her heart she wanted nothing to spoil these precious moments with him, for they would probably be their last together. Here they were, tucked away in a cozy cabin with soft rain pattering comfortingly on the roof and Ian's deep voice a soothing presence within. She let the moment for controversy pass without a struggle. For several minutes they sat in silence, looking into the fire. Both of them finished their coffee, and Ian placed the empty mugs to one side.

"After I finished reading your report," he continued, "I went out to find you." He reached for one of her hands. "I was so eager to see you, I looked everywhere."

He was speaking to her like a lover. His words, his gentle voice and his earnest expression confused her. He was behaving as if he was optimistic that they could sort out their differences and pursue the strong attraction they felt for each other. She drew her hand away from his and stared into the fire. It would only break her heart further to get her hopes up merely to have them dashed once again.

"Go on," she said softly.

Ian poked at the fire, sending sparks up the chimney. The orange coals cast their warm glow on his skin.

"I went back to my office," he said. "I couldn't think of where you could be that I hadn't already looked." He paused and smiled gently at her. "Then I finally figured it out. Where else would you be but at the seabird rookery?" He paused again. "I can't tell you how wonderful it felt to run up there and find you. I had just about talked myself into believing I'd never see you again. And that thought was killing me."

There was an awkward little silence in the cabin. Alex was very moved by what he'd just told her. Tentatively she placed her hand on his shoulder. A ripple of pleasure passed through her as she felt his smooth skin, warmed from the fire. The expression in his eyes was so full of longing and desire, she was nearly moved to tears. His next words were husky with emotion.

"I know you must dislike me, Alex, but I'm going to tell you something anyway. I'm in love with you. I started loving you the first time I saw you, that day you got yourself tangled up in the net. I've never wanted any woman as much as I want you. The thing that pulled me back from Kodiak, then out to the rookery, was the awful fear that I might never see you again.''

Were her ears deceiving her, playing a cruel trick? Or was she really hearing the only words in the world that could make her happy? Her heart felt as if it would burst, she was so overjoyed. She moved toward him. He raked her with an appreciative look that told her that his immense hunger for her had not diminished.

"Dear Ian," she exclaimed, "I don't dislike you. I've been terribly angry with you, and I've spoken harshly at times, but I could never dislike you. Oh, please forgive me."

The touch of his fingers was like a burning brand on her cheek. "There's nothing to forgive, sweet Alex." He laughed deep in his throat as he gazed into her eyes. "Just look at us. Two people alone together in this cozy cabin. We have the whole night ahead of us, sweetheart. Let's not waste it."

Suddenly they were pressed together on the soft rug, and he was kissing her in a dozen places at once. His mouth pressed against her throat, her earlobes, her cheeks, her eyelids. It was as if he couldn't get enough of her. Everywhere his lips touched, she felt a shiver of pleasure course through her.

"Ian, dear Ian," Alex cried out, "I love you so. Please hold me tighter. Don't ever let me go."

"I'll never let you slip away, my love," he murmured against her neck as he cradled her to him. "I've waited too long for you to come into my life. There's no way I'm going to let you go now that I've finally found you."

His eager hands flung aside Alex's clothing. Her breasts began to tingle and feel fantastically alive and warm as Ian pressed her against his hard chest. His hands slid along her back and down to her hips. She twined her fingers in his thick hair and turned his face toward her. His lips were slightly parted and curved in a faint smile. He gazed at her intently, the corners of his eyes creased with playfulness.

"Shall I kiss you, Alex? Is that what you want?"

He drew near and teasingly touched the corner of her mouth with his tongue. She moaned with desire as he brushed his lips against hers, then stayed just out of reach of her eager mouth.

"Yes," she groaned, "I want to get drunk on your kisses. Please kiss me, Ian, please."

She moved against him, and he slid one hand down to caress her bottom. Then he captured her mouth with his, and Alex experienced an explosion of pleasure as he hungrily ground his mouth down upon hers. His tongue probed the sweetness behind her willing lips. She responded in kind, nipping at his lower lip and thrusting her tongue into the warmth of his mouth. The passion of his kiss shattered her nerves and made her feel as if she were spinning weightlessly through space. A whirling kaleidoscope of colors exploded behind her closed eyelids. His hand fondled her breast, his fingers gently caressing the nipple, his touch light and almost painfully teasing.

"Mmm, I want to touch you everywhere at once," he groaned huskily against her moist, parted lips.

Dragging his mouth from hers, he lowered it to her breast, where the pink bud was standing up stiff and eager for his touch. He kissed it, then took the nipple in his mouth, sending a spasm of delight through Alex's entire being. He showered her breast with kisses, caressing and coaxing until Alex cried out in ecstasy.

She guided his mouth to her breast's twin, urging him on with eager hands and with hips that moved and strained against him. He sucked and nipped demandingly until her nipple was throbbing and as hard as a pebble. Sensations pulsed through her like rippling water, sending licks of fire to every part of her body.

His fervor increased as his mouth once again sought hers. She moaned against his lips as he kissed her possessively, claiming every part of her willing mouth. His touch was so agonizingly delicious, so full of hunger for her, that she felt as if she would faint.

With one hand he stroked her waist, then leaned back to look at her. She lay naked before his eager gaze. The firelight cast a million flickering golden lights across her shapely form. Slowly and deliberately, he ran his hand down the length of her, exploring the curves, dips and valleys of her body.

"What an exciting woman you are, Alex. You're so beautiful," he said in a voice that was ragged with desire. "I can't look at you enough."

He ran his hand lovingly over her smooth stomach and down to her thighs, which parted slightly, involuntarily, at his intimate touch. His hand was firm and warm. Wherever it touched her skin, she felt a flame flicker and grow. Her nerve endings ignited and burned brightly as he continued his exploration.

"Help me take these off," he said in a feverish voice.

He rose to his knees and guided her hand to his belt. Her hands were trembling from the overwhelming arousal of her senses. She loosened the plain brass buckle and unsnapped the top of his jeans. Slowly, teasing him in turn, she pressed her mouth to a spot just below his waist. She kissed the sensitive skin where soft hair disappeared beneath his jeans. He groaned in ecstasy, clutching her shoulder with one hand and her head with the other. His skin was clean and smooth, the hairs silken. She breathed in his faint male scent and reveled in it. Raising her head, she saw the desire that was written on his face. His lips were parted slightly, his eyes hooded in ecstasy, and a faint sheen gleamed on his upper lip. She was profoundly happy that she had the power to give him so much pleasure.

He caught her face in his hands and kissed her deeply.

"Tell me you love me, Alex. I want to hear you say it again, sweetheart."

"I love you, dearest Ian. I love you so much."

It was such a joyful release to say those words to him. She knew there was no turning back now. The intensity of her feelings was sweeping her away in a tidal wave of desire in which she would have gladly drowned.

He helped her remove the rest of his clothes. Then he was beside her. She gloried in the perfection of his body and in the proud form that greeted her hungry eyes. He folded her in his arms before the warm glow of the fire, pressing his length to hers.

She felt intoxicated from the kisses he pressed onto her mouth. Dipping his head, his lips burned a molten path to her breasts. She quivered as his tongue worked its magic on their throbbing buds. His dark head swooped lower, and he used his mouth and hands to caress her smooth stomach. Jagged moans of wanton desire escaped her parted lips as she realized his intention.

As his mouth trailed kiss after kiss down the length of her body, shafts of heat shot through her. Her fingers tangled in his hair as she threw her head back in eager supplication. His demanding hands possessively parted her legs, and he ardently caressed the satiny skin of her inner thighs. Low groans of ecstasy slipped through her lips as she hastened him on with encouraging hands.

She felt as if she might explode when he at last pressed the heat of his mouth to the heart of her. Like a bow flexed taut to launch its arrow, her body curved to meet the demands of his restless lips and tongue. Never in her life had she experienced such sweet, savage wantonness, and she greedily cried out for more.

Waves of heat from his intimate touch fanned through her, faster and faster until she was arching her body in an agony of pleasure. His expert lovemaking lifted her to heights of ecstasy she'd never dreamed possible.

Her body suddenly tensed as if she were teetering on the brink of a high cliff. Then she was toppling, falling, spinning, her mind in a whirl. Behind her closed eyelids, a sky full of rockets exploded in a multitude of colors. Time meant nothing in the vortex in which she spun. Through the fog of pleasure that clouded her mind, she was vaguely aware of the breathless cries that were torn from her throat.

Then an overwhelming need forced her to speak through the sweet haze. "Ian, I want you. Please come to me. PLease." Nothing would satisfy her now but the sensation of being filled with him, of merging their bodies in the ultimate expression of love.

Her hands reached for him, drawing him to her. She opened her eyes and looked up at his form above her. His skin glowed with a fine dew from the exertions of their lovemaking. On his face she read the extent of his desire. Again time stood still as she watched the flickering shapes of the fire on his bronzed skin. Then, with one swift, fluid movement, he entered her, causing her to gasp aloud. He lowered his chest to hers and feverishly kissed her love-swollen lips as his hips melded with hers.

"Oh, sweet Alex," he groaned against her mouth, "how I've wanted this. I can't get enough of you. Love me, Alex, love me."

He reached beneath her and grasped her bottom, pressing her up to him as if attempting to completely merge their dew-slicked bodies. She hung on to him as he moved, marveling at the strength of his muscles and the beautiful rhythm of his passion. Clasping his back, her lips sought the smooth skin of his shoulder. Together they found the tempo that melded their bodies into one.

She held her breath in sweet anticipation as she felt a greater tension enter his body. Muffled cries of ecstasy escaped his lips as tremors of pleasure began to shake him. He held her closer, and she threw her legs over his back, urging him on with whispered words. His breath was hoarse and ragged against her hair as the inferno of his passion claimed him. For what seemed like an eternity, Alex clung to him, amazed by the power of his release. Lovemaking, for her, had never before been this profound, and she was awed by the intensity of their passion.

They lay without moving for many minutes, their arms and legs still entangled. Slowly Alex's senses began to register her surroundings. Rain splattered against the windows. Shadows and reflected firelight danced on the sheltering walls and ceiling of the little cabin. A playful wind sighed around the corners of the building, whispering softly to the entwined lovers.

At last Ian eased off her, then tucked her curves neatly into his own contours as they nestled, spoon-fashion, before the fire. He reached over her and threw more

sticks onto the little blaze, causing the embers to flare
with renewed life.

An agreeable languor claimed Alex's body, and she felt
mildly and pleasantly drugged. Ian spoke to her in a soft
voice.

"Darling Alex, you've made me the happiest man in
the world." His hand rested on her hip, and he murmured near her ear. "There's something I want to tell
you."

"Yes," she responded lazily, "what is it?"

"I've decided to cancel building the crab plant near the
seabird cliffs." He paused. "I hope you'll accept my
gesture as a wedding present."

She was instantly alert. His words were so stunning, so
unexpected, she wasn't even sure she had heard him cor-
rectly.

"What?" she said. "I...I don't understand."

"As I was sitting outside Bennie's room this morning,
I got to thinking about how you and I had locked horns
over those seabirds. Neither one of us was ever willing to
give in. I could see I'd been pretty stubborn, and I wondered if I hadn't reacted the way I did because I was just
too close to the situation. I decided to call Dr. Harper and
get a fresh look at things. We were on the phone for at
least an hour, and we had a great talk. She explained a
few things to me about seabirds, things that made me
think. She didn't actually change my mind, because I'd
already heard most of what she said from you, but she
made me take a step back and look at the situation—the
big picture, I guess you'd say—from a different perspective."

Alex gave a chuckle of amused pleasure. "Ian, this is
really great. I was planning to call Dr. Harper myself,
tomorrow when I arrived in Kodiak. I'd been thinking

how stubborn I'd been, and how I hadn't tried hard enough to work out a compromise with you. Don't you think it's wonderful that both of us still believed there was hope for a solution?''

He kissed her on the neck. "Yes, it is wonderful." He paused. "Do you remember how I said your report was persuasive?''

"Yes.''

"Well, it persuaded me, Alex. Today when I read it with a more open mind, I could see that you're probably right. There is a very real possibility that the colony would decline, or maybe even be destroyed, if there was a development close by. So, rather than take that chance, I had Dan send a message canceling the project at that site. I'm going to expand the cannery at Chulinka Bay, instead. The designers will have to rethink the whole thing, and it'll be trickier this way, but I'm sure they can work out the details.''

Alex was bursting with happiness. The one obstacle that could have marred her contentment and joy had been removed. She was almost unable to speak, she was so deeply touched by his change of heart. She turned to face him.

"Ian," she finally managed to say in an emotion-laden voice, "I can't tell you what this means to me. Thank you so much.''

He pressed tender kisses on her eyelids and brow. "Believe me, Alex, it's my pleasure. I had already made up my mind about it when I went out to look for you. I wanted so badly to tell you how much you've influenced me, how differently you've made me see things. Now that I have you, I never want to let you go." He nuzzled her neck, then looked deeply into her eyes. "You haven't responded to my offer yet, sweetheart," he reminded her.

She was confused. "Your offer?"

He laughed throatily. "Darling Alex, the cliffs are my wedding present to you. I'm asking you to marry me."

And then everything became clear to her. This man, whom she loved so deeply and so utterly, was saying the only words that could make her happiness complete. Suddenly her world expanded and began to glow with perfection, and she knew she had come home at last. Her heart soared with the greatest joy she had ever felt in her life.

"Oh, yes," she cried out to him. "Yes, dearest Ian, of course I'll marry you."

Then with her whole body she repeated her answer as he once more enfolded her with the love and passion that would be forever hers.

Can anyone tame Tamara?

Life is one long party for the outrageous Tamara.

Not for her wedded bliss and domesticity.

Fiercely independent and determined to stay that way, her one goal is to make a success of her acting career.

Then, during a brief holiday with her sister, Tamara's life is turned upside down by Jake DeBlais, man of the world and seducer of women…

Discover love in full bloom in this exciting sequel to Arctic Rose, by Claire Harrison.

Available from May 1986.

Price £2.25.

WORLDWIDE

Silhouette Special Edition

COMING NEXT MONTH

SUMMER WINE
Freda Vasilos

Was she dreaming? Or had golden Apollo just decended from Olympus? No ... Nick was real ... too real for Sara Morgan. A summer affair wasn't on the agenda, even with a bronzed god whose passionate kisses were as potent as wine.

DREAM GIRL
Tracy Sinclair

Angelique was Vendome Cosmetics' Dream Girl and had many admirers, but none so attentive as the mysterious Claude Dupont. When she discovered that he was the Prince of Souveraine, his uncle insisted she pretend to be his 'friend' to avoid any scandal ...

SECOND NATURE
Nora Roberts

For Celebrity magazine reporter, Lee Radcliffe, tracking down writer Hunter Brown had become a personal quest. But when the master of the supernatural turned out to be a dark-eyed master of seduction, Lee knew that it would take more than just good interviewing skills to get her an exclusive...